Du

**Two brand-new stories in every volume...
twice a month!**

Duets Vol. #101

Popular Darlene Gardner serves up not one,
but *two* quirky stories this month in a very special
Double Duets volume. Join the fun as she focuses
on past loves—the One Who Got Away and the
One Who Never Left. Would *you* ever look for these
people? Darlene always spins "a delightful tale with
an engaging set-up and lovable characters," says
Romantic Times magazine.

Duets Vol. #102

Boxers or briefs? That's what every woman
wants to know about the sexy hunk in her life.
Talented Delores Fossen tells us the answer and
more in the hilarious *Truly, Madly, Briefly*. Joining
Delores this month is newcomer Katie Gallagher,
who hails from North Carolina, but has set her very
first story in *Tried and True*, Kansas. Enjoy this tale of
a runaway fiancée and the sexy sheriff who
nearly arrests her on the way!

Be sure to pick up both Duets volumes today!

"I bet you're thinking I'm going to start by talking about intercourse, orgasm and arousal!"

Zoe couldn't believe what she was hearing. Instead of the innocent dogsled author she thought would be lecturing tonight, here was Phoebe Lovejoy, sex therapist, extolling the virtues of hot and spicy sex.

Phoebe bellowed, "We need to connect with our partners, people. This is called intimacy. Look into his or her eyes and remember why you've chosen this person as a lover."

Zoe gulped as she gazed at Jack. Her palms started to sweat, her throat went dry and her heart pounded. She didn't need a spice-up-your-sex-life author to teach her how to want. She needed lessons about how *not* to want Jack.

And then everything went black.

"Sakes alive," Phoebe joked, "your gazes were so hot we blew a fuse." But Zoe hardly heard her because she couldn't stop herself. She kept moving forward, until her lips came in contact with the soft sweetness of Jack's mouth.

She'd thought about kissing Jack for so long that a part of her had been sure the fantasy couldn't live up to the reality.

But reality was better...sooo much better.

For more, turn to page 9

"Skating's not my thing," Matt explained.

"You've been doing pretty well so far," Amy offered, hoping he'd stick with it.

"Would you rather do something else, like catch a movie?"

"No!" Sitting beside him in the darkness with only an armrest separating her from all that gorgeous male flesh would be much worse than just skating alongside him.

She was about to make up an excuse when a wild-haired girl suddenly got up from the seat where she'd been putting on her skates and headed for them at full speed.

"Out of the way, people," she yelled. A demonic look glazed her eyes as she barreled through.

"You do realize," Matt explained, "that if we stay here we're going to be in the line of fire all day, don't you?"

In the Line of Fire," Amy said automatically. "Clint Eastwood, John Malkovich, René Russo."

And Amy Donatelli.

She hadn't been one of the stars of that movie, of course. But the way she was reacting to Matt, she very definitely was In the line of fire.

Fire that had nothing to do with combat and everything to do with chemistry.

For more, turn to page 197

HARLEQUIN DUETS

ISBN 0-373-44167-3

Copyright in the collection:
Copyright © 2003 by Harlequin Books S.A.

The publisher acknowledges the copyright holder
of the individual works as follows:

ONCE SMITTEN
Copyright © 2003 by Darlene Hrobak Gardner

TWICE SHY
Copyright © 2003 by Darlene Hrobak Gardner

Darlene Gardner

Once Smitten

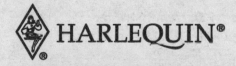

HARLEQUIN®

TORONTO • NEW YORK • LONDON
AMSTERDAM • PARIS • SYDNEY • HAMBURG
STOCKHOLM • ATHENS • TOKYO • MILAN • MADRID
PRAGUE • WARSAW • BUDAPEST • AUCKLAND

Dear Reader,

If you want to start a juicy conversation with a group of your friends, wait until their guards are down and dare them to tell you about the One Who Got Away.

You know, the person from your past you can't forget. The one who creeps into your mind when you least expect it and holds on tight. The one you'd dearly love to see just one more time.

Chances are that even the happily married among us have an OWGA, which is the acronym the trio of friends in my Double Duets novel use for the One Who Got Away.

Zoe O'Neill, the heroine of my first story, simply can't get Jack Carter out of her mind five years after she'd last seen him. So she accepts a dare to look him up.

Sure, most of us would probably rejoice that we let our OWGAs go if we met them again. Then again, maybe, like Zoe, others would discover that what they let go of was love.

I dare you to find out!

Darlene Gardner

Books by Darlene Gardner

HARLEQUIN DUETS
39—FORGET ME? *NOT*
51—THE CUPID CAPER
68—THE HUSBAND HOTEL
77—ANYTHING YOU CAN DO...!

HARLEQUIN TEMPTATION
926—ONE HOT CHANCE

To Lynette Revill and Adrienne Fritz,
who not only share the same parents as I do,
but are my sisters of my heart

1

THE TROUBLE WITH GOOD friends, Zoe O'Neill thought as one of hers launched into a tonsil-baring laugh, was that they never quit while you were ahead.

"So let's see if we understand this correctly, Zoe." Amy Donatelli's dark eyes danced as she laid a conspiratorial hand on Matt Burke's arm. "You're saying there isn't one man from your past you can't stop thinking about? Is that it?"

Zoe's mouth twitched when she tried to answer in the affirmative. Darn it. She wanted to lie, but it went against her blasted moral code to tell falsehoods to her two best friends. Evasion didn't.

She raised her voice to be heard over the conversation and the music inside the noisy Washington, D.C., pub where the three of them had a standing Wednesday night date to toss back a few in the name of friendship.

She'd been so eager to get here tonight that she'd powered through a job for a client who contacted her Clutter-Bee-Gone business with a closet emergency. Then she'd practically sprinted three blocks and hopped a crowded Metro train in a mad dash to get to Dupont Circle on time.

All for this!

"Just because my mailman tracked down his high school sweetheart and discovered he still loved her doesn't mean everybody has somebody who got away," Zoe said.

As she waited to see whether her comment had done the trick, she nervously caught her left earlobe between her thumb and index finger only to discover she'd neglected to put on her earrings. Unless...she touched the gold hoop on the right earlobe. Yep, she'd done it again. She'd put on only one earring.

"Everybody doesn't have someone who got away, honey," Amy said. Zoe's lips curved into a relieved smile as she covertly removed the right earring, noticing in the process that she'd painted the fingernails on only one of her hands. "But you do."

Zoe's smile disappeared faster than their first round of drinks. The color she felt flushing her face, unfortunately, seemed like it was going to stick around.

"Cut it out, Amy," Matt said in the slow, measured way he had of talking. "You're being too hard on Zoe."

Zoe could have kissed him smack on his sensible, analytical mouth, not that she had any romantic inclinations in that direction.

With light-brown eyes, dark-blond hair and

cheekbones a model would kill for, Matt was a looker. If you liked the clean-cut, suit-and-tie type. But he bore an uncanny resemblance to Zoe's only sibling, a half brother who lived in California and whom she saw far too seldom.

Until Matt had taken a job at a D.C. law firm and moved to the district a few months ago, Zoe hadn't seen Matt enough, either. In addition to looking like her brother, Matt was considerate, thoughtful and intelligent.

Not to mention a true-blue friend.

Matt took a swig of pale ale and raised his eyebrows. "If Zoe wants to pretend she never had a thing for Jack Carter, we should let her."

He was also lower than a pig in a mud bog.

"Ha!" Amy clapped her hands in obvious delight. "That proves it, because Jack Carter is..."

"...the man you were thinking of," Matt finished for her.

"Right," Amy said, nodding.

Zoe felt her face turning redder and wondered if she could talk her way out of this one. Considering she, Matt and Amy had met at the University of Maryland, the same place she'd met Jack Carter, it was doubtful.

"Since you bring up his name every couple of months, that's no surprise," Zoe told Amy with feigned aplomb.

"Uh, uh, uh." Amy wagged her finger for every denial she uttered. "You bring him up, honey. It's like he's always there in the back of your mind, waiting to jump into the conversation.''

"You're exaggerating," Zoe said, but her voice cracked and four eyebrows raised. She threw up her hands. "Okay, I might have mentioned him once or twice, but that's perfectly understandable. Don't you remember what he looks like?"

It had been five years since Zoe had seen Jack Carter, but she could still picture the way all female eyes swung to him when he sauntered into the college biology class they'd taken together senior year. Even though the campus had twenty thousand students, she still marveled that she hadn't noticed him before then.

He'd be wearing those blue jeans with the slight rip in the back. The rip she suspected he'd made deliberately because he was such a perfect specimen coeds couldn't help but want to reach out and trace the inches of powerful thigh it exposed.

As though Jack Carter needed any help in the sex-appeal department. Not only had he been the star pitcher on the baseball team, but all six foot two inches of him were gorgeous.

He'd looked his sexy best when he strolled into class fifteen minutes past the eight o'clock start time, his hair mussed and his face unshaven as though he'd just rolled out of bed. How could a biologically sound woman not want to hustle him back to his place and crawl into that bed with him?

Not that Zoe would have considered letting Jack

know she was susceptible to his bedroom look. Or the killer smile he'd flash her when he'd unsuccessfully try to bum her notes.

Amy waggled her eyebrows. "If you're trying to say Jack Carter had what it took to heat up your oven, why don't you just spit it out?"

"It's nothing to be embarrassed about, Zoe," Matt said when Zoe's face attained ovenlike temperatures. "Most people think about the One Who Got Away."

"But—" Zoe began.

Amy didn't let her finish. She squared her shoulders, shot an indecipherable look at Matt and blurted out, "I certainly think about my OWGA."

Zoe didn't immediately realize Amy had turned One Who Got Away into an acronym, but Matt had no such trouble.

"You have an OWGA? Who? The gum chewer? The knuckle cracker? The loud talker?" He rolled his eyes. "Those guys were losers."

"They were not!" Amy denied. "And it's not any of them anyway."

"Then who?"

Amy tossed her thick mane of long, dark hair and hesitated only slightly before replying, "Pierre… LeFrancois," a name so French that Zoe was sure Amy had never mentioned him before. Was he someone she knew from childhood? A family friend? A French chef?

Before Zoe could ask, Amy was grilling Matt.

"So who's your OWGA, counselor? The giggler? The eyelash batter? Don't tell me it's the exhibitionist."

"Wearing miniskirts didn't make Lori an exhibitionist," Matt said, then took only marginally longer to answer than Amy had. "It's a girl I went to high school with."

"What's her name?" Amy pressed.

"Mary… Contrary."

"The one in the nursery rhyme with the cockleshells?" Amy asked. "That Mary Contrary?"

"Of course not." Matt cleared his throat and rubbed the back of his neck. "We called her that because she's contrary. Her real name's Mary Contrino."

"And you've thought about contrary Mary all these years?" Amy asked, the pitch of her voice rising at the tail end of the question.

"Probably no more than you've thought about the dock guy."

Zoe scrunched up her eyebrows, wondering what Matt meant by that. Amy didn't have to scrunch.

"I didn't say his name was *Pier*," Amy said. "I said it was *Pierre*."

"Go on," Zoe said when her two friends lapsed into an unusual silence. She got an uncooperative look from Amy, so she turned her attention to Matt. "Why don't you tell us more about the cockleshell woman? What are cockleshells anyway? Did you ever ask Mary?"

"We weren't talking about me, Zoe," Matt pointed out. "We were talking about you."

"Hey, why can't we talk about you and Mary Contrary?" Zoe protested. She turned to Amy. "Or Amy and Pierre LeFrancois? Your OWGAs are probably much more interesting than mine."

When Amy's dark eyes widened, Zoe knew she'd made a mistake of grave proportions. Darn it. Why couldn't she have dim-witted friends instead of ones who picked up on every conversational slip?

"So you admit that Jack Carter is your OWGA," Amy said.

Zoe sighed, because denying the truth had been an exercise in futility. Since the three of them had become friends while members of the Snap To It photography club in college, Amy and Matt had developed a knack for unearthing her secrets.

"So what if he is my OWGA," Zoe said. "It's not like I'm ever going to see him again."

"Why not?" Matt asked. "The alumni directory's online. Look him up and give him a call."

"No way." Zoe shook her head so vigorously she feared she'd given herself whiplash. "Even if I was in the market for a man, which I'm not, it wouldn't be Jack Carter. For heaven's sake, he carried a scorecard around in college instead of a little black book."

"The scorecard was a rumor." Amy waved a dismissive hand. "Besides, you're five years older and wiser than you were then. You're better able to handle a man like him."

"You're forgetting that I'm building a business. I don't need someone like Jack distracting me."

"If he's stuck in your mind all these years," Matt drawled, "sounds like he's already distracting you."

"Well, yes, but—"

"But nothing," Amy said. "If you think about him so much, you need to get him out of your system. Maybe you won't even be attracted to him anymore. The only way to find out is to look him up."

Zoe's heart thudded in time with the bass beat coming from nearby speakers. Look up Jack Carter? It was unthinkable. She'd learned from her mother's gullibility to avoid empty charmers like rush-hour traffic in D.C.

With his good looks and effortless charisma, Jack was the epitome of an empty charmer. Still…she had to admit she was curious to see him again. Not that she planned to satisfy that curiosity.

"You don't honestly think I'll agree to look up Jack, do you?" she asked after a moment.

"Of course you will," Amy said, a brilliant smile crossing her face, "because you can have that photo from my Ugly Cube if you do."

Zoe stared at her friend in astonishment. A few years ago, after complaining that she threw away more photos than she kept, Amy hit upon the idea of displaying the worst of them in a plastic photo cube. Thus the Ugly Cube was born.

The cube, which displayed comically unflattering photos of the living things closest to Amy, was prominently displayed in Amy's apartment.

Zoe might have considered it an honor to be included on the Ugly Cube if the ugliest photo hadn't been of her.

"Nice try, but it won't work," Zoe said. "No matter how many times I take that photo of myself out of the Ugly Cube, you replace it with a copy."

"She meant she'd give you the negative," Matt said, and Amy nodded. "I don't know what the big deal is anyway. That photo of Speedy Gonzalez with his nose pressed up against his cage is way uglier than yours."

"Box turtles don't care how they look," Zoe said. "Doesn't it bother you to be on the Ugly Cube, Matt?"

"Nope," he said and took a swig of beer.

"Me, neither," Amy chimed in.

"That's because you look kind of pretty in your ugly picture," Zoe retorted. "I can't believe you couldn't have found an uglier one."

"Ugliness is in the eye of the beholder," Amy said. "If it weren't for those pink curlers and the bit of drool at the corner of your mouth, you'd look nice in yours, too."

"It's hard to control the drool reflex when you're asleep," Zoe muttered.

Matt laughed. "Sounds like a once-in-a-lifetime chance to get rid of that picture, Zoe."

"But it's extortion," Zoe complained. "How can you use the Ugly Cube against me like this, Amy?"

Amy looked pained at the charge and covered Zoe's hand with hers. "Oh, honey. I'm not using it against you. I'm using it *for* you. You know as well as I do that you hardly ever date. What if it's because you subconsciously compare every man you meet to Jack Carter?"

"I don't date because I'm busy, not to mention uninterested." Zoe had no intention of becoming seriously involved with any man until she was financially and professionally secure, the way her mother had never been, but that was another conversation. "It's not because of Jack."

"Then prove it by looking him up."

Zoe took her hand out from under Amy's so her friend wouldn't notice that her pulse rate was running wild. "But what if he's married? Or living in China?"

Amy pondered that for a moment. "You're off the hook unless he's single and living inside a hundred-mile radius."

Zoe chewed on her bottom lip, because she knew very well that Jack Carter was unmarried and living far closer than that.

But giving in to a whim and punching a couple of computer keys to find out what Jack Carter was up to was far different than getting up close and personal with him. Not that she'd ever let herself get *too* close or *too* personal. She was *too* smart for that.

On the other hand, what would it hurt? Amy was right. She thought about Jack Carter far too much. Maybe one more look at him would banish him from her thoughts forever.

And she did have the Ugly Cube to consider. She *really* wanted her photo off that darned cube. She looked toward Matt, who was silently regarding her.

"What do you think, Matt?"

He reached for some beer nuts, popped them into his mouth and said, "I think Amy won't give you any peace until you agree to look this guy up."

Zoe bit her bottom lip and returned her attention to Amy. "And I have your word that you'll give me the negative from the Ugly Cube if I do this?"

"Deal," Amy said quickly, sticking out a hand.

Zoe hesitated only slightly before grasping her friend's hand, aware as she shook that Amy had given her too much leeway.

Knowing Amy, her definition of looking up a man from the past meant phoning him or marching up to him and asking him out.

But Zoe wasn't going to do that. No, siree. She meant to jump through the giant loophole Amy had left her.

"Deal," she said.

She deliberately failed to mention that her meeting with the glib-talking, head-turning Jack would seem purely accidental.

2

"I'M TELLING YOU, JACK CARTER, this is not negotiable." The tone of the redhead's voice escalated along with her temper. "Either you come to the Adirondacks this weekend to meet my parents or...or else!"

Oh, Lordy, Jack thought as he glanced around at the once-active crowd populating the health and fitness center where he worked. Not a single exercise-bike wheel was spinning nor plate-loaded weight machine clanking.

"Now calm down, Fiona," Jack said in his most soothing voice. "You don't want to be having this conversation here where everybody can hear."

"Let them hear," she said, taking a step closer to him. "I want everyone to know I'm not the kind of girl who moves in with a guy before he meets her parents."

Move in with her? Jack could have pointed out he didn't yet know Fiona well enough to have memorized her phone number. Not only had they been on just three dates, but they hadn't even consummated their relationship.

But the way her eyes were sparkling, he didn't think she was in the mood to listen.

"I don't recall discussing us moving in together," he said carefully.

"Of course we discussed it. I told you that everyone in my family lives together before they get married. But not until they meet Mom and Dad."

Married? Jack took a step backward, raising his hands with his palms facing outward. "I don't know where you got the idea that we're getting m—"

Fiona didn't let him finish. She settled her hands on her hip and snapped, "Are you coming with me this weekend or not?"

"Not," Jack said softly.

"I should have believed what everyone said about you." She drew to her full height, which couldn't have been more than five feet two. "I need a man who can commit to a relationship. You're a...a serial dater!"

She spun on her heels and stalked away, stopping halfway to the exit to pull off one of her tennis shoes and pivot. Her release was so quick, Jack barely had time to dodge the shoe as it came hurtling through the air, tumbling sole over laces.

It glanced off his shoulder and thunked against the control panel of a state-of-the-art treadmill, sending the machine into sprint mode.

Despite himself, Jack was impressed. He knew pitching, and Fiona could really bring it.

When she was almost to the door, Fiona seemed

to realize she was missing a shoe and reversed directions. Jack bent to pick it up and met her halfway, holding the tiny white sneaker out to her.

"You realize, of course, that you just killed Billy and Sally," she hissed as she snatched the shoe from him.

He scratched his head. "Who are Billy and Sally?"

"The children we were going to have," she retorted as she shoved the shoe back on her foot and stalked away.

"Woman trouble, K-Jack?"

The large, beefy hand that captured his shoulder in a vise-like grip was at odds with the cartoon-mouse voice, but both belonged to Squeaky Hogan.

Jack had always wondered if Squeaky had accepted the nickname because, like the father of the boy named Sue in the Johnny Cash song, he knew it would make him get tough or die. It must've worked. At six foot six and nearly three hundred pounds, Squeaky was a brawny testament to might.

"I'll never understand women," Jack said, keeping a vigilant watch on Fiona's retreat to assure she didn't let loose another potent fastball. "Did you hear her? How do you suppose she got the fool notion that I wanted to marry her?"

Squeaky laughed, a tittering sound that had been known to frighten first-time visitors to the center. "Haven't you heard yourself talk, buddy? With that

Southern accent of yours, everything you say gives women the wrong idea.''

Jack let out a short, disbelieving laugh. ''C'mon, Squeaky. This is me you're talking to. You could trust me with your sister.''

Squeaky bristled, his thick dark brows drawing together under his smoothly shaven scalp. His heavy muscles tensed. ''Don't you be going near my sister.''

''It was a figure of speech, but you *could* trust me with your sister.'' Jack scowled. ''Jeez. I'm glad everybody around here doesn't think like you do.''

''You're kidding, right? You know why everyone calls you K-Jack, don't you?''

Jack affected a shrug, because K was baseball shorthand for strikeout. Once upon a time, he'd thrown them with ease. But strikeouts had become so rare when he reached the minor leagues that the Chattanooga Lookouts, the AA affiliate of the Cincinnati Reds, had released him a month ago after spring training. And his dream of playing in the majors had come to a crushing end.

''An old pitcher can't have a more flattering nickname,'' Jack said.

Squeaky snorted. At least, Jack thought the high-pitched noise was a snort. ''They don't call you K-Jack for striking out batters, buddy.''

Jack's brows drew together. ''Then why?''

''Here's a hint. Think about the way you treat the women you date.''

Jack frowned, not understanding. He admired and respected the women he dated. Because he didn't want to lead them on, he broke things off before they got too intense, usually after the first or second date.

The situation with Fiona had gotten a little sticky but it would have gotten nastier if he'd let things progress beyond date three...date three, his unspoken limit.

"Wait a minute," Jack said slowly. "You're not saying y'all call me K-Jack because I don't go out with a woman more than three times, are you?"

"Bingo." Squeaky gave him a tremendous slap on the back sure to leave a handprint. "You don't strike out batters anymore. You strike out women."

"That's not true!" Jack said. "Half the time, they strike me out. Like Fiona there. You saw it, Squeaky. She dumped me."

"Only 'cause you wouldn't meet her parents."

"I hardly know her!"

"You knew she already had three strikes," Squeaky said.

"Aw, c'mon. I hate that." The way Jack saw it, guarding against falling in love wasn't a sin. He'd learned from baseball that there was danger in letting himself want anything too much, and that included a woman. "Now how am I supposed to get folks to stop calling me by that awful nickname?"

Jack winced when he realized that he was complaining about being called K-Jack to a man nicknamed Squeaky. But the mountain of a man didn't seem phased by it.

"Easy," Squeaky said. "Go out with someone more than three times."

"And who's gonna go out with me that many times without wanting some kind of commitment in return?" Jack asked, throwing up his hands.

Squeaky's burst of laughter was so piercing Jack feared his eardrums would shatter.

"You have to ask, I'd say you deserve the nickname," Squeaky said, then paused meaningfully, "K-Jack."

ZOE CLUTCHED BOTH SIDES of her head as she stood on the busy sidewalk in front of the place where Jack Carter worked. Maybe that way she could ward off the headache she felt coming on.

Even if a steady procession of body beautiful types hadn't been entering and exiting the building, the sign over the glass double doors would have clued her in on her mistake.

The Lockerroom was lavishly scripted in bold red letters, but the small print below made Zoe's stomach churn.

Get Physically Phit!

She might have found the creative spelling clever if she hadn't been sick to her stomach for believing The Lockerroom was a storage facility instead of a health and fitness center.

What was she supposed to do now? Waltzing into

a storage place on the pretense of soliciting business for Clutter-Bee-Gone made sense. Offering a fitness center her services as a professional organizer did not.

What could she say? Would you like your rows of exercise bikes straightened? Can I suggest a new way to group your free weights? Can I interest you in a set of closet organizers for the lockers in your dressing room?

By trying to devise a foolproof way to approach Jack, she'd outsmarted herself. And now there was no way she was going into that gym. Not when she didn't have an excuse to be there.

No. She was going to turn tail and run like the wind before Jack saw her. She turned, fled and plowed into the warm, solid mass of a man's chest.

"Whoa, there," the owner of the chest said, reaching out long arms and catching her by the shoulders.

Her eyes were even with the strong, tanned column of a gorgeous, familiar neck. She slowly lifted her eyes. Past the cleft in his chin. Over the white flash of his sinfully attractive smile. Across his well-shaped nose and high cheekbones.

Her gaze finally settled on the eyes with the charming crinkles at the corners. The irises were dark green, like the grass on a baseball field after a day of soaking rain.

Her own eyes almost rolled at the absurdity of

her plan, because she already had the answer to one of her questions.

One look at Jack Carter was not going to banish him from her thoughts forever more. Especially not when she had the sensation of being zapped by electricity merely because he'd caught her by the shoulders. He'd already dropped his hands, but that hadn't completely cut off the flow of current.

"Zoe O'Neill, as I live and breathe," he said in a voice that dripped with the sounds of the South and cut through her like a knife in whipped cream. "Now if this isn't a surprise to beat all surprises."

The real surprise was that Jack looked even better than he had in college. His golden-brown hair was shorter, but just as luxuriously thick. The planes of his face more mature, but just as compelling. He'd added some brawn but his muscles weren't the overinflated type. They were long and ropy, exactly the type she preferred.

At least he was wearing sweatpants instead of leg-baring shorts. Probably because he'd torn them in the back to provide a tantalizing glimpse of hard-muscled thigh.

She forced her mouth to drop open, made herself put a hand to her lips and feigned surprise for all she was worth. "Oh my gosh. Jack Carter. This *is* a surprise."

His grin reached all the way to his crinkling, green eyes. "I'm wondering what's more surprising. Running smack-dab into you on the street or you recallin' my name.''

"Why wouldn't I remember it?"

"Oh, let's see." He tapped a finger against the side of his wide mouth. "Maybe 'cause you hardly gave me a chance to make your acquaintance back in college. I'd sit down and you'd get on up and scoot half a classroom away."

"That's because your never-ending crusade to bum my notes was distracting," she said. The way her heart tripped whenever he was nearby hadn't helped her concentration, either.

"It wouldn't have been if you'd given me the notes," he said softly, trailing his forefinger down the slope of her nose.

Her heart gave a ba-boom equal to any it had sounded in college, but with any luck the traffic noise on the street drowned out the ba-booming. To be safe, she moved a step backward and his hand fell away. The sun was shining out of a cerulean-blue sky, but the glare of his good looks was more blinding.

Never trust a golden boy, she reminded herself, *especially one with a silver tongue.*

"You wouldn't have needed my notes if you'd been on time for class," she said. "Besides, I never did understand why it was *my* notes you wanted."

Especially because every other coed in the class was all but panting to help him out—and probably with a heck of a lot more than just his homework.

"I'm no dummy. Not only were you easy on the eyes, but you made the best grades." He grinned his lady-killer grin and she tried not to drop dead. "So, tell me, what are you doing here?"

"What am I doing here?" she parroted because she couldn't think of any answer but the truth.

Trying to prove I was right to let the One Who Got Away go.

"Um...I was about to ask you the same question," she said, stalling.

"I manage the personal trainers at The Lockerroom."

"But what about baseball?" The question had been burning a hole in her mind since his name had stopped appearing on the Web page of the Cincinnati Reds' minor-league affiliates. Not that she checked the page more than a couple times a week.

"I got released after spring training." His tone was matter-of-fact, but she thought she saw him wince. "Have I told you yet that five years looks great on you? *Really* great."

His eyes traveled over her in a slow slide that would have been more distracting if she hadn't suspected he was trying to distract her. He transferred his weight from one foot to the other and returned to their previous subject of discussion: What the heck she was doing there?

"I'd like to flatter myself that you're here to see me, but that would be wishful thinking."

"Yes, it would," Zoe retorted automatically although there was a part of him she was dying to see.

She took a step backward and furtively craned her neck so she could look for a sexy tear high on the thigh of his sweats. Hmm. No tear. Her eyes drifted higher to his mighty fine posterior. Oh my, but he could fill out some sweatpants, she thought, just as her purse slipped out of her hand and landed on his foot.

"Ow," he yelped, jumping back so the purse toppled on its side and thudded to the sidewalk.

"Sorry," she said, biting her bottom lip.

He reached down to pick up the offending item and the muscles in his back and upper arms strained. "What do you carry in this thing?" he asked as he handed it back to her. "Cement?"

"Oh, no." She prepared herself to accept the weight of the purse, which was color coordinated to match her outfit. "I carry supplies. I like to be prepared for anything."

"I can see that," he answered, gingerly shaking out his foot. "So are you gonna tell me what you're doing around these parts?"

"I have a very good reason to be here," she announced, swallowing hard. She thought about saying she was interested in a membership, but The Lockerroom was in Silver Spring, miles north of the Maryland state line. At least a dozen gyms were closer to her Northwest D.C. apartment.

Out of the corner of her eye she noticed a teenage

girl approaching her with a petition before getting distracted by a long-haired boy on a souped-up motorcycle.

The girl had set down her clipboard on the bench closest to Zoe and seemed to have forgotten about it. Zoe marched right over and picked it up.

"I'm gathering signatures for a petition," Zoe said, waving the clipboard.

"Oh, really." Jack cocked his head charmingly. The sun brought out the golden highlights in his brown hair and the wind tousled it around his strong face. "Maybe I'll sign it. What group are you petitioning for?"

Zoe glanced down at the large black letters atop the position. "BLOT," she read.

Jack's smile was just as devastating as it had been in college. "Not the most attractive name for an outfit, but I reckon it's better than smear."

"No. It's an acronym. B-L-O-T. It stands for..." She paused to look down at the petition. "Oh my."

"Wouldn't the acronym for that be OM? Kind of sounds like a yoga chant, don't you think?"

She would have smiled at his silliness if her disbelieving eyes hadn't read more of the small print atop the petition. She should have recognized the name immediately. She'd surely spent enough time worrying about the group after reading last week's article in *The Washington Post*.

"You're going to wish BLOT had something to

do with yoga when you find out what this petition's for," she said.

His perfectly arched eyebrows shot up. "Why's that? What does BLOT stand for anyway?"

"Better Linguists of Tomorrow," she said.

"You're a linguist? And here I thought you majored in business."

"I did." She neglected to add that part of the reason she'd taken that career path was that she couldn't spell a lick. "I'm a business-minded linguist."

Who'd thought it was cute to name her business Clutter-Bee-Gone so she could decorate her business cards with worker bees spiriting away clutter.

She cleared her throat and forced herself to continue. "BLOT's mission is the obliteration of misspelled words and poor grammar."

A puzzled look clouded his handsome features. "What's that got to do with me?"

"It doesn't have to do with you, specifically. It has to do with the p-h in phit on your sign. The Lockerroom is BLOT's next target."

"You're joking," Jack said.

"Would I joke about language?" Zoe asked and tried to look like Miss Mitterwald, who'd scared the bejesus out of her in third-grade English class. But unlike Miss Mitterwald, Zoe didn't have a ruler to rap sharply on the nearest desk or a voice so resonant she was the stand-in when the fire alarm went on the fritz.

"BLOT's a force to be reckoned with." Zoe tried to remember the successful campaigns of linguistic terror the group had waged against other D.C. area businesses. "Ask the owners of *Kountry Kitchen* or *Ye Olde Towne Shoppe*."

She was about to repeat one of Miss Mitterwald's favorite sayings—We have met the enemy and her name is Miss Spelling—when she realized they weren't alone.

The legitimate petitioner, a petite girl of about eighteen, was suddenly next to them, gaping at Jack. She wore a pair of barely there shorts with a white T-shirt sporting a huge black blot and the saying, Blot Out Lousy Language.

"Well, helloooo there," the Blotted One said to Jack in a come-hither voice that sounded like it was patterned after an actress in a bad soap opera. "I'm Heidi."

"Hey, Heidi. That's a right pretty name," Jack said, giving her an easy smile. "It suits you."

The girl blushed and Zoe tried hard not to gag. Even though her hair looked like it had been dipped in shoe polish, the girl was pretty. That wasn't in question, neither was Jack Carter's oozing charm and the female race's susceptibility to it.

He leaned closer to Heidi. The girl stared at Jack as though he'd mesmerized her. And maybe he had. Maybe that's what he'd done to Zoe, too. Except she was going to fight the mesmerization.

"Something tells me you're another one of the BLOT people," Jack said.

"Blotters," Heidi said breathlessly.

"Excuse me?"

"We're called blotters, not BLOT people."

"Well, then, Zoe here's a blotter, too." Jack jerked a thumb at her. "She's been telling me your kind doesn't like the way we at The Lockerroom spell phit."

"Zoe?" The girl's puzzled eyes finally focused on Zoe.

"The BLOT powers-that-be sent reinforcements," Zoe explained hastily, giving a little wave.

"Didn't know we had enough recruits for that," Heidi said, then focused on Zoe. "But why aren't you wearin' the blot?"

She indicated Zoe's tailored, lemon-yellow power suit, matching purse and high heels. Zoe looked down at herself...and saw that her shoes didn't match. They were both white, but one shoe had two straps across the top while the other was decorated with a dainty white rose.

Darn. That was what she got for setting her alarm clock at the last possible second before she was due to arrive at her first appointment of the day. But she couldn't think about that now. Not when the girl was calling her credibility into question.

"You're supposed to be wearing the blot," the girl added, sounding tense.

"The blot blew up," Zoe said quickly. "It ran

something fierce when I put my T-shirt in the washing machine. It looks like a fountain pen exploded.''

''No way,'' Heidi said, her eyes round.

Zoe nodded. ''Way.''

The boy on the motorcycle revved his machine. Heidi stole a glance at him, then focused on Jack. ''Don't suppose you'd consider datin' a teenager, would you?''

He smiled. ''I'm right flattered that you asked. Like I said, you sure are pretty, but you're a little young for me.''

''In that case, gotta book.'' She cracked her gum and shoved a homemade sign at Zoe. ''BLOT doesn't need two of us hangin' 'round. 'kay?''

''Wait a minute,'' Jack said when the girl turned to leave. ''What kind of linguist says 'kay and gotta?''

''The kind whose librarian mom made her become a blotter.''

Heidi waved gaily as she rushed across the street to the boy on the bike. She swung her leg over the machine, wrapped her arms around the boy's midsection and held on as he pulled away from the curb with a loud screech.

''Get the hotty to fix the phit,'' the girl yelled to Zoe as the motorcycle whooshed by them.

Zoe smoothed back the hair that had blown in her eyes, but her mind wasn't on blotting out the p-h in phit.

It was on blotting out Jack Carter.

She'd seen enough to know he hadn't changed his charming ways. Women still fell all over him, the way she'd promised herself she'd never.

She'd fulfilled her mission, and the photo from the Ugly Cube was as good as hers. Now all that was left to do was to get out of there and try once again to forget him.

Jack might always linger at the corners of her mind, but at least she'd be secure in the knowledge that she was better off staying away from the One Who Got Away.

"What do you say we go inside and discuss this BLOT matter," he suggested, taking her elbow. A thrill ran up her arm but she determinedly ignored it.

"That's not necessary."

"Sure it is. The blot's bad business. I don't want you out here all afternoon chasing away customers."

"I wouldn't do that."

"You're doing it." He pointed to the sign Heidi had handed her. It was white with a huge black blot at its center. "Now are you coming?"

She wanted to tell him she was leaving but found that she couldn't. Not without revealing that she'd never been interested in fixing the phit in the first place.

"I'm coming," she said.

When the choice was between the blot and total humiliation, it wasn't much of a choice at all.

3

JACK WAS TOUCHING NOTHING but air.

Zoe and her very pretty back, which his hand had been in contact with only a moment ago as he'd ushered her toward the fitness center, were two steps ahead of him.

That marked the second time since he'd made Zoe's reacquaintance that she'd shied—no, jerked—away from his touch. It could only mean one thing.

Zoe O'Neill wasn't attracted to him.

"Hey, Zoe," he called as friendly as he could, testing his theory, "I'm all the way back here, you know."

She didn't even turn her blond head. "I know," she called.

Disappointment coursed through Jack like runoff from a heavy storm. That proved it. Zoe wasn't any more attracted to him now then she'd been in college.

That she'd found him lacking in college, however, had probably been a good thing. He'd been so rash back then he'd have done something stupid— like ask her out.

And she wasn't his type at all. Oh, he liked the

look of her with that strong jawline, slightly crooked nose and high, broad forehead. He liked the blond hair she wore in a smooth cap, that wide mouth and those hazel eyes, even if they did seem suspicious of him.

But she was button up to his button down. The kind of person who went through life with her ducks in a row instead of scattered every which way on the pond. The type who needed a computerized gadget because she'd planned not only the present, but the future. Unlike Jack, whose future was as cloudy as the sky before a storm.

He should be thanking the stars that appeared when the sky cleared that she'd made it known she found him unattractive. He was smarter than he'd been in college and far less likely to take a chance when he couldn't succeed.

He frowned. Too bad he hadn't known he wouldn't succeed at baseball. It would have saved him a lot of pain.

Jack opened doors for women, but Zoe's mad dash had gotten her to The Lockerroom ahead of him. She stood inches inside the door, holding it open for him, an anguished look on her face. As though she were in pain.

"Something wrong, Zoe?" he asked a second before shrill whistles hit his eardrums. The ruckus drowned out the soft strains of inspirational workout music that usually pervaded the club.

"It's that awful noise," Zoe said and shuddered.

The door swung shut behind them, offering them no escape from the sound. "What is it?"

He cocked his head, listening more carefully, but darned if he could make sense of it.

"Oh my gosh," Zoe said. "I think it's supposed to be the tune to 'Take Me Out to The Ballgame.'"

The next-to-last line of which had to do with striking out.

Jack's gaze shot to the massive man behind the glossy reception desk Jack's teenage sister was supposed to be manning. Squeaky's thick lips came out of their whistling position and then he smiled.

"Hey, K-Jack, you wanna introduce me to this lovely batter?" Squeaky smirked. "Uh, I mean lady."

Jack didn't want to, but he figured he didn't have a choice. "Zoe, this here's Squeaky Hogan. Squeaky, this is Zoe O'Neill. We went to college together."

Jack slanted the mammoth personal trainer a meaningful look as Zoe reached out her hand and shook Squeaky's. "Zoe's here on *business.*"

"Oh, yeah?" Squeaky's dark eyebrows lifted, then he snorted. "That's a good one, K-Jack."

"She's a blotter," Jack explained.

Mysteriously, Squeaky's eyes narrowed and a scowl darkened his usually cheerful face. "You weren't in on the *Jim's Jim* protest, were you?" he all but screeched at Zoe.

"Hey now," Jack said, taking an instinctive step

in front of Zoe. He doubted her quick negative response had even registered upon Squeaky. "No need to get hostile."

"But those rotters were out there every day in front of my buddy Jim's place until he agreed to change j-i-m to g-y-m." His scowl darkened and the pitch of his voice rose. "They couldn't see how cute it was spelled the other way."

"I think you mean *blotters*," Zoe corrected, sticking her head around Jack.

"Oh, no, I don't," Squeaky muttered. "That's a rotten bunch you're running with. A very rotten bunch."

"If you'll excuse us, we have business to take care of," Jack said, ushering Zoe away before it dawned on Squeaky that BLOT was trying to obliterate their p-h.

He'd have to ask his sister to get someone besides Squeaky to fill in at the reception desk when she took a break. Even in his best mood, Squeaky wasn't the receptive type.

"Sorry about Squeaky," Jack said when they were inside his office. "He shouldn't have called you a rotter."

He watched her take stock of his office. It was generic aside from a framed watercolor of a pitcher in motion, which hurt so much to look at that Jack usually averted his eyes from the wall. He'd long since tossed the autographed baseball he'd tried to keep on his desk into a drawer.

She brought her pretty hazel eyes back to him and lifted one of her elegantly shaped shoulders. "It wasn't sticks and stones. Everyone knows names can never hurt you."

He thought of the way the K-Jack nickname was damaging his reputation and hoisted himself up on the edge of his desk, letting his legs dangle. "That's a strange comment coming from someone who thinks misspelling is a fighting matter."

"Not really. I assume Squeaky can spell rotter."

"But it's slang."

She cleared her throat. "We at BLOT don't object to slang as long as it's spelled correctly."

"I still say he shouldn't have called you a rotter."

Zoe picked the chair in the office farthest from him, sat down as primly as Eliza Dolittle after Henry Higgins had gotten hold of her and crossed her legs at the calves.

And what fine legs they were. Slender but with great calf definition, tapering down to slim ankles and well-shaped feet. Feet wearing shoes that didn't match.

"Don't give it another thought," she said before he could comment on the curious fact that Miss Organization was wearing mismatched shoes. "Actually, I was more curious about why he calls you K-Jack."

Jack made a face. "You wouldn't be interested in that."

He expected her to question him further, but instead she folded her hands in her lap and said, "Okay." Exactly as though she *wasn't* interested in him, which, of course, he'd already figured out.

Zoe launched into a spiel about blotting out the p-h, but Jack hardly heard what she was saying. An idea formed in his mind, thrusting everything else aside.

Zoe O'Neill wasn't interested in him.

Unlike most of the women he ran into, Zoe didn't want anything from him but good spelling.

Earlier today, when he'd been talking to Squeaky about the hated K-Jack nickname, Jack thought he'd never be able to find such a woman. But she was in his office, sitting not six feet away, supremely unaffected by his presence.

"Jack," Zoe said, leaning forward slightly, her manner devoid of anything remotely akin to flirting. "Were you listening to me? You looked like you were thinking about something else."

"I was," he said readily as a smile spread across his face. "I was thinking that I'd sure be a happy man if you'd date me."

Jack watched Zoe blanch, as though he'd proposed something horrifying, like changing the sign outside to read Git Fysically Phit.

His stomach dropped even as he tried to tell himself it was a good thing she found him about as appealing as the Ks in the Kwik Kopy Kompany. Her very aversion to him made her the perfect woman to help him get rid of that annoying nickname.

Now all he had to do was figure out how to get her to say yes.

ZOE FELT ALL THE COLOR drain from her face and settle in the vicinity of her heart.

It was beating so furiously she was half afraid to look down for fear a heart-shaped cutout would zing in and out of her chest in the manner of cartoon tickers.

Jack Carter, who was so attractive she felt like shouting "oo-la-la" every time she looked at him, had just asked her out.

Say no, the sane part of her brain screamed. *He's too sexy, too charming, too much like the kind of man who could throw your organized existence into disarray.*

She composed her features, careful to keep any hint of pleasure off them. "Dating you isn't a good idea, Jack," she said. Good. Her voice sounded firm, composed, in control.

"Now don't go saying no until you hear me out," he said. "I could make going out with me worth your while."

Her zinging heart seemed to freeze while heat zoomed to another, lower part of her body. She closed her eyes, praying for strength. He was talking about sex. She was positive of it.

"I know what you're thinking," he continued

and she wanted to cover her face in chagrin. He *knew* she wanted to go to bed with him. "You're looking over at me and thinking, 'Jack, I can't imagine any incentive you could offer up that would make me want to date you.'"

"I am?" she asked, her mouth hanging open.

"You've made it clear as a mountain stream that I don't stir your coffee cup."

"I have?"

"To be honest, I wouldn't be asking you out if you'd given me any inkling you found me attractive."

"You wouldn't?" She bit her lip. "I didn't?"

"No, siree." He hopped from the desk, walked a few paces closer to her until she could smell him. But of course he smelled clean and sexy instead of sweat soaked the way a fitness center employee should. "That brings me back to the incentive."

Zoe was about to ask another rhetorical question, but she clamped her mouth shut. She'd find out what was going on sooner if she didn't speak.

"Phil Nickles, the owner of The Lockerroom, is an old fraternity brother of mine. That's how I got this job. He called me up out of the blue one day and said it was mine. He likes me, Phil does. I'm thinking that, with a little bit of persuading, I can get Phil to get rid of the *p-h*."

Following her new policy of silence, Zoe waited.

"In exchange," Jack said, "all you've gotta do is date me."

He looked inordinately satisfied with the plan. Pleasure shined out of those gorgeous green eyes and lit up the lady-killer smile she still saw in her dreams.

"Do you mean to tell me," Zoe said slowly, "that you're *bribing* me into going on a date with you?"

"Not one date, four dates," he said, holding up the requisite number of fingers. "I should have made that clear from the beginning."

"So you're bribing me to go on *four* dates with you?"

He frowned. "Don't think of it as a bribe. Think of it as a mutually satisfying agreement."

Mutually satisfying? Oh, no. She'd been right the first time. "You are talking about sex!"

A corner of his mouth kicked up along with his eyebrows. "Now where'd you get that idea?" he asked in that sexy drawl of his.

"From you. You said the dates would be mutually satisfying." Heat rose in her like lava in a pre-eruptive volcano. Her voice sounded strange, as if it belonged to some whiskey-throated siren. "What would you get out of it if not sex?"

He laughed, a rich, vibrating sound she felt clear to her bone marrow. She shivered in sexual awareness.

"Oh, come on, Zoe. Do you really think I'd suggest that knowing how you feel about me? I'm not blind. I know you don't want to go to bed with me."

"I don't?" Zoe asked, then realized she'd responded in the form of a question. Oh, darn. She tried again, this time forming a statement. "I don't." She paused. "And because I don't, I'm wondering why you're asking me on a date."

"Four dates," Jack corrected. He turned, paced to the door and back again. "I'm asking 'cause I want to get rid of that awful nickname they pinned on me."

"K-Jack?" she asked, and he nodded. "You didn't tell me why they call you that."

He let out a heavy sigh. "K's a baseball term for strikeout. Some of the people 'round here have gotten it into their fool heads that I strike out women."

"Oh, I get it," Zoe said. "You don't go out with anyone more than three times, do you?"

"That's about the gist of it," Jack said, but a frown marred those classic features.

Zoe couldn't figure out why he looked so downcast. Charmers like Jack were happiest when flitting from one woman to the next. Settling down with a single female went against their butterfly nature, which was why her parents' marriage hadn't lasted past her third birthday.

"What's wrong with this nickname again?" she asked.

"It's terrible," Jack said, appearing stunned that she'd asked. "It makes it sound like I don't like women."

Oh, he liked women all right. Zoe thought the K-Jack nickname proved it.

"Like I told Squeaky, half the time the women I date don't want to keep dating me," Jack continued. "Even when I call it quits, I'm not striking them out. I'm acknowledging things wouldn't work out between us in the long run."

Zoe tried to make sense of his words. He didn't dispute that he was in it for the short-term when it came to dating. Instead he seemed to be objecting to the semantics of the charge rather than the charge itself.

"So you're saying you don't want people claiming you strike out women?"

Some of the tension seemed to seep out of his broad shoulders. "Exactly. That's why I need you to go on four dates with me."

She looked at him doubtfully. "And you think that will get your co-workers to stop calling you K-Jack?"

"Sure will." He grinned. "A K is three strikes, not four."

Zoe didn't believe Jack would be proving much of anything if he managed to exceed his self-described limit by one date, let alone that he could sustain a relationship.

But what Zoe thought didn't matter, because she wasn't about to let herself get roped into his wacky plan. Prolonged contact with Jack hadn't been her objective when she'd strolled back into his life.

She'd meant to prove with one look at him that he no longer had what it took to ring her bell. Since it sounded as if Big Ben had gone off in her head, that objective hadn't panned out. But she wasn't stupid enough to abandon phase two of her plan.

That was to get out of his life, this time for good.

"So what do you say?" Jack asked. She opened her mouth to say no, when he continued, "Of course you'll have to promise to hold off on your petitioning until I talk to Phil, and that may take a couple of days."

"Phil? Who's Phil?"

"The owner of The Lockerroom. I already told you about him. He's the only one who can authorize taking the p-h out of phit."

Oh, no. She'd forgotten about blasted BLOT. How could she tell Jack she didn't care about the p-h without blowing her cover and revealing that she really was attracted to him?

She chewed on her lower lip, desperately trying to devise a way to get out of dating him.

"Aw, don't look that way, Zoe," he said. "I told you Phil likes me. I'm sure he'll take out the p-h."

She closed her eyes briefly, knowing she was trapped. She'd backed herself into a corner by claiming to be a blotter and now she'd have to pay for it. But she didn't intend to pay with her heart.

"I'll do it on one condition," she said and watched a wary look enter his grass-colored eyes. "I get to choose where we go on the dates."

His wariness disappeared, and he smiled his sexy smile. "Choose away," he said.

Zoe smiled back as she mentally patted herself on the back. Everybody knew the atmosphere had to be right for romance to bloom. On the kinds of dates she planned to arrange, neither Jack nor his smile would seem quite so sexy.

And romance would die on the vine.

4

JACK WALKED INTO The Lockerroom the next morning, feeling his lips curve into a smile the instant he spotted his sixteen-year-old sister behind the reception area.

Désirée was staring transfixed at the entrance as though waiting for someone. As though, Jack realized when she leaped to her feet, waiting for him.

"What took you so long? I've been dying for you to get here," she said when he was still twenty paces from her.

He glanced at the clock, noting that it was seven minutes past the hour, which technically meant he was still on time.

"Hello to you, too, little sister." He walked the rest of the way to the reception counter, glad he'd thought to recommend Désirée to fill the summer job. "You're looking especially lovely this fine summer morning."

She was dressed the same as always, in shorts and a T-shirt with her golden-brown hair pulled back in a ponytail, but she seemed…taller. He anchored a hand on the counter and peered over it at her neon-pink platform tennis shoes.

"Like them?" she asked, kicking up a heel.

She tottered and would have fallen if he hadn't reached out to steady her. She clutched at his arm, inadvertently clawing him with fake nails that could have been classified as deadly weapons.

"I like the girl who's in them, that's what I like," he said and kissed her on the cheek. Teenagers were such a contrary lot that he knew better than to say anything negative about her recent obsession with all things feminine. "Now why've you been waiting on me?"

"I heard that classy woman who was in here yesterday was your old college girlfriend and that you're going out with her today."

His smile vanished. Ten minutes after Zoe had left the center, he'd casually let it drop that he'd found a woman he wanted to date long-term. He'd aimed for the news to spread, but not to his sister. His impressionable, die-hard romantic sister.

"I didn't have any particular girlfriend in college, sugar," he said, using the endearment because he couldn't get past her insistence that she be called Désirée instead of Denise.

"Then you didn't make a date with Zoe?"

He regarded her curiously. "I hadn't realized you two were on a first-name basis."

"I talked to her before she left, because I thought she might want to join the center. She was real nice, Jack, and real sophisticated, not anything like the women you usually date." She gave him a look so hopeful it called to memory a basset hound. "You are going out with her, aren't you?"

He sighed. "Yeah, we do have a date."

"That's not what Squeaky says. He says you're all set to go on four dates because of the strike-out thing." She made a face. "He didn't seem too happy about it. He said something about her being a rotter."

Jack ignored that because it would take too long to explain. "You know why they call me K-Jack, too?"

"Doesn't everybody?" she asked rhetorically. "Anyway, I just saw this romantic old movie where this man gets arrested after robbing a bank. See, he didn't love anyone and thought money might buy him some. Turns out the prosecutor's a woman he used to know. After he gets out of jail, he realizes she's his Love of a Lifetime. Once she gets past the fact that he's poor and an ex-felon, she loves him back."

"What's that got to do with me?" Jack asked suspiciously.

"Maybe Zoe's your LOAL," she finished triumphantly.

"My what?"

"Your Love of a Lifetime. Heaven knows nobody else has been. Your romances have the life span of a mosquito. What if it's because you're still hung up on Zoe?"

"I'm not hung up on her and she's not my LO… Heck, I can't even pronounce it."

"LOAL. Rhymes with goal, not spool." She stared at him through slitted eyes, which could be because her eyelashes were weighed down with a heavy coating of navy-blue mascara. "And if you're not hung up on her, why'd you choose her to go on the date? I can't believe it's a coincidence."

Jack examined his sister, trying to figure out how to get her to stop talking. "No offense, darlin', but I don't feel like discussing my love life with my little sister."

"Why not?"

He tried a smile but the muscles controlling the sides of his mouth didn't seem to be working. "Oh, let's see," he said, then snapped his fingers. "Because it isn't any of your business."

"The heck it's not my business," Désirée exclaimed. "Since Mom died and we moved north to be close to dad's brothers, I've been the only female in the family. Do you know how sick I am of wiping whiskers out of the sink and watching *Sports Center?*"

"You're exaggerating. I don't live at home anymore, Scott and Bruce are away at college and Dad hardly watches TV."

"Our brothers come home on weekends sometimes, you know. Usually with their buddies. Then it's Testosterone City."

"It can't be as bad as all that."

"Yes, it is. I'm completely outnumbered, and I'm sick of it. Just hear me out, Jack. Keep an open mind about Zoe being your LOAL. It's about time I had a sister-in-law to go shopping with."

"Oh, no," Jack said, shaking a finger. "You can't decide Zoe's my LOOL—"

"LOAL," Désirée corrected.

"Just because you want to go to the mall with her," Jack finished.

"I'm not only thinking of myself, Jack. I'm thinking of you. You're already twenty-six. In another couple years, you'll be bald. Have you asked Zoe if naked scalps turn her off?"

Jack's hand went to the hair at the back of his head, which felt plenty thick to him. "It doesn't matter how Zoe feels about my scalp. I'm gonna go on four dates with her, and that'll take care of everything."

"We'll see about that," Désirée said cheerfully. She put her elbows on the counter, her chin in her hands and gazed up at him. "So where are you going on your date? I sure hope it's somewhere romantic."

"I love you to death, darlin', I really do," he said, tapping her affectionately on the nose, "but that's not something you need to know."

Especially since his ultraromantic sister wouldn't approve of a first date among the lions and tigers and bears.

PERFECT, ZOE THOUGHT AS SHE gazed at the pair of donkey-size animals in the grassy enclosure on the other side of the fence. She finally had her breath back after dashing the four city blocks from the Cleveland Park Metro station to make sure she was at the appointed place at the agreed-upon time. But the animals were so perfect they almost took her breath away again.

They had feet like rhinoceros, bodies like pygmy hippos and noses like elephants. Their legs were short, their ears small and their black-and-white bodies massive, probably upward of seven hundred pounds.

Nobody, and Zoe meant nobody, could look at the tapirs who lived at the National Zoo and think of sex.

Which meant she'd not only chosen the perfect location for a first date with Jack Carter, but by a stroke of luck she'd suggested they meet at the least sexy exhibit.

She intended to take great pains to assure that Jack didn't get the wrong idea on any of their four dates. She frowned as it occurred to her that the "wrong idea" would actually be the right one.

She couldn't look at Jack without thinking about sex, but she much preferred he didn't know that. If he was under the misconception that he didn't attract her, resisting him would be a snap. And resist him she must.

She wasn't the type to indulge in a frivolous relationship, and she didn't plan to have a serious one until her business was established and she was financially secure.

She didn't intend to end up like her mother, who'd scratched her plans to be a nurse and dropped out of college to get married. She'd divorced when Zoe was three and had been drifting from place to place and man to man ever since.

Why, just last night her mother had phoned from the West Coast about her ''great'' new man. They'd met in a bar after he'd sent a drink her way and claimed he was a sucker for redheads. Even though her mother was a natural brunette, she'd fallen for the line and was falling ever harder for the man.

Never mind that her mother didn't know whether he was unattached or what he did for a living. He had charisma, they had a connection and the rest would work itself out.

Zoe wasn't nearly as gullible, which was why she viewed her four dates with Jack as an opportunity to rid herself of the fascination he held for her instead of a chance to indulge in it.

One of the tapirs shrieked, a shrill sound that had Zoe stepping backward in alarm. Straight into something solid and unyielding. Strong hands gripped her shoulders.

''Hey, there, Zoe.'' A honey-rich voice whispered in her ear as soft breath sent goose bumps skittering over her skin. ''I love it when you throw yourself at me like this.''

Zoe whirled, freeing herself from Jack's grasp. She wanted to be angry at him for the suggestive comment, but the teasing light in his green eyes made that impossible.

His skin was freshly shaven, owing to the fact that it was just past ten o'clock in the morning. He was wearing a T-shirt that wasn't tight but still managed to call attention to his muscular chest. His shorts bared long, well-shaped legs dusted with hair the same shade of golden-brown as was on his head.

He looked, in short, gorgeous.

"You're early," she accused, searching for some reason to be miffed. Her back was to the tapirs, but she heard another strange noise. Like the wheezing of an asthmatic standing in front of a microphone.

"I'm early?" Jack seemed surprised. "And here I would have guessed I was late."

"Technically speaking, you are late." Zoe tapped the face of her watch. "But you're only ten minutes late. I expected more like fifteen or twenty."

He angled his body toward her, encroaching on her personal space by about a foot and a half. She shifted to put more distance between them, and her left arm bumped his right. Skin met skin, making Zoe's nerve endings go haywire.

"Everybody knows you're not late if you show up within fifteen minutes of when you're supposed to arrive."

"That's ridiculous," Zoe said. "You're probably

saying that because you forgot to set your alarm clock.''

''What alarm clock?''

She rolled her eyes, and he laughed. The laugh was low, rumbling and so darn appealing she was tempted to throw back her head and laugh with him.

''For the record, I've already been at the fitness center. If you'd met me there like I suggested, we could have come to the zoo together.''

''There was no need,'' Zoe said, striving for a businesslike tone. ''I understand you want your co-workers to know we're dating, but they already knew we were going out today.''

He leaned his dark head closer to hers. ''Sounds to me like you're discounting the possibility that I want to spend time with you purely for the pleasure of it.''

Zoe might have overdosed on a heady scent of shaving cream, shampoo and man if she hadn't been distracted by the series of wheezes and shrieks coming from behind her.

Grateful for a reason to change the subject, she asked, ''Why are the tapirs making that racket?''

The moment Zoe turned, she realized she shouldn't have. The tapirs were sniffing each other at a place on their bodies better left unsniffed. They began moving in a circular pattern, seeming unnaturally excited, as if... Oh, no.

Zoe wouldn't have willingly touched Jack a moment ago, but now she grabbed him by the hand and tugged.

"Let's go," she said, infusing false cheerfulness into her voice. "There's a lot to see at the zoo."

He cast a long look over his shoulder as they moved away from the circling animals. "But don't you want to wait to see what the tapirs are up to?"

He sounded innocent, but his sparkling eyes told her he was anything but.

"No," she said decisively, practically sprinting down the path that led to the main walkway through the zoo. "If anything comes up, I don't want to know about it."

ZOE'S EYES GREW TO SAUCERLIKE proportions as she watched the lioness rub and nudge the golden-maned lion before rolling over on her back and emitting a low guttural moan.

Like any male, he took the hint. Within seconds, he was behind her, biting her neck, his face comically contorted as he took his pleasure with a mighty roar.

Jack said something about the call of the wild, but Zoe pretended not to hear. She moved swiftly away from the Big Cat exhibit, her lower lip trembling.

How could this have happened? She'd chosen the zoo to keep her mind off sex, and she and Jack hadn't been able to take more than a few steps without witnessing it. Weren't the zoo animals aware of how difficult it was to get them to breed in captivity? Didn't they know that late summer was not prime mating season? Hadn't they ever heard of discretion?

"Hey, Zoe, wait up," Jack called.

She hesitated, then slowed and gave into the inevitable.

"Did you get a load of what those lions were doing?" he asked when he caught up to her, slinging a friendly arm over her shoulders.

"No," she lied, speeding up so his arm dropped away.

"Didn't last long. Twenty seconds tops. But that male was pretty vocal about the whole thing. You sure you missed it?"

"I told you. I didn't see anything out of the ordinary."

Jack shook his head. "I don't think it is out of the ordinary. Seems to me I remember reading lions in heat mate every twenty to thirty minutes." He paused. "Guess they make up in quantity what they lack in quality."

A giggle rose in Zoe's throat, but she swallowed it. Who'd have guessed that Jack Carter would know so many stray facts about the animal kingdom? Or that he could be so entertaining?

If it hadn't been for all the hanky-panky going on, she would have enjoyed his company. He'd even bought her an oversize stuffed panda when she'd remarked on how cute the animals were. He'd nicknamed it Pandamonium and had been lugging it around the zoo for her for the past hour.

"Must be something in the air," he continued, sounding thoughtful. "Why else would all the animals be behaving like that?"

Zoe cleared her throat, debating whether to keep quiet or feign ignorance. He seemed to expect a response, so she didn't have a choice. "I don't know what you're talking about."

His eyebrows rose. "You're joking, right? Haven't you been noticing a routine here?"

"No," she said, walking blithely on. If she ignored the subject, maybe it would go away.

"You didn't notice those prairie dogs kissing?"

"Nope."

"Or that honeymoon chamber for the snakes in the reptile house?"

"Uh-uh."

"How about those siamangs who looked like they were wrestling? Or the orangutans hanging upside down clutching at each other?"

"No and no," Zoe snapped, then immediately felt ashamed of herself. She was overreacting as badly as the mothers she'd seen spiriting their children away from the exhibits.

Jack wasn't coming on to her. He was merely calling attention to an evolutionary truth. So what if the animals were having sex? Denying their impulses to procreate would have been impossible, not to mention unnatural.

Just because sex was happening all around them didn't mean she and Jack were going to have it.

Sex might be in the air, but romance wasn't. And without romance, she was safe from Jack's dangerous allure. Which meant the zoo had been the perfect place for a first date, after all.

Sure, it was pretty. Bird songs and not traffic sounds carried on the breezes. Sunlight filtered through the tall trees, dappling the ground. The summer flowers still bloomed, providing splashes of color among the lush greenery that stretched on either side of the sidewalk.

But it wasn't romantic. No zoo was.

"What are those guys carrying?" Jack adjusted the stuffed panda in his arms and nodded at two men who were walking their way. Although one was a foot taller than the other, they were identically dressed in black slacks and white shirts.

"Violins, I think," Zoe said as the men got closer. She scrunched up her nose. "That's strange. Can you tell what it says on their shirts?"

"Serenade," Jack said after a few seconds.

The information had barely computed when the man in the lead, who had a full head of dark hair and a paunch worthy of a sumo wrestler, pointed at them.

"Those two over there. They are perfect," he told the smaller man, who had to scamper to keep up with the dark-haired man's ground-eating steps.

Although Zoe sensed what was coming, the incongruous sight of violinists at the zoo froze her feet in place. It was like seeing hippos at the symphony.

"Bonjour," the big man said with a French accent and a flourish. He bowed at the waist. "We represent Serenade, a new restaurant of the finest quality. We are on Connecticut Avenue not so very far from here."

They tucked their instruments under their chins and positioned their bows before Zoe found her voice. "Wait," she said. "What are you going to do?"

Jack grinned down at her and answered for the two men. "Why, I do believe they're gonna serenade us."

The larger of the men nodded at the smaller and the two musicians broke into a rendition of a popular love song that hadn't been composed for the violin. Beside her, she heard Jack chuckle. And why not? As love songs went, the song couldn't have been sappier.

It consisted, for the most part, of a single line about how the singer would always love the man she was serenading. The violinists performed an instrumental version, but inside her head Zoe could hear the singer wailing away.

The song had come over the radio once when she'd been with Amy. Her friend had listened for no more than a minute before shouting, "All right already. I get it. You'll always love him."

Zoe tried to summon Amy's annoyance with the repetitive lyrics and the melodramatic tune, but as always the beauty of the song made her throat constrict and her eyes tear.

She felt Jack's arm come around her shoulders, felt her head lean against his shoulder, felt her heartbeat speed up and couldn't force herself to move away.

Not while the violinists serenaded them with her favorite song, which could even make the zoo seem romantic.

5

JACK SHIFTED PANDAMONIUM to a more comfortable position in his arms, adjusted the strap on the purse he'd insisted on carrying and followed Zoe from the Metro station into the sunshine.

"It's not necessary for you to walk me home," she said in a familiar refrain.

It hadn't been necessary for him to unburden her of the purse, even though she claimed that carrying it had tired her out so much she'd been forced to use his shoulder as a headrest during the serenade.

Neither had it been necessary for him to buy her lunch, although he heard her stomach grumbling before they gobbled down sandwiches and French fries at an outdoor table at the zoo.

Accompanying her on the Metro was something else that hadn't been necessary. But no way would he have let Zoe, the stuffed animal and the purse get on the train without him.

"'Course it's necessary," he said as they walked with the flow of the crowd onto the city sidewalk. "Not only did I grow up in Tennessee, where men walk women home, but I'm toting quite a load here."

Jack moved closer to Zoe to make room for a harried-looking woman and a towheaded boy no older than six who were walking in the opposite direction. The boy's big blue eyes rounded as he stared up at Jack.

"Why's that man carrying a pink purse, mama?" he asked loudly. "Isn't that for girls?"

The boy's mother gave Jack a troubled glance and quickly looked away as she put an arm around the boy and hurriedly ushered him past them.

"Shush, Danny," Jack heard her say. "You know how we talked about there being all kinds of people in the world."

"Like I was going to say," Zoe said conversationally, but there was laughter in her voice, "I'm surprised you want to carry a pink purse."

"I don't necessarily want to," he said, even as he felt his shoulder sag under the weight of it. "I just don't want you carrying it."

"If you gave it back, you wouldn't have to walk me home." She increased her pace as if she wanted to shake loose of him. He walked faster to keep up.

"If you don't stop your protesting, I'm gonna get a complex here," he said when he was once again abreast of her. "I could get the idea you're not enjoying my company."

"Enjoying each other's company isn't the point. We have a business arrangement, remember?"

"Aw, come on, Zoe. We're talking about a date, not a board meeting. How am I supposed to keep my mind on business with a pretty lady like you around?''

Her shoulders tensed, the same way they'd been tensing for the past few hours. He frowned. Tense silence wasn't normally the reaction he got to his flirting.

She didn't break the silence until they'd walked past a sweet-smelling bakery and a New Age music store packed with teenagers. The look she gave him was so brief she probably would have gazed longer at a cornea-burning eclipse.

"As a matter of curiosity," she asked, "do you flirt with every female you see?"

"Only the ones I can get close enough to wink at."

He intended his comment as a joke, but she didn't laugh. The truth was that he did flirt with just about every female he came across, but he couldn't recall any who affected him the way Zoe did without half trying.

He'd had a flare of hope when Zoe snuggled against him during the serenade that he might be wrong about the way she felt about him, but then she straightened and blamed weariness on the snuggling.

He understood how her purse could make a body tired. He didn't understand why he kept flirting with her in the face of outright indifference.

"I was joking about the winking, but I'm not gonna apologize for the flirting." He gave her his best smile, which might have been more effective if she'd been looking at him. "People like flirting. If you want to find out how much, try it on me."

"No, thanks," she said as they turned off the busy thoroughfare onto a side street shaded with tall oaks. "I'm quite sure you already know how it feels to be flirted with."

"Not by you, I don't," he said, racking his brain for a way to get a rise out of her. After a moment, he grinned. "Gosh, the orangutans at the zoo were doing more flirting with each other than you do with me."

Her head whipped around. "Those orangutans were mating!"

"Gotcha," he said, pointing a finger at her. "And you said you didn't notice."

An adorable pink blush crawled up her neck and stained her cheeks. Maybe his strategy was working after all. Maybe she couldn't withstand relentless flirting.

"I only said I didn't notice so you wouldn't get the wrong idea," she said.

Or maybe her powers of resistance were as great as his determination to wear them down. He took in the length of her legs as she hurried home, the curve of her cheek as she kept her eyes averted from his and flirted on.

"You mean the kind of wrong idea those serenading violinists got?"

"It goes to show you how wrong first impressions can be," she said, sounding blithe.

"Oh, I don't know about that," Jack drawled, stung by the blitheness. His voice sounded a little thick. "Those guys thought we made a right pretty pair. Maybe they were on to something."

"I doubt it," she said quickly, but her jaw tensed.

He was proud of himself for being able to focus on her jaw when his eyes kept straying to the way her simple short-sleeved shirt clung to her breasts. But her reaction was important so he brought his eyes back up again and saw tiny white lines at the corner of her mouth.

Maybe he'd been wrong before. Maybe she wasn't tense because she found his flirtation annoying. Maybe he was unsettling her.

"Then why does talking about us being together make you nervous?" he asked.

"I'm not nervous." Her voice cracked. Just a little, but enough that he noticed.

"Sure you are. You're clenching your jaw so hard that any second now the enamel in your teeth is gonna crumble."

She opened her mouth. "I am not."

"Not now you're not."

"I wasn't before, either. And before you get any high-handed ideas, *you are not making me nervous.*"

He cocked his head and pressed on. "Then why

are you so tense? As a trained professional, I know stress when I see it.''

"You're trained in identifying stress?'' She sounded doubtful.

"Sure am. It was part of the phys. ed. curriculum in college.'' A minor part, to be sure, but he wasn't going to get into that. "Your shoulders are stiff, aren't they? And I bet your hands are clammy. I can hear your shallow breathing.''

"That's only because I'm walking fast,'' she said.

"Aha,'' he said with a flourish, "another sign of stress.''

"Walking fast is not a sign of stress!''

He laughed. "Maybe not, but you're still one stressed lady.''

"My mind's preoccupied, that's all.''

They'd stopped at a cross street and were waiting for a car to pass through the intersection. Jack pretended not to notice the driver giving him and the purse a double-take and then breaking into laughter.

"Preoccupied with what?'' he asked her.

She tapped a foot as another car followed the first down the street. "On work. I have a lot to do.''

Jack ignored the blaring of the horn and the whistles as the car went by. "At the library?'' he asked.

"I don't work in a library. Whatever gave you that idea?''

"I figured it'd be a place blotters work.''

Her eyes shifted and she took off across the street. Jack, Pandamonium and the pink purse followed.

"BLOT's just a sideline," she said after a minute. "I have my own business."

Jack's spirits sank, because the pressure of owning a business was a reasonable explanation for why she'd seemed so tense all day. So much for his hope that he was the reason she was nervous.

"What's your business called?" he asked when he had his disappointment in check.

"Clutter-Bee..." she said, then trailed off.

"Clutterby's? You mean like Sotheby's, the auction house? Is that what sort of business you're in?"

"It's not Clutterby's." She pressed her lips together. "It's...Clutter Bees. Two words. My idea was to call to mind worker bees who labor to rid your life of clutter. The same way I do."

"Then you own a housecleaning business?"

She shook her head and the blond strands of her hair rustled. "No. I'm what you call a professional organizer. I'm trained to survey a room or even an entire house and make the chaos and clutter go away."

"How do you do that?"

"It depends on the client, but I adhere by the adage that there's a place for everything. I use closet organizers and other tools, but the main idea is to help clients establish a routine for putting things in their place.''

"And thinking about all the de-cluttering you have to do is making you tense?"

"Yes," she said. "I'm a one-woman operation so I do everything myself. Have you looked around lately? The world is a messy place."

They'd reached her apartment, a two-story brick structure in a quiet, residential part of northwest D.C. She strode ahead of him and inserted a card in the slot beside the door. A buzzer sounded and she pulled the door open.

"I'll take Pandamonium and my purse now. Thank you very much for carrying them home for me," she said, sounding like she was dismissing him.

The thing was, he wasn't ready to be dismissed. Not when she was suffering the effects of job-induced stress.

"Unless you live on the first floor, I'm not going anywhere," he said, knowing perfectly well she was on the top floor from the glimpse he'd gotten of her last name on one of the mail slots.

"Why?" she asked, her brows drawing together.

"'Cause my Southern ancestors, God rest their souls, would rise up from their graves and hunt me down if I didn't carry this heavy burden up the stairs for you.''

He watched the breath expel from that gorgeous

chest of hers. "Oh, all right," she said after a moment and held the door open so he could get by.

He made sure to brush up against her as he passed, all in the name of flirting. But she merely pressed her back harder against the door frame, and he realized he'd been more affected by the body contact than she was.

Darn. He was starting to think he was fighting a losing battle here. Never mind why he was fighting it at all.

"After you," he said when the door closed behind her. He waited for her to precede him up the narrow staircase so that he could enjoy the view.

All too soon, they were in front of her door. She opened her mouth, no doubt to dismiss him once again, leaving him no choice but to blurt out the first thing he could think of.

"What do you say to having dinner with me tonight?" Once the question was out, Jack wondered why he hadn't thought of it before. It was only three o'clock, the night stretched ahead of them full of possibility.

The indentation appeared between her brows again. "Would it count as our second date?"

"Nope," Jack said quickly, not about to get roped into a two-for-one deal. "It'd be a continuation of the first. We could go to that restaurant the violinists were advertising."

She shook her head even before he finished the sentence. "No," she said. She sounded horrified.

He had a pretty fair notion that she was objecting to the date itself more than the place, but he indulged in willful misunderstanding. "It sounds like a fine place to go on a date to me."

The restaurant was probably one of those ultra-romantic places where all the tables were secluded and the only light came from candles. He pictured flickering shadows accentuating Zoe's cheekbones and making her eyes look like they belonged in the bedroom. *His* bedroom.

"No," she repeated. "I'm not free for dinner tonight. I told you I have a lot of work to do."

"On the weekend?"

"You can't take weekends off when you run a business out of your home."

"Okay." He hid his disappointment with a smile. He slid the purse off his shoulder, set down Pandamonium and leaned one shoulder against the wall. "Then we could go to Serenade another night. How 'bout tomorrow?"

"I'm busy tomorrow night, too," she said, her jaw clenching and unclenching again, "and I don't want to go to Serenade at all."

"Why not?" He reached out and brushed a piece of her hair back from her face.

She took a step backward, out of hair-touching range. "I get to pick the places for our dates, remember? I thought we could listen to Helga Moore talk about her new Iditarod book Wednesday night.''

"The Iditarod? But that's a dog-sled race." Jack couldn't keep the dismay out of his voice. His mind was on romance and hers was on the frozen tundra of Alaska.

"I know," she said, turning her back on him and unlocking the apartment door. "It's the perfect date because it won't take much time. An hour or two at the most. And time matters. I'm a busy woman."

Her comment sent a wash of guilt through Jack. In his eagerness to get her to commit to another date, he'd forgotten that her job was stressing her out.

It was especially disturbing because he had the means to relieve some of that stress.

"Aw, heck, Zoe, I'm sorry," he said. She hadn't yet turned all the way back around so he softly laid his hands over each of her shoulders.

"What are you doing?" The tone of her voice spiked at the end of the question.

"Giving you time to get used to me touching you. Gosh, you're as tense as a stretched rubber band. This'll work better if you can relax."

"How am I supposed to relax with you touching me?"

"Me touching you is the whole point," Jack said, although there was no way all this touching would enable *him* to relax. "How else am I going to give you a massage?"

"I don't need a massage."

"Sure you do. Even your voice sounds strained," he said, although it didn't sound nearly as strained as his own. "Now turn around."

Now that his hands were on her, he couldn't seem to break all contact, so he let his left hand slide over her back and her right shoulder as she turned.

The top of her head was roughly level with his nose. Slowly she raised her big hazel eyes to his. He cleared his throat. Warmth spread under the hand he'd kept on her shoulder and radiated throughout his body with lightning speed.

"Okay, now, give me your right hand and let the weight of your arm drop." He flexed her elbow, extended her arm away from her body and rocked it gently back and forth. After a moment, he switched the position of his hands and did the same thing on the other side of her body.

"Do you feel yourself relaxing?" he asked, his eyes still on hers.

She blinked. Once. Twice. Three times. "No," she said, wetting her lips with the tip of a pink tongue.

"You gotta trust me for this to work." He realized how ridiculous his statement was when he wanted nothing more than to pull her into his arms and ravage that moist mouth of hers. ''Maybe you should turn around.''

He figured it would be easier to fight the urge to kiss her when she wasn't facing him. He concentrated on using soft, sure movements to massage her upper back and shoulders, but touching her only made him want to explore more of her skin. Preferably when it was naked.

Oh, brother.

''Where did you say you learned this?'' The husky purr in her voice was hard to read. Was it due to relaxation? Awareness? An oncoming cold?

''Massage was part of the curriculum when I got certified as a personal trainer,'' Jack answered, fanning out his hands to gently clasp the rounded shape of her shoulders.

She felt soft and warm and unlike any other woman he'd ever massaged. Even as his hands kneaded her flesh, his mind dwelled on the huskiness he'd heard in her voice.

''I didn't know there was such a thing as stand-up massage,'' she said. There it was again. That little rasp in her voice.

He brought his mouth closer to her ear. ''It'd work better if you were lying down,'' he said thickly. ''How 'bout we take this inside your apartment?''

He held his breath as he waited for her answer to

his question, which had been about so much more than massage.

"There's no need for that," she said finally, stepping away from him and breaking the physical contact. The smile she gave him looked unnaturally bright. "I'm all relaxed now."

His protest, like his disappointment, was automatic. "How can you be relaxed when I just started?"

"Must be your magic fingers," she said cheerfully, wiggling hers.

He couldn't stop himself from reaching out for her again. The pads of his thumbs kneaded her shoulders, slowly applying and releasing pressure as his eyes bored into hers. "You sure you relaxed?"

She didn't say anything for a moment, and he could see his hot gaze reflected in her pupils. The flirtation had gotten out of hand the instant he'd touched her and he wanted nothing more than to kiss her.

All he needed was one sign from her. One sign that she wanted him even a fraction as much as he wanted her.

"I'm as limp as a rag doll," she said even as her shoulders tensed.

What she wanted, Jack realized miserably, was for him to stop touching her. Accepting the inevitable, he stepped back.

"Very good," she said, reaching down to pick

up Pandamonium and her massive purse. "I'll call you about Wednesday, okay?"

"Sure," he said a moment before she slipped through the door. He stood staring at that closed door for a long time after she'd shut it in his face, letting the disappointment flood through him.

Yep, he'd been right all along.

Zoe O'Neill was not now, and never had been, attracted to him. And the last thing he'd ever do was set himself up for failure by making a move on an indifferent woman.

No matter how much he wanted to.

6

ZOE TORE INTO THE SMALL package as soon as she'd shut her apartment door on the FedEx man, spurred on by Jack Carter's return address and the withdrawal pains she'd been suffering. For three whole days, she hadn't heard a word from him.

She came upon a note first, written in a bold, slanted hand: *Thought you could use this. I bought it on deep discount on the way home Saturday. Don't sic BLOT on the street vendor. He's getting new ones made. 'til Wednesday. Jack.*

Puzzled, she put the note aside and reached into a small box until her hand fastened on something round, soft and squishy. She pulled out a spongy blue ball and rotated it until she could read the green lettering stenciled on it.

Squeeze away you're stress.

She scrunched up her nose, wondering what the ball could possibly have to do with BLOT and why Jack had sent it in the first place.

The doorbell sounded before she could figure out either puzzle. Still holding the ball, she pulled open the door. Amy barely waited for Zoe to step aside before she trudged into the apartment and threw herself onto the nearest sofa.

"Hey, Zoe." Her friend let her oversized shopping bag drop to the floor with a thud and massaged her upper arms. "Wow, those Rollerblades sure are heavy. I bought some for my nephew, then decided I wanted them, too. You don't think I can talk Matt into skating with me, do you? He can be such a stuffed shirt.

"Of course, maybe he'll be off with his OWGA." Her voice dripped with disdain as she kicked off her shoes and tucked her legs under her. "Can you believe Matt has an OWGA? I'd like to meet…"

Amy's voice trailed off, possibly because Zoe was paying more attention to the squishy ball than to her. "What have you got there?"

"A Stress Squeezer," Zoe said and tossed the ball to Amy so she could get an up-close-and-personal look. The snag was that both of Amy's hands were still busy rubbing the soreness from her upper arms.

"Look out!" Zoe yelled, but the ball was already smacking her friend in the forehead.

"If you don't want me to drop in on you unannounced, just say so," Amy said, rubbing at the spot the ball had struck.

Zoe's hands covered her mouth. "I'm sorry."

"Oh, don't worry about it. I'm hardheaded and that ball's as soft as mush." Amy picked the ball up from her lap and examined it. "Cute. But it has a misprint. The contraction's wrong."

"Let me see that again," Zoe said, coming across the room to stand in front of her friend. Amy handed her the ball and again Zoe read the message. *Squeeze away you're stress.*

"But you're *is* the contraction for you are."

Amy rolled her eyes. "I swear, Zoe, you're hopeless at grammar. It shouldn't be a contraction. It's like saying, 'Squeeze away you are stress.'"

"Oh," Zoe said lamely, glad there wasn't a blotter in sight. She'd be unceremoniously kicked out of the group.

"I guess that explains why he sent it to me," she said, thinking aloud. "He must've thought the misspelling would make me squeeze harder."

"Why would you squeeze harder because something's misspelled?" Amy asked, but didn't give Zoe time to answer before scrunching her brow and asking another question. "Wait a minute, who's the he we're talking about?"

"Jack Carter, that's who."

Amy let out a little squeal before she reached for Zoe's hand and yanked her down on the sofa cushion next to her. "You've seen Jack Carter and you didn't tell me? Spill it, girl."

Zoe chewed the inside of her bottom lip. "There's nothing to spill. Not really. I looked him up and now you owe me that photo from the Ugly Cube."

Amy's brows rose. "If you think I'm giving up that photo before I've heard every last detail, you're delusional. Now give it."

"Okay, okay." Zoe leaned back and sank into the sofa. "I did like you said and looked him up, we went to the zoo—"

"That explains the panda in the living room," Amy interrupted, nodding toward Pandamonium, who had a place of honor in a wing chair. "Go on. Finish the story."

"There's not much more to it. We went to the zoo and then he sent me this ball." Zoe let out a heavy sigh. "Oh, Amy. Do you think he's toying with me? Do you think he knows the real reason I was so tense Saturday?"

Amy's brows drew together. "Sorry, honey, but I can't make heads or tails of what you're talking about."

"The massage he gave me to relieve the tension."

"A massage! That's great!" Amy took both of Zoe's hands and squeezed them. "Did you get naked before the massage or after?"

"We didn't get naked at all!"

A sharp indentation appeared between Amy's brows. "This doesn't compute. The guy you've been thinking about sleeping with for five years gives you a massage and you don't get naked with him."

"But the point is to keep from getting naked with him."

"Why?" Amy peered at her through narrowed eyes. "Nothing happened to that handsome face of his, did it? He used to be a pitcher, didn't he? Did a ball smack him in the kisser?"

"Of course not," Zoe said. "His kisser's fine."

"Did you try it out?"

"No! I'm trying to say he's as gorgeous as ever. Maybe more so."

"Then what's wrong with his personality?"

"Nothing's wrong with it," Zoe confessed. "He still has that dreamy voice and that Tennessee charm. And he's considerate. Like a Southern gentleman."

"I don't get it then. Why don't you want to sleep with him?"

"I swear, Amy, you're not listening to a word I say. I do want to sleep with him. That's why I was so tense. I spent the entire date with my muscles clenched so I wouldn't reach out and grab him."

Amy threw up her hands. "So why didn't you?"

"You know why. He's a charmer, just like all those men my mother falls for. I didn't tell you about her new one. They haven't been going out a week and already she's making excuses for why he keeps standing her up."

"How many times do I have to tell you that you're not your mother? And unless I missed something, Jack didn't stand you up."

"That's beside the point. I can't let someone like him distract me from what I want out of life. Before you know it, I'll be involved with him."

"Sounds like you already are involved."

"Oh, no, I'm not."

"Then you're not going out with him again?"

It was on the tip of Zoe's tongue to tell Amy about BLOT and the four fake dates, but she swallowed the words. Amy was the most bullheaded person she knew, and her friend had already conjured up a fantasy in which Zoe couldn't live without Jack.

If Zoe confessed she was temporarily dating Jack as a direct result of her posing as a blotter, Amy was bound to attribute false motivation to her masquerade. She wouldn't accept that Zoe had been forced into the unfortunate situation. She'd probably accuse Zoe of perpetuating the myth to get dates with Jack.

"I'd rather not go out with him again," Zoe said slowly, hoping it was true. They had three dates left, but she liked to think she'd opt out of all of them if he'd let her.

"Oh, for pity's sake, Zoe. How can you say that when drool forms at the corner of your mouth every time you say his name?"

Zoe's hand immediately went to the edge of her lips to wipe away any telltale moisture, and Amy laughed aloud. "See? That proves I'm right."

"All it proves is what I've admitted all along.

Yes, I'm attracted to him. But no, I'm not going to do anything about it.''

"What if he's the one who acts on the attraction?''

"He won't," Zoe said confidently. "As long as he doesn't know I want to get naked with him, I'm perfectly safe.''

"I don't know about that," Amy said. "You might be safe from Jack, but you're forgetting this man is your OWGA. Maybe you're not safe from yourself.''

ZOE TOOK A DEEP BREATH and pulled open the door to The Lockerroom, telling herself she was not nervous.

No, siree. Absolutely not.

Her pulse might flutter and the blood might rush to her nether regions every time she laid eyes on Jack Carter, but she could deal with the sensations now that she knew to expect them.

As long as she kept reminding herself of the overwhelming reasons she couldn't get involved with him, she could stay calm and in control.

That's why she'd settled on a pantsuit in an icy-blue, which she considered the most placid of colors.

The donning of the blue had helped her calm down after Jack had talked her out of meeting at the downtown auditorium where the Iditarod author was slated to speak.

So had the knowledge that Jack's motive for meeting at the center had everything to do with getting rid of the K-Jack nickname and nothing to do with spending more time with her. No matter what he'd suggested in the midst of one of his flirting jags.

If they weren't seen together, after all, what good was fake dating?

The reception area was empty, so she wandered over to the entranceway of a large room filled with at least three thousand-square feet of bench-press and plate-loaded machines.

She noticed Jack immediately and had to brace a hand against the wall to withstand the force of his sheer masculine beauty. Was it really necessary for him to look so buff in a T-shirt that wasn't even tight? His eyes did the charming crinkle thing at the corners, but he wasn't looking at her.

A blonde so buxom it was a wonder she didn't pitch over from the great weight of her breasts had her hand on his arm as she smiled up at him.

Zoe's clenched fingers wanted to peel him from the other woman's clutches and she watched the scene with sick resignation. Of course Zoe wasn't the only woman Jack was dating. Monogamy, even the fake kind, was anathema to a man like him.

The woman leaned closer to Jack, who to his credit didn't leer down at her cleavage. But then he didn't have to. It would be his for the asking as soon as he made a date with her.

The irresistible smile never left Jack's face as he listened to the woman, but then his head shook. Not up and down, but back and forth. His shrug seemed apologetic.

A moment later, the woman turned away from him, her shoulders rigid, her mouth cast downward as though...

"What's so interesting?"

A face suddenly appeared next to hers. Zoe turned slightly and recognized the teenager who'd tried to sell her a membership the last time she was in the center.

Sparkles dusted the girl's cheekbones along with the rouge she'd applied with a heavy hand. Hot-pink streaks ran through her long, golden-brown hair.

"No one," Zoe denied, then caught her bottom lip in her teeth. "I mean nothing."

The girl peered into the weight room in the general direction in which Zoe had been staring.

"Cool. You were gawking at K-Jack." Zoe tried to utter another denial, but the girl didn't take a breath before she continued. "Don't be embarrassed. I'm glad you're hung up on my brother."

A number of responses pingponged inside Zoe's brain, but the one that came out of her mouth was, "Jack Carter's your brother?"

"Désirée Carter." The girl thrust out a hand. Every one of her nails had a different floral appliqué. "I would have told you I was his sister the other day, but I didn't know you were hot for him."

"I'm not ho—"

"'Course I hadn't seen you looking at him then. I'm really good at figuring out who has the hots for who. 'Cept for Jack 'cause he flirts with everyone. But don't worry about that."

"I'm not wor—"

"Although I can understand you're nervous about this four-date thing." Désirée's voice lowered to a whisper when Zoe's mouth dropped. "I know all about it. But like I said, don't worry. You know you're perfect for each other, and I know you're perfect for each other. Jack will figure it out."

"But we're not per—"

"Not that anyone who looks at you could tell. I mean, Jack usually dates bimbos and you're so classy. But that's why his relationships don't last the way this one will."

Finally, at long last, Désirée stopped talking. Now was Zoe's chance to set her straight. Zoe cleared her throat.

"You forgot to take out one of your hot rollers." Désirée reached around Zoe and unfastened the offending article from the hair at the back of her head. "How'd you do that?"

Zoe remembered her mad scramble to get out of her apartment in time to catch the Metro train that would deposit her at The Lockerroom at the time she said she'd be there. "I must've only combed out the front."

"It still looks pretty." Désirée examined the

roller before she handed it back to Zoe. "Do you think these things would work on my hair?"

Zoe would have preferred to talk about the girl's delusions, but Désirée was whirling to show off her flagpost-straight hair. Zoe unzipped her oversize blue purse, popped the roller inside and gave in to the inevitable.

"Your hair looks great that way, but hot rollers would give you some lift and body. It'd be a nice change."

"Really?" Désirée's eyes lit up. "Maybe you could show me how to do it if I come over to your place."

"Why, sure," Zoe stammered.

"I have next Monday night off. How 'bout then?"

The girl was looking at her with such hope that Zoe didn't have the heart to tell her she didn't want to get any more involved in Jack's life than she already was.

Zoe forced a smile. "That'll be fine."

"Great." Désirée clapped her hands and then grabbed one of Zoe's. "Come on. Let's let Jack know you're here."

"By the way, I wasn't staring at your brother," Zoe said as she trailed the girl in the direction of where Jack was standing over a teenage boy doing bench presses. "I just didn't want to interrupt him when he's busy."

"Yeah, right," Désirée said absently, then sighed. "Isn't he all that?"

Zoe watched Jack bend over to adjust the plates on the weight machine, which caused his biceps to bulge and Zoe's breath to hitch. "Well, yeah," she admitted.

"All the girls at school think so, too."

Zoe stopped in her tracks, causing Désirée to come to a halt, too. "Jack hangs out at your school?"

"Not Jack, silly, Devin Clark. The guy with Jack."

Twenty feet still separated them from the two males, who were absorbed in the boy's workout. It was easy to understand why Désirée was attracted to Devin, who had dark, spiked hair and a slender, athletic build.

"Devin pitches for the high school baseball team. Jack's still a legend there so Devin got it into his head Jack was the guy to help him get better. I'm not sure Jack's convinced of that yet."

Jack stood over the youth, extolling him to work harder. The boy was breathing hard and sweat glistened on his exposed skin area, but he pushed himself to do whatever Jack asked.

"It looks like Jack's doing a good job to me," Zoe said.

"Oh, he is. I just wish Jack would agree to do more than weight training with him. I've seen him work with some young pitchers when he was still playing, and he's great with them.''

Zoe was about to ask Désirée why her brother didn't pursue a job in the sport when the girl tugged so hard on her hand she nearly fell.

''Come on. They're done.''

By the time Zoe had regained her center of gravity, they were a few feet from Jack and Devin. The boy grinned as Jack clapped him on the back and complimented him on a workout well done. Zoe waited for Désirée to insinuate herself into their conversation.

Instead from the girl, she heard… silence. Or possibly the sound of her swallowing really hard.

''I, uh, need to go do some recepting,'' Désirée muttered and took off in the direction of the reception desk like she'd been shot out of a cannon.

Zoe's inclination was to take off after Désirée, but Jack had already spotted her. ''Hey there, Zoe. It's one fine workday that ends with the sight of you waiting for me to finish up.''

He slid her a grin so infectious she couldn't help but return it, darn her weak-willed smile muscles. Not that a simple smile verified Amy's ridiculous suggestion that she couldn't control her response to him.

''Hi, Jack.''

''Zoe, this here's my man Devin, who's going to be one of the finest pitchers Baldwin High has ever seen.'' Devin had been straining his neck, possibly to follow the path of Désirée's abrupt departure, but at the sound of his name he politely turned toward Zoe. "Devin, Zoe O'Neill, my...girlfriend."

Before Zoe could puzzle over the term, the boy's dark liquid eyes seemed to lighten a shade. He transferred his gaze from Zoe to Jack and blurted out, "Your girlfriend? You mean you've been out with her more than three times?"

"Well, not yet," Jack said, looking injured as he put an arm around Zoe. She reminded herself he was putting on a show and commanded her pulse rate to behave. "But we're heading in that direction."

"Oh, yeah. Sure, K-Jack," Devin said, smiling as he told Zoe it was nice to meet her before excusing himself to head for the locker room.

"See what I'm dealing with here?" Jack asked when the teenager was gone. "Nobody in this whole danged place has the slightest faith in me."

Including her, Zoe thought. His right hand was idly playing with her hair and she could feel the warm weight of his arm through her pantsuit jacket but still she shivered.

"He's gone, Jack. You can take your arm away now."

"That's not such a good idea," he said, looking down into her upturned face. "There are lots of people around here we've got to convince and this is sure a pleasing way of doing it."

He smiled at her again, like the incorrigible flirt

he was. Zoe knew he was putting on an act, knew that he'd smile at any female within fifty feet, but she still couldn't stop herself from smiling back. He reached out and touched the corner of her upturned mouth.

"Does that smile mean you're not mad at me?" he asked.

His eyes traveled over her face, looking for what—Zoe didn't know. She searched his eyes, trying to figure out what he'd done that should make her angry.

"Because I've been trying to get in touch with Phil, truly I have. But, darn it, he's been out of town." His finger trailed upward, over her cheek.

"Phil?"

"The owner of The Lockerroom." The rest of his fingers joined the one on her cheek, creating sensory overload.

"Why are you trying to get in touch with him?"

"Don't tell me you've gone and forgot about the *p-h?*" His palm cupped her cheek, making her want to yank on his other hand and put it on another, more sensitive part of her body.

"What p-h? The p-h in Phil?"

The grin on his lips reached his green eyes and Zoe became so lost in them she could have been in the middle of a vast, never-ending meadow.

"I'm talking about the p-h in phit," he said. "The one you blotters want us to get rid of."

Blotters? Zoe dragged her eyes away from Jack's,

focused on a spot on his shoulder and forced herself to think. Oh my gosh. Blotters! With a supreme act of will, she stepped away from him.

"Yes, of course," she said in her most authoritative voice. "I want that p-h taken care of at the earliest possible date."

"Aye aye, sergeant." Jack saluted her, his smile never fading. "But now can I have permission to take a quick shower so we can go on a date?"

"Go," she said, mostly because she wanted him to turn around so she could see if this pair of sweatpants were torn.

Her eyes immediately traveled downward as he walked away, lingering on his mighty fine rear before falling to the spot she hoped would give her a glimpse of bare thigh.

Darn it! If that man didn't rip his pants soon, she'd have to do it for him.

7

___

JACK SWALLOWED A GROAN as he looked over the Kennedy College lecture hall from the top of the staircase.

Fluorescent lights beamed down on a small lectern that backed up into a large blackboard. Rows of identical tiered seats spanned out from the floor-level stage, broken only by regularly spaced aisles.

Nothing about the room or the musher scheduled to talk about the tribulations of guiding a dog-sled team over Alaska's frigid landscape were the least bit sexy.

Which made Jack's spirits sink lower than the below-ground dugouts at the stadium where he'd thrown his final pitch.

"You sure you don't want to go somewhere else?" he asked, examining Zoe's face for any sign of encouragement. "It's not too late to give Serenade a try."

"I've already eaten dinner," Zoe said crisply.

Jack had, too. But he was up for seconds if it would get them away from the auditorium's impersonal atmosphere.

"There's a comedy club around the corner."

Laughter, after all, could be an aphrodisiac. "How 'bout that?"

"I want to stay here." Zoe gave him an uncompromising look before she descended the stairs. There was a dicey moment when her big blue purse bumped an aisle seat, but he caught her elbow before she could go sprawling. The purse, thankfully, hit nothing but seat.

Zoe had her choice of seats because the auditorium was nearly empty, but she kept descending the steps until they reached a spot directly in front of the lectern.

"Aww, Zoe. Why'd you go and pick a seat in the first row? Everyone knows you can't get away with anything all the way down here."

"That's why I picked it," she said primly as she sat down. He slouched into the seat next to her, extending his long legs in front of him. He should look on the bright side. At least he had some leg room.

He waited for Zoe to follow up on what he'd said, but after a few moments it became clear she wasn't going to.

"Don't you want to know what I'd like to get away with?" he asked.

"Not particularly," she said. But he thought, hoped, the flicker in her eyes wasn't disinterest.

He reached across the seat, fingered a strand of her hair and slid it through his thumb and forefinger.

"Good," he said, "because if I told you, you'd accuse me of flirting with you again."

He looked straight into her hazel eyes and her gaze shot away from his, the same way it used to all those years ago in this same kind of classroom.

Even back when they were college students, he'd known she hadn't wanted him this close to her. But that hadn't stopped him from scanning the classroom for a glimpse of her blond hair and plopping down in the chair next to hers.

Something about her had always drawn him, and it wasn't only the pretty picture she made. He liked the way she cocked her head when she was absorbed in a lecture, the way she bit her full lower lip when she was concentrating, the way she softly expelled breath through her nose when something puzzled her.

The way she made his pulse jump.

"Could I have my hair back now?" she asked.

He didn't like the way she had no feelings for him.

He let her hair slide through his fingers, exactly the way he would let Zoe slide out of his life once they'd gone on the four dates. He'd just have to ignore the way she made his hormones hum.

He was a big boy, one who'd dreamed of success but instead tasted the bitter flavor of failure. He wasn't about to reach for Zoe when he knew she'd pull away. He dropped his hands in his lap and leaned back in his seat.

"This should be a very interesting talk," she said after a moment. Her hair smelled like vanilla bean, and he tried not to picture her in the shower, lathering the scented shampoo into her wet hair.

"I agree," he said. "Why, I could hardly get through the day for wondering how the musher kept those sled dogs from getting frostbite."

"Are you being sarcastic?"

He was hardly ever sarcastic but realized she was on the mark, which made him feel a little guilty. While he was forming an apology, he noticed that couples sat to their right and left. He turned around. The auditorium had begun to fill and every last person in the room was part of a twosome.

"Sorry," he said, bringing his attention back to Zoe. "I thought this was a mighty strange place for a date, but looks like I was wrong. Everyone in here seems to be on one."

Zoe braced an elbow on the back of her seat and turned to examine the crowd. "Hmmm. That's strange," she muttered.

"Pardon me, do you have the time?" A round-faced woman sitting behind them asked Zoe. She had curly red hair and a pinched, worried expression.

Zoe told her it was five minutes before the hour, and the woman nudged the bored-looking man next to her. "Why didn't you remind me to call, Edgar? I don't have time to find a pay phone and it's the sitter's first time with Austin."

"How many times do I have to tell you to quit worrying about her?" The man's patience was obviously wearing thin.

"How can I not worry? She's only six months old," the woman replied in a hurt voice. "And she's yours, too."

"You can use my cell phone to call your sitter," Zoe cut in.

"That's not necessary," the man replied at the same time the woman offered a heartfelt thank-you.

"It'll just take me a second to find it," Zoe said, reaching down to where she'd set her purse on the floor. Jack helped her lift it and watched in fascination as she unzipped the monstrosity and dug through its contents.

"I know my phone's in here somewhere," she said, pulling out in turn an electronic organizer, a slim blue wallet and a super-size hairbrush.

"Ever think about decluttering that purse?" Jack asked with a grin as he took the items from her and piled them on his lap.

"You can't declutter a purse," she said, biting her bottom lip as she foraged. "Every item's essential."

A CD of classical music, an empty Tupperware container and a traveling alarm clock later, Zoe finally produced the phone.

The grateful woman quickly punched in a number, fired questions at the baby-sitter and then whispered words of love to six-month-old Austin before handing the phone back to Zoe with a gushing thank-you.

The man rolled his eyes. "Did it ever occur to you, Millie, that we might not have to be here tonight if you paid as much attention to me as you do to that dog."

"Austin's a dog?" Jack asked.

"A Pomeranian," the woman said readily. "Prettiest animal you ever did see."

The man let out a harrumph. "That squishy face of hers is not pretty."

"How do you know? You barely look at her."

"That's because I can't see her under all that hair."

Jack and Zoe shared a laughing glance and turned around in unison. "Wonder what she's doing here," Zoe whispered to him as he helped repack the purse. "Alaskan malamutes pull sleds, not Pomeranians."

"I do believe she thinks Austin can do anything," Jack said, and she laughed, leaning her head toward him and meeting his eyes.

"Put those hands together because I'm here, people!"

At the announcement, a petite dynamo of a woman in a hot-pink suit and dark hair so big it overwhelmed her small, pert face bounded up to the lectern.

"She doesn't look like my idea of a musher," Jack said out of the side of his mouth.

The woman grabbed the microphone from its

holder and paced to the front of the room in her four-inch heels. "I'll skip the foreplay and get right to the good stuff."

She windmilled her right arm like a coach signaling a base runner to head for home. "Who's ready to talk sex?" she shouted, bouncing up and down with glee. The audience erupted into applause.

Zoe leaned close to him, but Jack still had to strain to hear what she was saying above the cacophony. "That can't be Helga Moore."

Jack grinned. "Not unless we're about to get a play-by-play on the intimate habits of the Alaskan Malamute, it isn't."

"In case you haven't guessed, I'm Phoebe Lovejoy," the woman continued in the same chipper voice. She held up a book with a cover as pink as her suit. "And I'm here to talk about my fantastic new book: *Spice Up Your Sex Life.*"

Zoe grabbed her head, which had begun to pound. This couldn't be happening. Beside her, Jack chuckled softly. All around them, people hooted and applauded. She yanked on the sleeve of a woman two seats away to get her attention.

"What happened to Helga Moore and her book about the Iditarod?" she asked, hearing the desperation in her voice.

"That was last week," the woman said quickly, then turned away and gave a great whoop. "Let's get it on," she yelled.

Mortified, Zoe sat back in her seat. She felt Jack's eyes on her and wondered what he must be thinking.

"I didn't plan this," she said. "I must have mixed up the dates."

"Don't apologize," he said, wiggling his eyebrows. "I think I'm gonna enjoy every minute of this."

"We could leave," she said hopefully.

"Not when we're sitting in the first row, we can't. That'd be rude, don't you think?"

Zoe slumped back against her seat, knowing he was right. Some members of the audience were still murmuring excitedly, but the noise had died down enough for Phoebe to continue.

"I'm not only an author, I'm a sex therapist who specializes in working with couples." Phoebe surveyed the room and gave a thumbs-up. "I see you've all brought your partners. Now let's get to work heating this place up!"

Zoe tilted back her head and gazed at the ceiling. Only a higher power could rescue her from the coming hell.

"I bet you're all thinking I'm going to start off by talking about intercourse and orgasm and arousal." Thinking about who was sitting next to her, Zoe felt heat flood her body. Nope, arousal wasn't going to be a problem for her. "But I'm not. Because before you can view your partner as a sexual animal, you have to feel like a sexual animal yourself."

Zoe kept her eyes carefully averted from Jack as Phoebe bounded around the stage like somebody who'd been sitting in front of a computer for too long.

"Do you know that during mating season a lion can have sex up to sixty times a day?" Phoebe asked.

"We knew that," Jack whispered, making Zoe picture the amorous big cats at the zoo.

"Now there's a sexual animal! Let's get in the mood by imitating them." Phoebe laughed. "No. You there in the back, let go of your woman. I meant we should purr, not plunder. Okay, everybody, at the count of three I want you to purr. Or roar if you'd rather. One, two, three..."

The Pomeranian-owning woman behind them sounded like she was barking, but the rest of the audience let out such a collection of roars and purrs that Zoe longed to cover her ears. Or disappear. Disappearance would be better, especially when Phoebe skipped across the stage to stand directly in front of her.

"Purr," the author extolled. "Come on. You can do it. That good-looking man of yours is counting on you to become a sexual animal."

Phoebe pumped her fist and leaned forward, making it clear she wouldn't go away until Zoe purred.

"Purr," Zoe said feebly.

"Louder!" Phoebe shouted.

"Purrrrrrrr," Zoe shouted back just as the room quieted.

"Allll right," Phoebe said. "That's getting in touch with your inner sexual animal. Some of you may require more work on this." She indicated Zoe with a toss of her head. "But not our lioness over there."

Everyone except Zoe laughed.

"Let's move on to the next exercise. Human sexuality involves all the senses but for right now we'll focus on sight. Turn to your partners, people, because this one's called the Look of Love."

Because she didn't want the specter of Phoebe Lovejoy haunting her again, Zoe had no choice but to comply. She expected Jack to be smiling, his eyes dancing. But his lips were slightly parted, those grass-green eyes strangely intense.

He was looking at her as though she were the most important, desirable woman on earth.

"We need to connect with our partners, people," Phoebe bellowed. "This is called intimacy. Look into his or her eyes and remember why you've chosen this person as a lover. Nothing is sexier than looking at another person as though you want them."

Zoe gulped as she gazed at Jack. Her palms started to sweat, her throat went dry, her heart pounded. She didn't need a spice-up-your-sex-life author to teach her how to want. She needed lessons about how *not* to want Jack.

She felt herself move and realized with terrible certainty that she'd shifted closer to Jack and the heat in his eyes. She wanted that warmth, craved the intimacy his gaze promised.

The expression in his eyes didn't so much change as it did brighten. He moved forward, too, incrementally but as surely as her heart was beating.

And then everything went black.

"Sakes alive, your gazes were so hot we blew a fuse," Phoebe said, but Zoe hardly heard her. The room was so dark that she could no longer see Jack, but she knew where he was…knew the exact location of that sexy mouth that was always smiling at her.

Because she couldn't stop herself, she kept moving forward. Slowly, so slowly until her lips came in contact with the soft sweetness of his mouth. She tasted the texture of his lips, breathed in his clean scent, felt his heat pour through her. She kissed the corner of his mouth, the center, the other corner.

And then he was kissing her back, his mouth slanting over hers, his tongue playing with hers. She felt his arms come around her, felt safe in their circle. Her hands crept up his shoulders to his nape where his thick hair nestled against his warm skin.

She'd thought about kissing Jack for so long that a part of her had been sure the fantasy couldn't live up to the reality.

But reality was better…so much better.

She ran her fingers through his hair while his

mouth moved over hers and his heart hammered against hers. And then the world went crazily, blindingly white. For long moments, she and Jack kept kissing. But then she heard a tangible throat clearing that definitely wasn't coming from Jack, and she could no longer ignore the white light.

Puzzled, she drew back and looked into Jack's dazed eyes. Which she could see. Because, she realized, the lights had come on. Phoebe Lovejoy was just a few feet from them. Obviously she was the one who had cleared her throat.

"Well, well, well, would you look at what this couple down in front was doing?" Phoebe said with awe in her voice. "Either my tips are already working or their sex life is already spicy enough!"

JACK RELUCTANTLY TURNED HIS car onto the street where Zoe lived, knowing that the closer he got to her apartment, the sooner the evening would end.

"You sure you don't want to head on over to Dupont Circle for a nightcap? I know a place off the main drag that's not so loud you can't hear your self think."

"I'm sure," she said and inched closer to the passenger-side window.

She'd been shying away from him for more than an hour now, ever since Phoebe Lovejoy had made that crack about their spicy sex life.

She'd scooted to the far side of her seat when Phoebe advocated that couples spend time each day naked so their bodies learned to communicate. And she'd pretended to be asleep when Phoebe assigned audience members to locate three erogenous zones on their partner's body.

She'd been acting, in short, exactly as though that kiss they'd shared in the darkness had never been.

But Jack could still call up the feeling of her soft, warm body in his arms, still relive the wonder of kissing her and the astonishment that she'd kissed him back.

"I've been puzzling on the fact that you seemed to like kissing me back there in the auditorium," he said, hardly realizing he'd said the words aloud until she started.

All of the legitimate spaces in front of her apartment building were taken, so he pulled along the curb in a no-parking zone and left the engine idling. He kept his hands resting on the steering wheel so they wouldn't reach for her.

"I've gotta confess this whole thing's got me as confused as a June bug in January. You've always made it pretty darn clear you didn't want me coming around. So why, I've been wondering, did you respond to me like that?"

Even though the night was dark, the streetlights put out enough of a glow that Jack could clearly make out Zoe's features. Her top teeth were worrying her bottom lip so hard he was afraid she'd draw blood.

"You misunderstood," she said finally, flicking

a glance at him before looking away again. "I was responding to the situation, not to you."

He frowned, not liking the sound of that.

"I mean, come on, Jack. Phoebe Lovejoy's trained to get men and women to respond to each other. That's the whole purpose of the Look of Love."

Jack's frown deepened. "So let me get this straight. You're saying it wouldn't have mattered who was sitting across from you when you did that exercise?"

"Exactly." She sounded relieved. "I'd have responded the same way to any male. Why, I'd probably have kissed Jed Clampett from that old *Beverly Hillbillies* TV show if he'd been there."

The blow to his ego was swift, but Jack strove not to overreact. He'd seen reruns of the show a time or two and Jed was a good-looking son-of-a-gun, but he couldn't stop himself from pointing out the obvious.

"After the kissing, you probably wouldn't have much to talk about considering Jed was dumb as a post."

"That wasn't Jed, that was Jethro. Jed was the old father."

Jack's ego took another battering. He didn't have anything against Jed, but he preferred thinking that Zoe found him more attractive than a hillbilly who'd been a geezer back in the 1960s. But her logic was off somehow.

"If your theory's right, about circumstances leading us to kiss the way we did," he said, "I guess you'd suppose I'd have responded the same way to Granny Clampett."

He could have sworn a shadow of doubt passed over her face, but then she smiled and said brightly, "Exactly. I'm glad we figured that out."

"Now wait a minute there," he said, stroking his chin, "considering that Granny Clampett doesn't quite do it for me, I'm having some trouble with your theory."

"I'm sure it'll make sense if you sleep on it," she said and he thought he detected a nervous quality to her voice underneath the bluster.

"I don't know about that—" Jack began, but she didn't let him finish.

"Can you believe how late it's gotten? I really should be going. Thanks for driving me home, Jack."

Her sentences came out in a rush, giving Jack no chance to point out it was only nine-thirty before her hand was on the door handle.

He reached across her body, covering her right hand with his left so they were face-to-face. "Wait," he said.

He felt her body stiffen, heard her breath catch, saw the trapped look in her hazel eyes. Her voice, when she spoke, was whisper soft.

"I know you have this Southern-gentleman compulsion to walk me to the door, but this is a no-parking zone. I'll give you a little wave when I get to the door.''

''This doesn't have anything to do with parking,'' Jack said, then had to laugh, although that's the last thing he felt like doing. ''Well, I'm gonna have to take that back. 'Cause I've heard what I'm proposing called parking a time or two.''

He watched her swallow and felt the hand under his tremble. Or was that his own hand doing the shaking? He could feel the pulse in his neck jumping, his throat growing thick, his blood running hot.

She ran her tongue over her lips and his blood quickened. ''What exactly are you proposing?'' she asked.

What I've been wanting to propose since the first time I saw you, he thought.

She'd been hurrying along on the University of Maryland campus, carrying a backpack so heavy it made her look like the hunchback of Notre Dame's beautiful, blond sister.

He'd kept walking in the opposite direction, stunned by the rush of emotion that had surged through him at the sight of her, before he'd turned and hurried after her. Except he couldn't find her, hadn't been able to find her in three months of taking the same route at the same time of day.

He thought he'd never see her again until he'd walked into that biology class and there she was, the massive backpack at her feet. He'd wasted no time in making her acquaintance and would have asked her out if she hadn't treated him with chilly indifference.

She wasn't looking at him with indifference now. Her eyes were wide, her pupils dilated, her lips parted.

"I'm proposing an experiment," he said softly, "to see whether it really was circumstances that made us kiss the way we did."

He let go of her hand and switched off the ignition, half expecting her to jump out of the car and hightail it inside.

But she didn't move, possibly didn't even breathe. He shifted sideways, wishing automobile manufacturers hadn't done away with bench seats. Gently he reached out and touched the soft skin on the side of her face, turning her head so she had to look at him.

The air around them felt thick and hot, but still he smiled because looking at her gave him pleasure.

"We don't have to do this," she breathed. "We both know why we responded to each other."

"Is that so?" Jack moved forward as he spoke. Softly he laid his free hand on her shoulder. "Well then, how 'bout you humor me 'cause I'm not so sure I kissed you because some sex therapist wanted me to."

"But—"

"Tell you what," he said, further closing the gap between their mouths. "Why don't you be quiet for the next little while so we can get on with the experiment? We can figure it all out later.''

The moment their lips touched, he was as lost as he'd been in the darkened auditorium. Zoe's lips were softer, her breath sweeter, her skin smoother than any woman he'd ever kissed.

His heart had never pumped this hard, his blood never run this hot, his soul never strained this much to be close to a woman. The way she seemed to be straining to be close to him.

Her hands, which had been in her lap when he'd started this, were at the back of his head, cradling his scalp, as though she were afraid he'd draw back.

As though he would, Jack thought as he deepened the kiss and breathed in the fragrance of her hair, her skin, her heat. What was it about this woman that had captured him five years ago and never let him go?

His body had hardened the instant their mouths met, proving that a man didn't have to get naked to communicate his needs. He moved his mouth to Zoe's neck and nuzzled until she moaned, thinking inanely that he'd found one erogenous zone and that he had two more to go.

Except he didn't want to stop at two. He didn't want to stop at all. She was too sweet, too responsive, too much of exactly what he wanted. And that was precisely the reason he needed to back away from her, the way he thought he wouldn't be able to a moment before.

Because if he didn't back away, they couldn't move forward.

No way would he make love to her for the first time in a car parked in a No Parking zone.

From somewhere he found the strength to detach his mouth from hers, and then he smiled. Zoe's fingers clung to the material at the back of his shirt, her mouth was slightly parted and her eyes were dewy and dazed.

"I guess that proves it then," he said, smoothing the hair back from her flushed face, letting his fingers linger on her smooth skin.

He watched her nod, swallow and blink, as though trying to regain her bearings. "Yes. It does."

He smiled. "That first kiss—" he began.

"—was a fluke," she finished.

The word barely registered. "A fluke?"

His hands fell away and she moved out of touching range, shaking out her fair hair and smoothing her clothes. "That's right. I didn't feel anything this time."

He swallowed past the lump in his throat. "Nothing?"

"Some pressure against my lips but nothing of consequence anywhere else."

Jack's mouth wanted to drop open but he clamped it tight. Had he been so lost in his own sensations that he'd misread Zoe's reaction? By getting ready to confess his longtime fascination with her, had he been on the verge of opening himself to the kind of rejection he'd vowed never to risk again?

It was plenty bad that he hadn't been good enough for baseball. It would be worse if he wasn't good enough for Zoe.

"Whew," she said, theatrically wiping a hand across her brow. "I'm glad we got that experiment out of the way. Wouldn't want to wonder if we were missing out on anything great."

"Nope. Sure wouldn't," Jack heard himself say. "Good thing we didn't feel anything special."

Except what he had felt transcended special and ventured into the territory of extraordinary. But he couldn't let her know that. Not when she was distancing herself from him faster than a home-run ball from the plate.

"G'night, then, Jack. I'll let you know when I decide where we should go on the next date," she said and opened the door. He forced his numb legs into service so that he was out of the car and at her side by the time she shut it.

"You forgot the poster," he said, handing her the rolled-up, life-size likeness of Phoebe Lovejoy that the author had insisted every couple take home.

He expected her to shove the poster back at him, saying she didn't want to be reminded of a kiss she'd claimed was a fluke, but she took it.

"I'll walk you to the door," he said.

She tipped her head, and her hair looked golden

in the streetlight. "You really have this Southern gentleman thing down pat, don't you?"

"Yep, I surely do." He forced himself to smile through the disappointment of her rejection. "That's why I'm gonna leave the kissing up to you next time."

Her lips parted invitingly and he almost kicked himself. What had made him go and say a fool thing like that? Kissing her again shouldn't be on his agenda.

"The experiment proved no more of that will be necessary," she said briskly while she lugged the poster and her big, blue purse up the sidewalk to the security door of her apartment building. She inserted her card. "'Night, Jack."

And just like that, she was gone.

He stood in the darkness, confused by the disappointment that shrouded every inch of him.

He'd embarked on the four-date scheme with Zoe precisely because she wasn't attracted to him. So why did it hurt so much when she confirmed what he already knew?

"Hey, buddy," came a voice out of the darkness. "Is this your car?"

A policeman stood by the door of his car, writing him out a ticket. Jack sighed and went to face his fate. "Yeah, it's mine," he said.

"Can't you read? It's a No Parking zone."

"Yeah," Jack said. "That's the message the lady just gave me, too."

8

ZOE RAN A THICK BRUSH through Désirée's burnished-brown hair and stepped back from the mirror while the girl peered at herself through rounded green eyes that reminded Zoe of Jack.

"How do I look?" she asked anxiously, touching the softly curling strands.

"You look lovely. You're going to wow the boys at school," Zoe said and was unprepared for the way Désirée swiveled on her platform tennis shoes and launched herself into Zoe's arms.

Zoe's back slammed against the bathroom wall and she saw stars, but Désirée didn't seem to notice. "Oh, thank you, thank you. It's way cool to finally have a sister."

"But I'm not—"

"I know I'm jumping the gun. But I hope you'll feel like we're sisters when you and Jack tie the knot."

"But Jack and I aren't getting—"

"Although it'd be cool with me if you lived together for the first couple of years. I know it's tough to feel like you really know a person even when you're as perfect as you and Jack are together."

"I wouldn't say we're—"

"But you don't have to worry about Jack. Talk about a nice guy. He's like the Cadillac of nice guys. If they had a state fair for nice guys, he'd get the blue ribbon."

Zoe laughed, momentarily abandoning her mission to deny that she was marrying Jack. "Did Jack hire you to do his PR?"

"No, but he should. I know you think I'm just saying all this because he's my brother—"

This time Zoe was the one to interrupt. "Actually I think you're saying it because you want me to like your brother."

"You already do like him," Désirée accused.

Because Zoe couldn't deny it, she escaped from the grip the girl had on her shoulders and walked to the kitchen. She was so flustered by Désirée's comment that she mistakenly yanked open the cabinet where she kept plastic containers. Quart-size and pint-size receptacles rained down on her.

"Wow. It sure is messy in there," said Désirée, who was suddenly beside her picking up plastic from the floor. "Hey, don't you organize closets for a living?"

Zoe took the containers from Désirée, shoved them back in the cabinet and shut the door before they could fall out again. "Other people's closets."

Désirée stood in the middle of the room, surveying her surroundings. Zoe removed two glasses from the appropriate cabinet, took a liter bottle out of the refrigerator and poured caffeine-free diet soda for both herself and Désirée. Then she got out the chocolate cake she'd made the night before and cut two thick slices.

"This is a cool room," Désirée said. "I like those pretty flowered drapes and the way you hung those copper pots. But what's with the poster of the woman with the big hair?"

Zoe put the sodas and cake on the kitchen table and sat down before glancing at the wall Désirée indicated and the poster she'd foolishly hung there. It showed Phoebe Lovejoy running in the ocean, kicking up spray with her dainty feet. The caption read, Sexy Is As Sexy Does.

Zoe felt her face flame. "That's just an author Jack and I went to hear the other night."

"So it's like a memento?" Désirée asked, joining Zoe at the table. Zoe gave a reluctant nod. "Whew, that's a relief. Understand I wouldn't normally care if you had pictures of sexy women on your walls, but I have such high hopes for you and my brother."

"You shouldn't."

The girl gulped some soda, took a huge bite of cake and considered Zoe while she chewed. But then she closed her eyes and moaned. "This cake is really great. What brand is it?"

"It didn't come out of a box," Zoe said. "I made it from scratch."

"Then you have to give me the recipe."

"I don't follow a recipe. I throw in a little of this and a little of that. It comes out different every time."

"You need to feed this to Jack," Désirée said, leaning forward and grabbing her arm. "I was watching one of those cable cooking shows the other day and the chef said men love women who can cook."

"Maybe I don't want Jack to love me."

"Of course you do," Désirée said, digging into the cake again. After some more chewing, she said, "You only have two more dates until you break the record. When are you going out again?"

"Eventually." Zoe needed at least one more Jack-free week to rebuild her defenses after that last, soul-shattering kiss. Five days had gone by since she'd seen him and she still hadn't set up their third date. "But they're just dates, Désirée. Not a lifetime commitment."

"I can hope, can't I?" Désirée said, swigging soda to wash down the cake. "He needs to make a commitment. I'm tired of watching him date all those women."

Zoe's stomach pitched to her shoes, making her examine why. Had she actually hoped she was wrong about Jack's womanizing ways? Had she really duped herself into believing that the teary phone call she'd gotten last night from her mother, who'd called her new love at home only to have a woman answer the phone, didn't relate to her? Zoe tried to make her voice sound casual. "There've been that many women?"

"Oh, yeah. Dozens." Désirée rolled her Jack-green eyes. "As soon as I learn someone's name, she's outta there. How am I supposed to bond with anyone when his dating door's revolving like that?"

"I don't know," Zoe said absently. She'd been right all along to guard against falling for Jack. So why did the knowledge sting so much?

"Not that I wanted to bond with anyone until you came around. Most of those women were bimbos with a capital B. Considering Jack graduated with honors, I never could understand what he saw in them."

Zoe thought of Jack coming to class late and trying to bum her notes, of herself shielding her tests so he wouldn't copy from her. "I didn't know Jack made good grades," she mused, but Désirée wasn't listening.

"What Jack needs is an antibimbo. Like you. You are so totally not a bimbo."

"Thank you," Zoe said.

"I feel like I can talk to you about things and that maybe Jack will, too." She paused. "You do realize he's still hung up on baseball, don't you?"

Zoe nodded. She'd seen the clues everywhere, from the way he winced whenever someone mentioned the game to his reluctance to work on pitching with Devin.

"Dad told me once that Jack was a star from the

first time he picked up a ball. That being good at baseball was something he could always count on even when other things weren't going so well."

"What other things?" Zoe asked, eager for this glimpse into the experiences that had helped shape the man Jack Carter was.

"Our Mom was sick with cancer for a long, long time. Dad took off so much work to be with her that he eventually lost his job. Jack was sixteen when she died, but I was only six."

"That must've been hard," Zoe said, wanting to take the girl into her arms.

"It was. I was too young to understand how much I'd lost, but Jack took it hard. Not only was Mom gone, but Dad couldn't manage by himself, especially because he was struggling to build a new career."

"What did you do?"

"Moved north to be close to Dad's family. It was right before Jack's senior year of high school, which must've been the worst possible time for him. But he managed. Dad said it was because he had baseball. The thing he could always depend on having."

Until the Reds released him and he couldn't anymore, Zoe thought.

"Did he tell you about the head coaching job that's open at our old high school?" Désirée asked, then frowned. "No? I hoped he had. He'd be perfect for it, but I can't talk him into applying."

Zoe took a long pull of her soda while she

thought about that. "Baseball burned him once, so he's not going to let it happen twice," she said, voicing her theory aloud.

"That's probably it, which is a bummer because he'd make such a good coach. You've seen him with Devin." The moment Désirée said the boy's name, her concerns about Jack seemed to evaporate. She put her soda down and her elbows on the table. "Remember when you said that thing about wowing the guys at school? Well, there's only one guy I want to wow."

"Devin Clark?"

Désirée let out a gasp. "How'd you guess?"

Zoe smiled. "Intuition."

"Isn't he hot? Those dark eyes of his are like so radical." Désirée put her chin in her hands and got a dreamy look in her eyes. "Anyway, there's a dance coming up and I can't figure out how to get him to ask me."

"Then ask him."

Désirée put her hands on either side of her reddening cheeks and shook her head. "I can't. You saw me, Zoe. I head right for him whenever I see him, but then I lose my nerve. When I try to speak, it's like I'm a mime or something. No sound comes out of my mouth."

"We all feel like that around guys we like, honey," Zoe said, laying a hand on the girl's arm. "It's one of those things we women have to learn to overcome."

SQUEAKY LEANED AGAINST the wall a few feet from the treadmill, his arms crossed over his massive chest. "What were you doing, boss, running away from your troubles?"

"I don't have…any troubles," Jack gasped out, trying to get his breathing back under control.

"How 'bout that rotter you were dating?"

"You mean *blotter*. And what about her?"

"Did you strike her out already?"

"Of course I didn't strike her out," Jack snapped, stepping down from the machine.

"Then why haven't I been seeing her around?"

"She's been busy with work. It doesn't mean we're not seeing each other anymore." It sounded credible, but Jack didn't know if it were true. He'd stopped himself from calling Zoe at least a dozen times since their date seven days ago, and she certainly hadn't contacted him.

He walked across the weight room, eager to get away from the other personal trainer, but Squeaky was having none of it. Jack could tell he was shadowing him by the heavy footsteps behind him.

"I don't think you are seeing her anymore." Squeaky finally said when they reached the reception desk where Désirée leaned with her back against the counter, watching Richard Simmons prance around in short black shorts on the overhead television. "I think you sent this one back to the dugout after two strikes."

"Zoe and I are still dating, Squeaky," Jack said once more.

"Then when are you hooking up again? Huh, K-Jack?"

Jack faltered. From the way Zoe had thoroughly dismissed him on their last date, the possibility existed that he and Zoe would never hook up again.

"Jack's meeting Zoe and her friend downtown for happy hour today," Désirée announced, her eyes never leaving the television screen. "Zoe's there every Wednesday, and of course Jack's always welcome."

"I am?" Jack asked, then caught Squeaky's suspicious look. "I mean, I am."

"What's the name of this place?" Squeaky asked, and Jack was sunk. For some reason Désirée had fabricated a story to get him out of hot water, but she was only sixteen. She couldn't be expected to know of any downtown nightspots.

"Brewster's," she said. "They get there at six-thirty. It's about that now so you better hurry on over, Jack, or they'll think you're not going to show."

He hadn't realized his baby sister was so good at lying. Or that he'd be glad she was.

"I was planning to head on over as soon as I take a shower," Jack said and prayed Désirée wouldn't embellish her lie any further.

"How 'bout I go with you?" Squeaky said. "I'm done for the day, and I'm thirsty."

"I don't think—" Jack began.

"Oh, go on and take him, Jack," Désirée interrupted. "Zoe will be cool with it. She let me talk her into doing my hair at her place, didn't she?"

Zoe had done his sister's hair? Why hadn't Jack known about this? And why had Zoe invited Désirée into her apartment when he'd yet to get past the front door?

"Okay," Jack said and tried to catch Désirée's eye. But she was still looking at the television as though transfixed with the prancing man leading a group of senior citizens in their exercises.

"How do you think somebody like Richard got as far as he did?" she asked. "Do you suppose it's because he went after what he wanted?"

She looked at him then, as though the answer was important, but Jack didn't puzzle over it.

He was already heading for the shower, hoping Zoe would give him a smile instead of an eye-roll when he showed up at Brewster's.

9

ZOE COULD READ THE I-told-you-so gleam in Amy's eyes from clear across the bar, an expression that grew sharper the closer Zoe got to the booth they were sharing.

"Matt can't make it, right?" Amy said even before Zoe could sit down. "He tried to get away but work was too important. He would have called but he was too wrapped up in quid pro quo and liability to worry about the gross negligence of his friends."

"That's not fair, Amy." Zoe settled into the booth, noticing with a frown that she'd put on navy-blue pants instead of the black ones that matched her black-and-white shirt. She really needed to replace that burned-out lightbulb in her bedroom. "He did try to call but you know how bad cell phone reception is in a place like this. We'll be here for him next week, but if he blows off this job his client won't be."

"I know," Amy said, running a hand over her untamed hair, "but the way he's so focused on making money drives me nuts. He should draw the line somewhere. He couldn't make it last week, either, remember?"

"Neither could I," Zoe said, because that had been the evening she'd spent with Jack. Had it really been only a week ago? It seemed so much longer since she'd seen him, touched him, kissed him... She forced herself to cut off the thought. "Look at it this way. Without Matt here, we can get in some girl talk."

Amy angled her body forward, and her dark eyes sparkled. "You mean you want to talk about Jack Carter?"

"No," Zoe denied. Talking about him would only make not thinking about him harder. "I want to talk about...*your* OWGA. We never got a chance to do that. Pierre. Wasn't that his name?"

"Why don't you want to talk about Jack? You went out with him again and didn't tell me, didn't you?" Amy asked, peering at her as though she could see into her mind. "Where'd you go?"

To hear a pushy sex therapist tell us our sex life was on the right track, she thought. "Nowhere sexy. I mean, nowhere special."

Amy grinned. "What non-sexy place are you going to next time?"

"There's not going to be a next time."

The moment she blurted it out, Zoe knew she'd stumbled across the solution to her problem. It would be disastrous if Jack found out she'd been hiding behind BLOT but even worse if he discovered the extent of her attraction to him.

Even if Jack wasn't the womanizer she knew him

to be, she couldn't get involved with him. She could support herself in relative comfort but she had years yet before she'd feel financially secure enough to embark on a serious relationship.

Once she did, she planned to proceed step by careful step. Meet a nice man. Date him for at least two years. Settle in for a long engagement to make sure they were suitable for each other. Then on to a lasting marriage.

"I've heard you say there wouldn't be a next time with Jack before," Amy pointed out.

Zoe bit her lip. "I mean it this time."

"What's the matter? Did he slobber when he kissed you?"

"Of course he didn't…" Zoe stopped and glared at Amy. "You tricked me, didn't you?"

"I knew it. I knew he'd kissed you." Amy beamed. "So I gather it was fantastic?"

"So what if it was? It's over between us."

"Oh, come on, Zoe. You admit he's your OWGA. You admit his kisses are incredible. How can you expect me to believe you aren't going to see him again?"

"Because I'm not," Zoe said firmly.

"Hey there, darlin'. Sorry I'm late."

Zoe's head swiveled at the familiar, drawling voice and would have keeled over if she hadn't been sitting down. Jack Carter was coming toward her as though out of one of her dreams.

His dark hair wasn't quite dry, as if he'd recently

showered, and he was wearing a casual short-sleeved shirt in a dark green that hugged his pecs and accentuated his eyes. His jeans were the snug, faded kind he'd worn in college.

She wanted to know what he'd meant by his comment, but her throat went so dry she couldn't ask. He lowered himself into her side of the booth, propelling her into action.

But before she could move too far away, he anchored her to him by hooking an arm around her shoulders. Then he dropped a light, devastating kiss on her lips.

As though they were a couple. As though she weren't the latest in the flock of women who poured in and out of his life like rain. She stared at him in aroused shock.

"I'd have gotten here sooner, but a client came in for some extra weight work at the last minute," he said as if she knew what he was talking about. Heck, she didn't even know how he'd found her.

With the hand that wasn't gently caressing her shoulder, Jack gestured at the man getting into the booth beside Amy. Oh, no. The personal trainer with the a cappella voice who had it in for BLOT. How had she missed him?

"You remember Squeaky Hogan, don't you, sweetheart?"

Squeaky's small eyes flared as he gave a high-pitched grunt in acknowledgment. Zoe murmured a greeting as Jack turned the full force of his charm on Amy.

"It's Amy Donatelli, right?" He held out one of the long-fingered, well-formed hands Zoe had been dreaming about touching her. "You probably don't remember me. I'm Jack Carter."

Amy slanted Zoe a questioning look before taking Jack's hand and returning his smile. She was already charmed, but what woman wouldn't be? "I'm surprised you remember me."

"There's not much I don't remember about my girl here." As he called her his, he gave Zoe's shoulder an affectionate squeeze. It felt like he was compressing her heart. "Zoe introduced us at the campus bookstore right after she knocked over a display of dictionaries. I got that right, didn't I, hon?"

Hon? Sweetheart? Darlin'? The endearments should have offended Zoe but instead gave her a traitorous thrill. The same type of thrill she'd gotten years ago when she'd tried to hustle Amy out of the bookstore after spotting Jack.

She hadn't spotted the dictionaries, which had tumbled down in an avalanche and rendered escape impossible.

"You *are* right," Amy said. "My toe throbbed for a week after getting crushed by Webster's Third."

Squeaky guffawed. "Aw, get outta here, K-Jack.

You can't expect me to believe you and the rotter had a thing going all the way back in college.''

Zoe stomach pitched as Jack's motivation in showing up at Brewster's became as transparent as the pale ale in her mug. Jack was putting on a show for Squeaky, all in the name of getting rid of that stupid nickname.

Zoe could have kicked herself for believing, even for a second, that his interest had been genuine. And, worse, for hoping it was.

"Rotter?" Amy slanted an unfriendly look at Squeaky. "Why'd you call my friend a rotter?"

"He meant a blotter," Jack cut in.

"What's a blotter?" Amy asked.

"Do you mean you don't know about Zoe's work with Better Linguists of Tomorrow?" Jack asked.

Amy, drat her, burst into peals of laughter. "Get outta here. I doubt she even knows how to spell linguists.''

Zoe gulped as all eyes turned toward her, aware she had to dredge up yet another cover story. "Amy's laughing because I've never been very good at spelling.''

"Or grammar," Amy pointed out. "A grammarian she ain't.''

"That's why I didn't tell her I was a member of BLOT," Zoe continued, absurdly glad she wasn't being entirely dishonest. She'd felt so miserable about lying that she'd joined BLOT and had been refusing missions to fight misspelling ever since.

Amy's dark eyebrows shot up. "But how can you crusade against bad spelling when you can't recognize it?"

"I can't always recognize evil either and it offends me." Zoe winced. Now she not only sounded like a good spelling zealot, but a hypocritical one to boot.

Jack ran his hand up and down her arm, giving her goose bumps and turning her brain to mush. "I'm wondering how you know which misspellers to target?"

"My pocket dictionary," Zoe declared, indicating her large purse, which was checkered today to match her outfit. "I carry one around to check if words are spelled wrong."

"Of all the highfalutin' things to do—" Squeaky began but Amy's exclamation drowned out the rest of what he was going to say.

"You've got to be kidding." Amy extended a hand across the table. "Let me see the dictionary."

Zoe tossed her head the way she'd seen Amy do countless times and deliberately ignored the request. She'd packed so much stuff in her purse it might actually contain a dictionary, but she couldn't chance it.

"It doesn't matter whether we're seven or seventy," Zoe said with feigned fervor. "We must constantly strive to better our spelling."

Squeaky glowered at her. "I don't care what you

do, but you should leave the rest of us bad spellers alone.''

"Hey," Amy said and shook a finger at him. "Don't you pick on her."

Squeaky looked chagrined. "She's the one who's picking on people who can't spell. I just think she should stop."

"She can't. She's proactive," Jack said, squeezing her shoulder again and gazing at her in an imitation of a besotted suitor. Her heart *ka-thumped*. His acting was so good he should try his luck in Hollywood. "That's why she's the gal for me."

Jack's touch was making Zoe's pulse rate zing so much she feared heart failure so she tried to pull away. He applied slight pressure, keeping her firmly within his grasp. *Careful,* his eyes said. *Don't give away the charade.*

Amy put her elbows on the table and gazed from Jack to Zoe and back again. "This is great. I always knew you two were perfect for each other. So when did you figure it out, Jack?"

Jack cast another warm glance at Zoe. "Probably when we went to hear Phoebe Lovejoy."

"The sex goddess?" If Amy's ears hadn't been covered by her fall of hair, they would have stood at attention. "Didn't she write a best-selling book about free love?"

"She's a sex therapist," Zoe corrected. "And her book's about how couples can keep their sex lives interesting."

"Zoe took me to hear her talk last week," Jack said before Zoe could explain about the mix-up with the Iditarod.

Amy sent Zoe a pointed look. "So that's where you went on your nonsexy date?"

"You didn't think it was sexy?" Jack frowned as he regarded Zoe, who was having a hard time fading into the background when his arm wouldn't let her. "I'd have to say I disagree. Especially about the part of the date when the lights went out."

Mortification set so deep that Zoe thought she'd never be able to wade out of it.

"I don't get it," Squeaky said to Jack. "If you're getting along so well, how come you needed to hear this sex-talk lady?"

"Sex therapist," Zoe said. "She's a sex therapist."

"Apparently we didn't need to." Jack slanted a bad-boy smile at Zoe. "She said it looked like we were getting along just fine, didn't she, darlin'?"

"What exactly were you doing when she said this?" asked Amy, who never missed a thing.

"Jack, would you like to dance?" Zoe interrupted with a tinge of desperation in her voice. He gazed around the room.

"I surely would, sweetheart, but this place is missing a dance floor. I'd suggest dancing in the aisles but it's so crowded in here that wouldn't go over too well."

Zoe swallowed while she tried to think of a credible reason to get him away from the table. The tune filling the bar provided one. "Then help me pick out some new songs. Sounds like someone's stuck in the seventies."

Jack cocked his head, obviously trying to figure out the tune. Zoe watched recognition dawn on his face, probably because of the oft-repeated do-ya-think-I'm-sexy line. *Yes*, she wanted to answer.

"You don't like the song?" Jack asked Zoe.

Zoe shook her head, refusing to let him know how sexy she found him. "Have you ever heard of stuck-song syndrome? That title's one of the songs that gets stuck in your head. The only way to get it out is to play another song."

"Then by all means, darlin'," Jack said as he got out of the booth, "let's play one."

As they navigated through the crowd, the song got around to the if-you-want-my-body lyrics. Zoe had a vivid mental picture of the magnificent way Jack would look unclothed.

Yes, she thought helplessly. *She did want his body.*

JACK'S HAND RESTED protectively at the small of Zoe's back as they winded their way through the bar. The building was roughly the shape of an L and the jukebox was around the corner and out of the sight line of their booth.

Despite the show they were putting on for Squeaky, Jack had the impression Zoe would have jerked away if she'd had jerking room. But too many people crowded the aisles for that.

She turned to face him when they reached the jukebox, and he couldn't figure out what was going on in her eyes. The same way he couldn't tell what had been in their depths after he kissed her.

"What are you doing here?" she asked abruptly.

"Did I mention you look darn pretty in red? The color brings out the flush in your cheeks."

He reached a hand up to touch the reddish spots on her cheeks, not sure why he was flirting with her. She probably thought it was because he flirted with everybody, but that wasn't it.

Every time he told himself he was glad she didn't want a real relationship, something inside him rebelled. Considering how he felt about rejection, it was darn confusing.

She batted his hand away, but it seemed to take her an effort to do it. Unless, once again, he were indulging in wishful thinking.

"If there's color in my face, it's because I'm angry," she said. But she didn't sound angry. She sounded...breathless. "How did you know I'd be here?"

"Don't tell me you haven't figured out my sister has a mouth like a kitchen faucet turned on full blast? She told me. If she was over at your place the other day, she must've told you she thinks we're LOALs."

"LOOLs?"

"LOALs. Rhymes with bowls, not pools."

"What are LOALs?"

Oops, Jack thought, and dodged the question. "I thought you wanted to know what I was doing here."

For a moment, he thought she might argue but then she let out a breath that sounded like a huff. "I do want to know."

He leaned closer and couldn't help smiling in pleasure as he breathed in the scent of her shampoo and subtle, fruity perfume. "I'm joining my girl and her friend after work for a couple of drinks."

"But I'm not your girl." This time her dismay was hard to miss. So was her determination.

"You're supposed to be my girl for two more dates. That's the agreement."

"I didn't agree to pretend I was crazy about you in front of your friends!"

His breath whooshed out on a sigh, because he didn't want her to pretend, either. He wanted it to be true. To keep from reaching for her again, he rested a hand on the jukebox, which was warm to the touch.

"I apologize," he said. "I didn't mean to bring Squeaky, but he was quizzing me on when we were getting together again. The next thing I knew, he was coming with me to Brewster's."

She pressed her lips together, lowered her eyes, lifted them. "This isn't working out, Jack."

Although he'd braced himself for her words, they

still hit harder than a heavyweight boxing champion. They were also unacceptable. "Oh, no. You can't back out now. We have a deal."

Her eyes were huge and imploring as she gazed up at him. "But this playacting is more than I can handle."

"Then let me handle it." He smoothed out the frown lines at the edge of her mouth. "We need to be alone, is all. Then we wouldn't have to playact. How 'bout you go out to dinner with me tomorrow night at Serenade?"

Even as he issued the invitation, Jack realized he was flirting with her again. What would it take to get him to stop? *I'm Not Interested, Jack* tattooed on her forehead?

"I'm not interested in going out with you again, Jack."

He should leave it at that and find some other woman to help him counteract the K-Jack nickname, but Jack couldn't do it. Not when he had the means to get Zoe to go on two more dates with him.

"If you don't date me again, I'll see that Phil doesn't change the p-h. I don't suppose BLOT would look too kindly on that."

Ah, jeez. Now he was resorting to blackmail to get his way. A way he was sure he shouldn't want in the first place. What kind of a man was he? She looked crestfallen, prompting him to consider compromise.

"Tell you what. We've been on half the dates,

so maybe I could talk Phil into dropping one of the letters. Either the p or the h. Your choice.''

She frowned. ''But then the sign would read either Get Physically Pit, which makes no sense. Or Get Physically Hit, which is mean.''

And dumb. Really, really dumb. But Jack couldn't very well admit that now. He shrugged. ''Then I guess you're gonna have to go on those last two dates with me after all.''

Jack's heart pounded so hard as he waited for her answer that he couldn't distinguish between his heartbeats and the drum beat on the jukebox song.

''Okay,'' she finally said, causing triumph to surge inside him, ''but remember we agreed I get to choose where we go.''

''Where are we going?'' he asked, pressing his advantage.

She pursed her lips and seemed to think for a long time before she said, ''How about an Octoberfest celebration?''

''It's September, Zoe,'' he said. ''If we don't go somewhere by this weekend, Squeaky's gonna get suspicious again.''

''I've got it.'' She genuinely smiled for the first time since he and Squeaky had walked into the bar, lifting his spirits. Maybe she didn't consider dating him again so distasteful after all. ''One of the Realtors I'm working with gave me a pair of complimentary tickets to Monticello.''

Jack barely stopped himself from groaning.

"Isn't that where elementary school kids go on field trips?"

"Not George Washington's Monticello. The Monticello Speedway."

Normally, a day at the races would appeal to Jack. But not now. Not when he was fairly certain Zoe had chosen the venue to ram home the message that romance wouldn't be part of this date.

"Do you really want to sit at a track and watch cars go 'round and 'round?" he asked, trying to sound discouraging.

"Not cars. School buses."

She looked so pleased about the buses that Jack felt as though he'd been hit by one. He summoned a smile. "School buses. Sounds great."

"I'm glad that's settled," she said, not looking quite as miserable as before. "I should be getting back to Amy. She's terribly loyal. If Squeaky calls me a rotter again, she might slug him."

"Squeaky can take care of himself until we pick out those songs you were talking about."

"I never wanted to pick out songs," she confessed. "That was an excuse to get you alone."

"You don't need an excuse," he said softly, looking deeply into her eyes. She took a step backward, then another, before she wrenched her gaze from his and practically sprinted away.

He rapped the jukebox with the heel of his hand, which caused it to abruptly switch to a song about staying at the Y.M.C.A. The jukebox, ironically, seemed to be full of songs that stuck in your head. The way he was stuck on Zoe. Who wasn't stuck on him.

A few minutes later, after making his song selections, he walked back to the booth to find it empty except for Amy.

"Squeaky had to leave," she told him when he sat down. "He had choir practice at his church. He says if you don't show up for practice, you don't sing at the next service."

Jack imagined that Squeaky's absence from choir practice would probably be the answer to a congregation's prayers, but he didn't feel like discussing Squeaky. "Where's Zoe?"

"She had to make a phone call. Something about verifying an appointment for tomorrow before she forgets."

"Zoe never forgets anything," Jack said.

Amy laughed. "Are you kidding? She only painted half her fingernails again. And she forgot to put on a belt. She's great at being a professional organizer but organization doesn't extend to her personal life."

Jack thought about Zoe confusing the dates in the series of author lectures and foraging through the items in her giant, untidy purse. Amy was right. Zoe wasn't quite as together as she liked to pretend, or as he'd originally believed her to be, which was only one of the reasons he found her so compelling.

"I think Zoe's perfect just the way she is." He

hadn't meant to say the words aloud, but the truth had a way of making itself known.

"So do I." Amy smiled at him and laid a hand on his arm. "You're a nice guy, Jack Carter. No wonder Zoe hasn't been able to get you out of her mind all these years."

Jack's heart stopped in midthump. "What did you say?"

Amy examined his face, which surely mirrored his shock. Then she grimaced and covered her mouth with a hand. "Nothing. I said nothing."

"Yeah, you did." His voice held wonder. "Something about Zoe having had a thing for me for years."

Amy's hand dropped, revealing the misery in her face. "Please tell me you already knew."

"I didn't know." Jack shook his head, trying to make sense of it. Were they really talking about the woman who'd once asked their college professor to assign seats so she wouldn't have to sit next to him? "Do you think I should ask her about it?"

Amy leveled him with a frosty look. "I like you, Jack. But if Zoe finds out I let on that you were her OWGA, I'll have to hurt you."

"Her OWGA? What's that?"

Amy covered her mouth again. "I didn't say that, either."

"You might as well tell me what it is," Jack said and pressed his advantage. "You wouldn't want me to ask Zoe."

Amy's lips flattened. "You wouldn't do that. You're too nice of a guy."

"You're right, I wouldn't," he admitted. "And that's why you're gonna tell me what an OWGA is."

"All right, all right, but I'm only telling you because I know you care about Zoe," she said finally. "OWGA stands for One Who Got Away.

"You're the man from Zoe's past she can't forget."

10

JACK LET ZOE PRECEDE HIM up the creaky wooden
bleachers that bracketed one side of the oval race
track. He noticed that only her lips were smiling as
she sat down, folded her hands in her lap and announced, "This should be fun."

Such horror filled her eyes that she could have
been watching zombies resurrect themselves from
the dead instead of the prelude to a school-bus race.

A chain-link fence stretching ten feet into the sky
separated the bleachers from the dirt track where a
few buses took the last of their practice laps. Exhaust fumes scented the air. An announcer broadcast
from a loudspeaker but the roar of the buses
drowned him out.

Zoe lifted the corners of her mouth into a smile
more false than the one Jack gave the managers who
came to the mound to yank him from baseball
games.

A night at the bus races, he decided, was pretty
much Zoe's idea of hell on earth.

"We can go somewhere else if you're not in the
mood for a bus race," he offered.

"Oh, no." Her pretend smile grew to unnatural

proportions as she placed a hand over her heart. "I love a good race. Of course I want to stay."

He let his gaze linger on her rosy lips. "I'm all for giving you what you want. Just give me a holler whenever something strikes your fancy."

"Okay," she said, missing his innuendo as her eyes darted around faster than the moths hovering around the overhead lights. Her posture was vintage touch-me-not and she was acting like she'd rather be anywhere but with him.

Her behavior caused Jack to wonder all over again whether Amy had been wrong about Zoe having a hankering for him. She certainly hadn't acted like she was pining for him during the hour drive from her D.C. apartment. She'd spent more time watching the Northern Virginia countryside roll by than she had responding to his flirting.

She tilted her chin, pointed those eyes skyward, and he looked up, too. "Oh, great," he heard her mutter while he was appreciating the golden beauty of a full moon.

Her chin slanted downward in the rough direction of her lap. She let out a little gasp, raised her hand and inspected the fluorescent-green letters the bleached blonde at the gate had stamped onto the back of it.

"What kind of sick thing is this to brand somebody with?" she asked.

The last of the buses had disappeared into the pits in preparation for their grand entrance, lowering the noise level considerably so that her shocked voice was clearly audible.

Puzzled, Jack took her hand and examined the letters. "It says 'six,' same as mine. Probably because Saturday is the sixth day of the week. What did you think it said?"

She was silent, but her face flooded with color, which was an answer in itself. She'd thought it said sex. He smiled, long and slow. Amy's claim that he was her OWGA seemed more likely if she had sex on the brain.

"You really aren't much of a speller, are you?" he teased.

"The i looked like an e," she mumbled. She was so adorably embarrassed that he laughed, pulled her to him with one arm and kissed the top of her head.

He caught the exasperation in the glance she sent him. "Do you have to keep touching me?"

He pondered that for a moment. Whenever she was in the vicinity, he had to admit to a nearly insatiable urge to reach for her. He gave into it, taking her hand in his, pulling it to his lips and kissing the backs of her very pretty knuckles.

"I don't suppose I have to keep touching you, but I want to," he said in a low voice and watched her eyes darken.

"What if it's not what I want?"

"Now if you didn't want me touching you, you wouldn't let me, would you?"

She frowned, staring down at their entwined

hands. He expected her to yank her hand from his grasp, the way a woman who'd never been attracted to him would. But instead of a yank, he got a shiver.

His eyebrows rose as he took note of her pretty pink pullover, which was made of such thin cotton it wouldn't have kept an Eskimo warm. "You cold?"

She shrugged. "I forgot my jacket."

Not one to pass up an opportunity, Jack shifted until his left side pressed against her right and draped an arm around her shoulders. "I didn't bring a jacket either, but I do have some body heat I can share."

He waited a beat, expecting her to shy away, but she stayed still. He turned to look at her, trying to read her expression in the glow of the moon, trying to figure out why she was staying put.

"Suppose you tell me who we're rooting for," he said. "I've got a favorite NASCAR driver, but the last bus driver I knew banished me for throwing spitballs."

"Are you trying to distract me from the fact that your arm is still around me?" Before he could admit he was guilty as charged, she continued. "Because I know it's still around me. I wouldn't let it stay there if you weren't right about the body heat."

So it was his body heat she wanted? He'd have to think on that for a while, specifically whether a woman had to be attracted to a man to crave his heat or whether any old heat would do.

He wasn't going to come up with a definitive answer any time soon, so he gave up puzzling over it. "I'm still waiting to hear what big, bad bus driver we're cheering for."

"Big and bad?" She laughed, and he felt her relax against him. "Marty's small and slight, the kind of guy who fades into the background. He jumped a full foot in the air when I came up behind him the other day. You'd never think he raced buses."

"Maybe it's not that hard."

"According to Marty, it is. They do a couple six-lap qualifying heats to whittle down the field and then a twenty-lap main event."

He made his eyebrows dance. "I can't wait."

A tremendous roar sounded off track, signaling he wouldn't have to wait long.

"The buses are coming, the buses are coming," he said into her ear, and she giggled.

And then they came. Although the field included the familiar yellow-and-black vehicles used to transport students nationwide, other buses were more colorful. There was a tritone bus in shades of black, red and yellow; a bright blue bus and a "bat bus" upon which somebody had painted the legendary comic-book superhero.

The seats had been gutted from all of the buses, the drivers wore crash helmets and most of the vehicles had air where their back panels should have been.

"This is wild." The noise had picked up again

so Jack had to speak directly into Zoe's ear. "The front end is mostly missing off that black bus, and the roof of that yellow bus over there is bashed in."

She had to move her mouth close to his ear to answer, and her breath was warm in contrast to the cool, night air. "With so many buses on the track, Marty says crashes are inevitable."

"Which bus is Marty's?"

"He said his is orange—oh, my gosh. There it is."

Bursting out of the pit area was the only orange bus in the field, except orange seemed a pale description of its actual color. Even though numerous collisions had robbed the bus of a good deal of paint, the overwhelming impression was of a bright, fluorescent tangerine. Yellow and red flames blazed down its banged-up sides.

Along the length of the bus, in garish lime letters, were the words, The Krazy Kid.

All around them, people jumped to their feet, their shouts adding to the general cacophony. "Krazy, Krazy, Krazy," they chanted in unison.

"I thought you said this guy faded into the background," Jack said, grinning at her expression of disbelief. He wondered if it was because Marty was a celebrity or because he couldn't spell any better than she could. Marty had so many fans that, if Zoe turned BLOT against him, they'd probably revolt.

"Go crazy for the Kid!" The woman in front of them bellowed while raising both arms. Jack stood so he could see what was happening on the track and Zoe followed suit.

Marty zoomed his bus around the outermost ring of the track, passing up five or six other buses in the process. Never mind that the race hadn't started yet.

"Your crazy friend's a celebrity," Jack shouted down at her. Remarkably, the woman in front of them heard him. She turned, a rapt expression on her round, freckled face. Her tangerine sweatshirt read, Krazy 4 U.

"You know The Kid?" she shouted at Zoe with a booming voice. If she were the track announcer, she might not need a microphone. "He's *so* brave."

Zoe's gaze flew to his. Jack raised his eyebrows to silently signal her not to tell the woman that Marty jumped at shadows. Why ruin the Kid's mystique?

"He takes so many risks he puts Evel Knievel to shame," Zoe yelled back, but Jack could barely make out what she was saying.

The woman gasped. "You're the one who should be ashamed. The Kid's not evil!"

Zoe's head shook like a panicked metronome. "I didn't say he was evil. I said he was like Evel, the motorcycle daredevil."

"How dare you." The woman's face turned a color to match her red hair. "The Kid's not a devil."

"I said a daredevil," Zoe shouted.

"You're daring me?" She bounced on the soles of her feet and raised her fists. Her eyes narrowed to slits, alarming Jack. The redhead had at least three inches and fifty pounds on Zoe. "Wanna take this behind the bleachers?"

"How 'bout I take her to sit someplace else?" Jack angled his body so he was between Zoe and the redhead, leaned down and said the first thing that came to mind to pacify the woman.

Relief poured through him when she smiled. She sent another glare Zoe's way, but turned back to the track without another word.

"Let's go," Jack said, enfolding Zoe's hand in a secure grip and leading her a section over and a dozen rows higher.

By the time they sat down again, the starter had waved the green flag to signal the start of the heat. The wooden platform he stood on seemed to shake as the buses barreled past it, and he held fast to his ear-protection gear.

"What did you say to that woman?" Zoe asked, moving closer to Jack. He wondered if it was because of his body heat, the protection he offered from the crazy redhead or the claim Amy had made.

"I told her she didn't have to worry about you and Marty, because you're mine."

"I am not." Zoe made an outraged noise and smacked him on the arm, but the blow wasn't hard. He couldn't help himself. He laughed.

"Hey, be grateful," he said, slinging his arm

around her again. "I'm the guy who rescued you from the wrath of the redhead."

Again Jack expected Zoe to pull away, but again she stayed exactly where she was. Exactly where he wanted her. Exactly where he was starting to think she wanted to be.

Down on the oval track, Marty was a bus length behind two of the other drivers, who took the laps side by side. The lead buses neared a turn and Marty must've stamped down on his gas pedal, because his tangerine bus gained on them.

"He's gonna try to go between them," Jack yelled, leaping to his feet with the excited crowd.

"There's no room," Zoe said but the chant of the crowd swallowed her cry.

"Krazy, Krazy, Krazy."

Marty drove straight for a narrow space between the two lead buses until they were three abreast. The eerie scrape of metal on metal resonated as the trio of buses careened around the turn with no more than a hand's width between any two of them. Exhaust fumes spewed into the night sky while engines emitted mighty roars.

"They can't keep this up," Jack shouted.

The back wheels on all three of the buses seemed to let go at once. The Bat Bus veered toward the plywood wall that lined a length of the chain-link fence.

"He's going to crash," Zoe yelled, but the rest of the crowd just screamed.

The Bat Bus slammed into the wall with a thud while the driver of the tricolored bus stood on his brakes. Marty's tangerine bus bumped the tricolored bus hard. Marty fishtailed but must have kept his pedal to the metal because he squirted through an empty space. A second later, the tricolored bus slid across the track directly into the Bat Bus.

Metal crunched metal, producing a deafening roar. Well out of the path of danger, Marty shot comfortably to the lead. Chaos reigned behind him. The three buses that had been trailing the field were going too fast to avoid a five-bus pileup.

"Krazy, Krazy, Krazy," the crowd exalted as the bangs and clangs of the crash filled the air.

The starter raised a red flag, stopping the race. Marty and the only other driver on the track who hadn't been involved in the pileup slowed their buses to a halt.

As sirens blared, Jack watched the drivers of the five wrecked buses climb out of their vehicles. A fire truck and ambulance arrived on the scene while workers picked up pieces of bus off the track.

"I know The Kid's a celebrity, but you better stick with me," Jack said into Zoe's ear. "If Marty drives as crazy as that all the time, he's not long for this earth."

Zoe seemed to be in post-race shock, so he put an arm around her waist and pulled her to him. He heard her soft gasp, which seemed to indicate she was as affected by him as she had been by the commotion down on the track.

He almost snapped his fingers at the simplicity of it all. Physical proximity was the key to unlocking the mystery of whether he was indeed her OWGA.

Before the night was over, he vowed, he was going to test his new theory.

The question remained about what kind of smack Zoe would give him for his troubles.

11

"KRAZY, KRAZY, KRAZY."

The chants of the crowd followed them as they left the bleacher area and headed for the pits, where Marty had invited them to stop by and say hello. The race fans were celebrating Marty's win in the feature race, but they could well have been directing the comment at Zoe.

Why else had she spent most of the night snuggled with Jack under a garish souvenir blanket decorated with tiny school buses? And why was she letting him hold her hand as they weaved through the crowd departing the speedway?

She was crazy, all right.

"I guess being crazy has its advantages." Jack's thumb absently rubbed her palm, igniting pockets of pleasure inside Zoe. "After the way Marty squirted through those buses in the heat, nobody would get within two bus lengths of him in the feature race."

"I'll tell you who was crazier," Zoe said, thinking back on the silly games the announcer had played during breaks. "That guy who won the most-tattoos contest by stripping down to his boxers to prove he had twelve of them.''

"Thirteen if you take his word about having a moon in a place the sun don't shine." Jack's face brightened as he chuckled. "But I don't think he was crazy. He got a hot dog and a soda out of the deal. I'd strip for you for free."

The thought of Jack's magnificent body bared for her viewing pleasure was so appealing that Zoe nearly took him up on his offer. But then she noticed the glint in his eyes.

"You're flirting with me again," she accused, feeling much too warm under the blanket that was now draped around her like a cloak.

"That depends on your definition of flirting." Jack brought her hand to his mouth and kissed the back of it. "If you think a flirt doesn't mean what he says, then I'd have to argue that I'm not flirting with you. 'Cause I'm telling the absolute truth."

She swallowed the nervous lump that rose in her throat and pretended to give all her attention to the security guard who granted them admittance to the pit area. But she was aware of Jack's hot, green gaze even as they located Marty by following the tangerine glow of his bus.

"Great race, Marty," Jack said after Zoe made the introductions, pumping the smaller man's hand enthusiastically.

Zoe read panic in the look Marty sent her as his already pale face whitened. He was half Jack's size, a balding man in his forties with spindly arms and legs and a retiring personality.

"I need to go." Marty took a quick step backward as he rubbed the hand Jack had released, mumbling something about a victory party. "Feel free to look around."

Marty disappeared into the darkness, leaving them alone in the shadow of the bus.

Jack frowned. "Was it something I said?"

"Marty's just shy," Zoe said, reaching out to give him a comforting pat on his arm. Awareness zapped her and she drew back her hand, making a show of examining the bus. The moonlight illuminated metal shining through the paint as well as a generous collection of dents. "He's also crazy as a loon to get in this thing and race it."

Jack hoisted himself onto the first step of the bus and braced his hand on the rearview mirror, which shifted a couple of inches. He offered his other hand to her. "Are you coming?"

"I'm not sure it's safe," she whispered, but she wasn't referring to the structural soundness of the bus. One side of his mouth kicked up, as though he knew that.

"Come on," Jack cajoled, his hand still outstretched. "What could happen?"

I could have my way with you, Zoe thought with a little shiver of unease. But she couldn't resist temptation and let him help her into the bus, which was little more than a metal shell with a driver's seat.

The night air drifted through spaces where windows had once been and blew through the gaping hole that had been an emergency exit door. Their shoes made eerie metallic noises as they walked the length of the bus.

"I always dreamed of getting a girl like you in the back of a bus." A teasing gleam entered Jack's eyes as he sat down and dangled his feet out the open back. "Come sit beside me."

Jack held out his hand and tried not to sigh with relief when she took it. She lowered her long limbs and nestled against him the way a woman didn't nestle unless she was attracted to a man. He put his arm around her and together they gazed at the stars twinkling like diamonds in the sky.

"I must be spending too much time around you," she murmured, "because I think the full moon looks like a baseball."

He started, because it always reminded him of one. But then, many things did.

"That reminds me," she said. "I've been meaning to ask why you don't apply for the coaching position Désirée says is available at your old high school."

He felt his body tense a moment before he removed his arm from her shoulders and ran a hand over his face. "I swear, that girl has a mouth that runs faster than a horse that's been penned up in a barn.''

"You didn't answer my question.''

He hadn't answered because baseball was something he never talked about. "I didn't apply because I'm through with baseball, simple as that. End of story.''

"How can you be finished with a game you still love?''

He sighed, recognizing she wasn't going to drop the subject. "The game finished with me. Don't you get it, Zoe? I failed.''

She took his hand and raised serious eyes to his face. "A high school player's chances of playing pro ball are nearly a thousand to one. I'd hardly call a pitcher who makes it to Triple A a failure.''

He cocked an eyebrow. "How'd you know that stat?''

"I looked it up online,'' she said. Before he could ask why, she rushed on. "Most minor leaguers don't make the majors. That doesn't mean they can't be good coaches.''

Jack laughed shortly. "Did you look up any stats on how often coaches get fired? The game chews up coaches and spits them out.''

"What makes you so sure you'd be one of the coaches baseball spit back out?'' She squeezed his hand. "I believe you'd be one of the successes.''

Such sincerity shone out of her eyes that he narrowed his. "Do you now? What I'm wondering is what caused this sudden shift in your opinion of me. I always got the idea you didn't think much of me."

Instead of denying the truth in what he said, her eyes seemed to cloud over until she looked well and truly confused. He watched her, waiting for an answer.

"I don't think much of the way you flirt with everybody female," she said slowly, "but I always knew you could succeed at anything you put your mind to."

She looked so lovely in the moonlight that he couldn't let her comment pass. "Anything?" he asked, arching his brow. "Is that an invitation?"

Before she could answer, the speedway lights shut off, shrouding the track in sudden darkness. They'd been so wrapped up in each other they hadn't noticed the place shutting down for the night.

"We should go," Zoe said, moving to jump down from the bus.

He restrained her with gentle pressure on her arm. "I vote we stay. I think it's kind of romantic to be marooned at a deserted speedway."

The night was moon bright, allowing him to read the nervous expression on her face.

"The only romantic thing about Monticello Speedway is its name," she said.

"I don't know about that. There's a full moon, we're alone and we're inside an open-air vehicle."

"It's not like we're in the back seat of a convertible. We're in a bus, for goodness sake."

"Yeah, but the speedway just went to the top of my list of all-time favorite places to be marooned. You want to know why?"

She wet her lips and his heart turned over. "Why?"

"Because you're with me."

Instead of acknowledging the attraction simmering between them, she gazed up at the sky. The stars sparkled even more boldly now that the speedway lights were banked.

"Once when I was about seven years old, my father drove me out to the country on a night like this." Her voice was soft, like she was sharing secrets in the darkness. "He parked in this empty field and we looked up at the sky through his car's sun roof.

"He said the stars were magical and timeless. Then he pointed out the brightest star and named it the Zoe Star. He said from that day on, whenever he saw that star, it'd remind him of how much he loved me."

Jack dropped a kiss on her soft, golden hair. "Sounds like you and your dad have a pretty special relationship."

Her smile was bittersweet. "That was the last time I saw him. He calls every two or three years to say he misses me and promises to visit, but he never does. They're just pretty words, like the ones he used when he made up the Zoe Star."

Jack was silent for long seconds, because he

sensed that she was talking about much more than her father. "Not every man says things he doesn't mean."

"My mother would agree, but gullibility's always been her problem. She's been divorced from my father for twenty-two years but she falls for him again and again. Because each man looks different, she doesn't realize she's falling for the same one."

Quite suddenly, all the pieces of the puzzle fell into place. Zoe hadn't avoided him in college because she wasn't attracted to him. She'd avoided him because she thought he was like her father.

He took her hand, a link in the darkness, and kissed the back of her palm. "I've never said a single word to you that wasn't true," he whispered.

"I don't know whether to believe you," she whispered back.

He moved her hand to his heart, which beat hard and heavy against his chest. "Believe this. No other woman has ever done this to me."

As she searched his eyes, he saw his own awed self reflected in her pupils. He cupped her face with both of his hands, leaned forward and kissed her very gently on the mouth.

"If you don't want this," he said, valiantly holding on to his control, "tell me now."

"My problem is that I've always wanted this," Zoe said as she put her arms around him to draw him close. He breathed in her sweetness and claimed her mouth.

They kissed for a few mindless moments before he traced a section of her upper lip with his tongue. He felt her body react, felt the sharp intake of her breath, the momentary hesitation. He moved his attention to her lower lip and thought he heard her groan before she fused her body against his and slipped her tongue inside his mouth.

Jack moaned, a harsh sound that was carried away by the rush of wind. Her blanket had fallen away, leaving her exposed to the cool weather, but her skin was burning, kindling the heat inside him.

No sooner had he willed her hands on his body than they were there, tracing the muscles of his back, holding him to her, inflaming him further because of the incredible fact that Zoe was finally touching him.

Zoe's pink sweater was so thin that it wasn't much of a barrier. He reached down to rid her of the obstacle, and his hands tangled with hers. With their mouths still clinging, essential components of their clothing somehow became undone. The zipper of his jeans. Her panties. His underwear.

Somehow, they were on the blanket. Somehow, he managed to take the condom from his wallet and sheath himself. She gasped against his mouth when his questing fingers found her moist center. She grabbed his buttocks, wordlessly telling him she didn't want to wait any more than he did, and he slipped inside her as though she were fashioned of the finest silk.

They moved in tandem, as though already one. Jack had rolled over so she could be on top but he was only dimly aware of the hard floor of the bus beneath them.

His body was finally doing what the rest of him had resigned itself to: loving Zoe O'Neill. Nothing had ever felt so complete, so right, so awe-inspiring. So beautiful.

So earth-shattering.

A loud bang sounded, and the world seemed to tilt on its axis as they slid toward one end of the bus.

His eyes were open, focused on her face, when the fireworks went off inside her, an explosive blaze of delight that filled every inch of him. Moments later, he cried out with his own release.

He laid there for a moment, not speaking, before he realized they were flush against one side of the bus.

"What happened?" Zoe asked.

"My guess is that the axle was cracked and our, uh, cavorting broke it the rest of the way. Then the rear wheel must have come off."

"Are you saying that we broke the bus?"

"'Fraid so," Jack said.

He expected her to cry out in horror and regret at what they had done but instead she buried her face against his neck. He felt her tears against his skin.

"Do you think we can convince Marty it collapsed on its own because of that crazy race he ran?'' she asked between gasps, and he realized she was laughing instead of crying.

Relief flooded him. He laughed, too, then kissed her as the truth of the matter hit him. Marty wasn't the one who was crazy. He was, too.

Not only would he take the blame and pay Marty for whatever repairs the bus needed, but he'd do it because he was in love with Zoe.

12

ZOE'S NERVES JANGLED as she walked into The Lockerroom the next day, hardly believing she was stepping foot into a fitness center on a Sunday afternoon.

She reserved Sundays for paying her bills, straightening her apartment and planning her work week. How had she let Jack talk her into going on their fourth date on a Sunday? To a late lunch at Serenade, no less?

She rolled her eyes. Probably the same way he'd talked her into making whoopee in the back of a bus, not that there'd been much talking involved.

Looking back on it, the entire night seemed surreal. After they'd driven back to town, the two of them had made out in his car like a couple of hormone-crazed teenagers. They'd probably still be making out if Zoe hadn't agreed to see him today.

"Zoe! I think I love you!"

One of the Carter siblings blindsided her, enveloping her in a hug, but it wasn't Jack. Désirée squeezed her tight, squealing all the while. She'd traded her platform tennis shoes for stiletto heels and wore so much perfume Zoe barely stopped from sneezing.

"I went for him, just like you suggested, and I got him!" Désirée said. "I almost chickened out when he disappeared into the locker room, but then I thought it's now or never and followed him. Not only did he say yes to the dance, but we're going on our first date this afternoon to the zoo."

Zoe examined Désirée's outfit, which consisted of the heels, a scarlet miniskirt and matching blouse. Typical zoo wear it wasn't, but Zoe didn't deign to damage the teenager's newfound confidence.

"I'm happy for you, honey, but why are you going to the zoo of all places?"

"Because that's where you and Jack went on your first date, and it worked for you."

"We're hardly a model couple," Zoe mumbled.

"Are you kidding? You're a great couple. You two go together like fingernails and polish, like hair and rollers, like gum and teeth."

Zoe looked away, hoping Désirée couldn't guess how well she and her brother had fit together last night. "We're only dating so Jack can get rid of his nickname."

"Ha," Désirée said. "You're with him because you're LOALs."

Zoe remembered Jack using the word. "What does that mean?"

"Love of a Lifetime." Désirée was too busy snapping her fingers and heading around the reception counter to notice Zoe's thunderstruck expression. "I almost forgot. I printed out a copy of Jack's résumé like you asked. I didn't tell him, either."

"Good," Zoe managed to reply as Désirée handed her the résumé. She folded it and put it in her purse with nerveless hands.

"Jack's in through there." Désirée pointed to the weight room at the same moment Devin came through the front door. "Oooh, gotta go."

She blew Zoe one last kiss as she hurried over to the boy, tripping on her high heels halfway there and ending up falling into his arms. Désirée's giggles trailed after Zoe as she walked to the entrance of the weight room.

She stopped in her tracks. A beautiful blonde had hold of Jack's hands as she smiled up at him. He said something with that silver tongue of his and the blonde laughed, a tinkling sound that grated on Zoe.

Jack was flirting with the woman, the same way he'd flirted with Zoe last night. The blonde raised on tiptoes and kissed him on the cheek, and the laugh lines at the corners of his eyes crinkled.

Zoe stared at the pair of them, waiting for the jealousy to well up inside her. But it didn't happen. She knew Jack wasn't interested in the blonde, just as she knew he couldn't help attracting women the way light attracted moths. Just as he'd attracted her.

Except she hadn't wanted to be attracted. Everything in life had a time and a place and this was neither the time nor the place in her life for a man.

Jack's eyes lifted and locked on hers. He smiled

in that charming way he had and raised a hand in greeting, but she'd already made up her mind.

She turned and walked out of the gym.

He caught up to her by the park bench in front of the fitness center, the bench she'd stood beside a few weeks before while she'd gathered the courage to approach him.

Why, oh why, hadn't she walked away then?

"Hey, Zoe, where you going?" Jack wore a puzzled smile. "We have a date, remember?"

Because looking at him weakened her resolve, Zoe averted her eyes and walked in the direction of the Metro station. The cool, crisp air did nothing to alleviate the feeling that she was suffocating.

"I'm canceling the date," she said as she walked. "I don't think we should see each other again."

Jack was silent for long moments as he kept pace with her but she could almost hear his confusion. "In my book, what we did last night is reason to keep seeing each other, not to break up," he said finally.

Because Zoe sensed he wouldn't let her go without an explanation, she seized on his mention of the previous night. "I saw you just now, Jack. I'm not the kind of woman who sleeps with a man one night and watches him line up a date the next."

He made an incredulous noise and reached out to stop her with a gentle but firm grasp. He ushered her off the sidewalk to an alcove that led to the entrance of an apartment building and said in a low, insistent voice, "That wasn't what I was doing."

Because she believed him, she went on the offensive. "So you deny that you were flirting with that blonde? That you flirt with every woman you see? That you keep a scorecard?"

"A scorecard? Of course I don't keep a scorecard." He ran a hand through his rich brown hair. "Look, I can't deny I was flirting with that woman. But I wasn't making a play on her. You're the only woman I want, Zoe."

She made her eyes hard although she could feel tears swimming behind them. "For how long, Jack?"

"I don't believe this." Jack shook his head as he regarded her with such intensity she felt herself squirm. "And you know what? You don't believe it, either. You won't even look at me."

At his challenge, she made herself meet his eyes but he looked so crestfallen she felt the ache clear to her heart and couldn't hold his gaze.

"Aw, Zoe," he said, his voice gentling. "Don't you see what's going on? You're afraid."

He was so close to the mark that it took a supreme effort for Zoe to toss her head and lift her chin. "Why would I be afraid?"

"Because I don't fit into your plans," he answered and she swallowed her gasp. "That's it, isn't it? That's why you keep resurrecting that tired claim that I'm a ladies' man, even though you don't believe it anymore."

"Of course I believe it!"

"Then look me in the eye and tell me you believe I was coming on to that woman."

"This is silly," she said because she couldn't state what wasn't true. "I don't know what you're trying to prove."

"That you're using this womanizer thing as an excuse not to fall for me, the same way you did in college."

At the mention of college, she raised her chin and forced out a short, humorless laugh. "You flatter yourself. I don't need an excuse. Not now and certainly never in college."

"Oh, really?" He raised his eyebrows and his green eyes bore into hers. "Then why do you think of me as your OWGA?"

Her mouth dropped open at his use of the acronym and the blood seemed to drain from her veins. "Who told you that?"

"Doesn't matter who told me. All that matters is if it's true." His hands, which had been at his side, clutched her shoulders. "Am I your OWGA?"

Yes, her brain screamed, but she couldn't say the word. Not when the future she'd mapped out for herself was at stake. Her heart felt as though it were cracking as she desperately cast about for some way to keep from telling him the truth.

Because if she confirmed he was her OWGA, he might use the knowledge to chip away at her already weakened defenses. The next thing she knew, he'd be far too important to her.

"I wasn't aware you wanted a relationship," she

said, once more going on the offensive. "You haven't said word one about going out past the fourth date."

It was true. He hadn't. Jack tried to tell her he loved her, but he couldn't get the words out. Not when she hadn't admitted he was her OWGA. Not when he wasn't sure of how she'd react to a declaration of love. Not when he was so accustomed to denying himself the things he most wanted.

"See, Jack, you can't say it." Her lower lip trembled as though he were the one hurting her. "This has all been a big game to you, hasn't it? Well I don't want to play anymore."

"You can't walk out now." He searched for a reason and came up with their bet. "We haven't been on the fourth date."

"So what?" Her voice sounded more strangled than flippant.

He leaned toward her, tightening his grip on her shoulders as though that would keep her with him. "If you back out on the deal, I won't get Phil to change the spelling of phit. It'll be grammatically wrong forever."

"I don't care."

"How could you not care? What will the people at BLOT say if you fail at your mission?"

"With any luck, they'll kick me out of the group." She sighed, a low, sad sound. "Do you really think I came to The Lockerroom that first day to yell at you about misspelling?"

He thought back on that day and wasn't sure

about anything except his pleasure at seeing her again. "You were real insistent about getting rid of the phit."

"I was bluffing. I think creative spelling is cute. Heck, the name of my business is Clutter Bee Gone. B-e-e. I only joined BLOT because I'd already told you I belonged."

His hands dropped away and he brought them to his head, which was pounding along with his heart. "If you didn't come to the gym to get rid of the phit, why did you come?"

She paused before she answered. "To see you again."

Through his despair, hope flickered, like a candle in the darkness. "So you're saying you were trying to prove that I was your OWGA?"

"No." She shook her head, extinguishing the flickering hope. "I was trying to prove that you weren't. And now that I have my answer, we don't have anything more to say."

She walked away before he could protest that he had plenty more to say. But he couldn't take the chance, not when he couldn't be assured of the outcome.

So why did he feel as though he'd already lost?

13

EXHAUSTED FROM HIS RUN, Jack collapsed into one of the kitchen chairs his father had designed in the early days of his woodworking business and ran a hand over his lower jaw. Normally he'd be surprised to find it bristly, but he hadn't shaved since Zoe had given him the brush-off three days ago.

He hadn't done much of anything except work, work out and brood. He leaned back in his chair and his eyes fell on the one piece of baseball memorabilia he kept in his home. It was a framed photograph of himself on the mound, his left arm cocked as he prepared to deliver a pitch.

He looked away. How long would it take for him to accept that Zoe didn't want him any more than baseball had?

Hope flared in his chest when the doorbell rang until he remembered that Zoe had never been at his small Silver Spring house, the one he would have loved to share with her. She probably didn't care enough to find out where he lived.

Still, the hope didn't die until he opened the door to his sister and father.

"We brought beef stew, the same kind Mom used

to make,'' Désirée said through shockingly pink lips, holding up a plastic container of the stuff as she shouldered past him.

''I've got the bread and beer,'' his father said. He didn't wait for an invitation, either, but followed his daughter into the house. Nearly as tall as his son and with a full head of hair that had turned prematurely gray, Charles Carter still cut a handsome figure at fifty. ''Your sister said she didn't think you were eating right.''

''That's why we're here.'' Désirée rummaged through his cabinets until she found a pot where she could dump the stew. She turned on one of the oven burners. ''Stew's comfort food, and I figured you needed comforting. What with the way you blew it with Zoe and all.''

Jack crossed his arms over his chest and scowled. ''Did it ever occur to you that Zoe might have blown it with me?''

''No,'' Désirée said and stirred the stew. ''Now why don't you take a shower while Dad and I get dinner ready?''

Fifteen minutes later, Jack tore a hunk from the loaf of French bread and dipped it into his stew. He chewed, swallowed and waited for comfort to engulf him, but it didn't happen.

He still felt miserable.

''I got some tickets to the Orioles game this Saturday,'' his father said between mouthfuls of stew. ''Thought you might want to go.''

"Thanks, but I'm not interested," Jack said.

"If you'd rather go with that lady of yours Denise is always talking about, that's okay with me," he said.

"Désirée," his sister corrected. "Not Denise."

"Zoe's not interested," Jack answered. *In me,* he silently added.

"But how do you know—"

The ringing of the phone interrupted what his sister had been about to say. She half rose, but Jack told her to let the machine pick up and listened to his recorded voice instruct the caller to leave a message.

"Hello, Jack. This is Dirk Matthews over at Glen Eagle High calling to schedule an interview at your earliest convenience." He rattled off a phone number while the blood flowing through Jack's veins froze. "I'm looking forward to talking with you about the coaching job. Your résumé is highly impressive."

"Well I'll be darned," his father said after Dirk Matthews had rung off. His face was bathed in a smile as wide as the Potomac River. "This is great news. I didn't know you'd applied for that coaching job."

"Neither did I," Jack said, leveling a dangerous look at his interfering sister.

"It is great news." Désirée beamed at him, apparently oblivious to his unhappiness. "You'll make a wonderful coach, Jack. Dirk Matthews would be a fool not to hire you.''

Jack ran a hand through his hair, wanting to rant at her but unable to bring himself to. Yelling at his sister would be like yelling at a puppy because it had chewed up your slipper on the way to bringing it to you.

''If I'd wanted the job,'' he said as calmly as he could manage, ''I'd have sent in a résumé instead of having my sister do it for me.''

''I didn't send in your résumé, Jack.'' Honesty shone out of her clear green eyes along with a mischievous glint.

Jack's accusing gaze swung to his father, who put both palms up. ''Me, neither,'' he said with conviction.

''Then who?'' Jack asked.

''Zoe, I imagine,'' Désirée said. ''I suspect that's why she asked me to sneak into your computer and print one out.''

Jack dropped his spoon, which clattered against the end of his bowl and fell into his stew. ''Why would Zoe send Dirk Matthews my résumé?''

''Probably because she says the only way to get what you want is to go after it,'' Désirée said. ''She must've realized you wouldn't take a chance unless she goaded you into it.''

''But why would she care if I took a chance or not?''

''As a man whose wife once insisted that losing

my job at the factory was a blessing, I've got some insight into that one," his father said, a soft smile on his face. "Did you two know that your sick mother talked a bank loan officer into fronting me the money for my woodworking business? She said she did it because she believed in me. My guess is that your Zoe believes in you, Jack."

Zoe had said as much a few nights before, when they'd shared confidences beneath the stars, but Jack had trouble believing it after she claimed she didn't want to see him again.

But what if he'd been on the mark when he accused her of shying away from him because he didn't fit into her plans? What if she truly did believe in him?

"Say something, Jack." Désirée stared at him with concern, her pink lips pressed tightly together. "Oh, please say you're going to do the interview."

"You'll never get the job if you don't," his father pointed out.

"I might not get the job if I do."

Désirée blew out a heavy, dramatic sigh. "Oh, Jack, you're not getting it. But maybe I wouldn't have, either, if I hadn't gotten so tongue-tied around Devin and told Zoe about it. She's the one who helped me realize."

"What did she help you realize?"

Désirée hesitated as though she wanted to get the wording exactly right. "That the things in life worth having are the things worth taking a chance on."

The way Jack hadn't taken a chance on Zoe. He swallowed, amazed that a message on his answering machine had opened his eyes to what he should have always seen.

"You are going to do the interview, aren't you, son?" his father asked, looking unsure of the answer. "Because I agree with your sister. You'd make a wonderful coach."

"I'm going to do the interview all right," Jack said and endured Désirée's yelps of delight as she got up from her seat and launched herself into his arms. "But that's not all I'm going to do."

"Do you mean what I think you mean?" Désirée asked, drawing back to look at him with a conspiratorial smile. Her pink lipstick was smudged, which meant most of it had probably come off on his neck.

"I reckon I do," he said and hugged her to him. "But I might need a little help from someone who's good at tracking down information."

"I know a receptionist who'd be happy to track down anything you need," Désirée said.

"Then maybe she can find the phone number of a guy named Marty Peobody. Sometimes goes by the name The Krazy Kid. There's something he's got that I need to borrow."

HOW HAD HER APARTMENT gotten into such a sad state?, Zoe wondered the next evening as she surveyed the disorder from the middle of her living room.

The place was so messy she was ashamed to call herself a Professional Home Organizer. If there was a place for everything, why hadn't she kept everything in its place?

She'd come home late the last few nights, packing her days with work so she'd be too exhausted to think about Jack Carter. But today it hadn't taken her as long as she'd planned to measure the closets for custom-designed organizers in a newly built home.

Good thing, too. She couldn't live with the mess in her apartment a minute longer. She launched herself into the task of cleaning, moving swiftly around the apartment, picking up newspapers and glasses, determined not to think about Jack and the things he'd said.

So what if she'd convinced herself he was a womanizer so she wouldn't have to admit how she felt about him?

How she felt about him didn't matter. Tears rolled down her cheeks and she dashed them away. What mattered was that he didn't fit into either her life or her plans. Exactly as he'd guessed.

Two hours of cleaning later, when the apartment was nearly up to her standards and she'd gone through a dozen tissues, she opened the door and Amy waltzed in.

"The Ugly Cube is officially devoid of its main attraction," Amy announced, handing her an envelope. Inside was the photograph that had been on display for the past year. It showed Zoe asleep, her blond hair in pink sponge rollers, her mouth agape. "The negatives are there, too."

"Thank you," Zoe said, walking to her kitchen table and setting down the envelope. "How are you going to fill my spot?"

Amy indicated the camera she had slung over her shoulder. "Easy. Wait for an opportunity and snap."

She went to Zoe's refrigerator, poured herself a glass of iced tea and strolled around the apartment with the drink in hand. "You've been cleaning, I see." She scrunched up her nose. "I hate it when you do that."

"You know I like an orderly home, Amy," Zoe said. "Just like I like an orderly life."

"Which is why you're no longer seeing Jack Carter," Amy said, repeating the explanation Zoe had given her. "Because he doesn't fit neatly into your plans."

"I like my life fine the way it is. I won't have the time for a serious relationship with a man for years yet. There's a time for everything just like there's a place for everything."

"Oh, really?" Amy walked over to the tacky poster of Phoebe Lovejoy that Zoe hadn't the heart to take down and tapped it with a short fingernail. "So you're saying the place for this poster is a prominent spot on your kitchen wall?"

Zoe swallowed. "Yes."

Amy moved to the living room, fingering the ugly gold blanket from the school-bus race that Zoe had draped over the back of her sofa. She nodded at the giant stuffed panda bear sitting in an armchair as though waiting for someone to turn on the TV.

"And the blanket and King Panda over there? You're saying their place is in your living room?"

Zoe bit the inside of her lower lip. Any professional organizer worth her weight in plastic containers would suggest she stash the items in a closet.

"I like them where they are," Zoe said defensively.

Both of Amy's eyebrows lifted. "Don't you think they make your place look messy?"

Zoe took stock of her apartment, which could have been featured in a house beautiful ad if not for the poster, the blanket and the panda. So why were those three possessions the ones she most treasured?

Jack, her heart answered. *She treasured those possessions because they reminded her of Jack.*

"I think they make my place look lived in," Zoe said.

"Exactly." A smug note entered Amy's voice as she crossed her arms over her chest and regarded her friend with a knowing smile. Zoe's blood pressure shot up.

"Oh, no, you don't." Zoe waved her index finger. "I can see through you, Amy Donatelli. Remember, I haven't forgiven you yet for telling Jack he was my OWGA. And now you're trying to get me to say that the mess is what's important."

"I am?"

"Yes, you are." She threw up her hands. "You want me to admit that things don't always go according to the way we plan."

"I do?"

"Uh-huh." Zoe marched over to her friend and poked her in the chest with a forefinger. "You want me to say that the mess is what touches the heart and that love is something you can't organize or arrange."

"And here I thought I was just paying you a visit," Amy said, going to the refrigerator to pour herself some more iced tea.

"You mean you're not trying to get me to admit I was wrong in denying I love Jack because loving him messes up my plans?" Zoe asked.

Amy didn't say a word, just tapped her foot and waited for Zoe to think about her question. As though there was anything to think about.

Loving Jack did mess up Zoe's plans. It made her want things that she couldn't afford to want until her business was established and she was self-sufficient, the way her mother never had been. What if he asked her to marry him? What if he became more important to her than her business? What if she got pregnant?

She shook her head even as her heart leaped with joy at the thought of the baby she and Jack could have together. A baby wasn't in her plans for years yet.

"My mother never had a plan," she pointed out to Amy, who still watched and waited. For what? For Zoe to realize that her mother had planned to be happy and done whatever she thought necessary to achieve her goal?

For Zoe to recognize the folly of turning down Jack because her carefully laid out plans dictated that it wasn't yet time to be happily in love?

For it to dawn on her that the mess was what mattered.

"Oh, my gosh. You're right." She gasped and covered her mouth as realization struck like a bolt of lightning in a clear blue sky. "The mess *is* what matters."

She ran to the kitchen table and picked up the envelope containing the photograph that had always bothered her because in it she looked, well, a mess. She thrust it at Amy. "I want you to put this back in the Ugly Cube."

"That's the spirit," Amy said, snatching it out of her hand. "If people can't appreciate you when you're a mess, they can't appreciate you at all."

"Yes. The mess is best," Zoe said as she yanked open a closet door and took out two shoes. She was in such a hurry she didn't check to see if they matched.

"What are you going to do now?" Amy asked.

Zoe wasn't rash. She thought things through before deciding upon a course of action. It was nearly nine o'clock on a weeknight, just two hours before her bedtime. Her modus operandi would be to sleep on what she'd discovered and make a decision in the morning.

"I'm going after Jack," she announced.

But before she could reach the front door, she heard a loud, familiar rumbling on the street outside her window. She stopped, hardly daring to hope that she'd correctly identified the noise.

Amy ran to the window, pulled aside the shades and peered into the night. She let out a whoop and yanked open the window.

"Did I tell you I'm thinking of doing an Ugly Cube of inanimate objects," she said while she lined up her camera for a shot. "And that bus isn't only ugly, it's orange."

"OKAY, NOW." JACK positioned himself next to the bus, stretched his arms until they ached and gripped the roof with his fingertips. "On the count of three, give me a push."

He hoped that the smaller man who had hold of his right leg was stronger than he looked. The big man gripping his left leg, he wasn't worried about.

"One...two...three," he yelled and felt his right side shoot up the side of the bus. He clawed at the roof, trying to drag his left side up the bus along with the rest of his body.

"Sorry, man," the big man called up to him. "I

thought you wanted us to push *after* the three, not *on* the three.''

"That's okay," Jack said while he teetered on top of the bus on his hands and knees. He'd never experienced a bus from this perspective before, which was possibly why he hadn't taken into consideration that the roof would be sloped.

"I should never have let you talk me into double parking," Marty Peobody's shrill, nervous voice carried to the bus top from the sidewalk. "What if I get a ticket?"

"Don't worry about it, buddy. If you get a ticket, I'll pay for it. I was good for the damage to your axle, wasn't I?"

"You made loaning you my bus a condition of your payment," Marty wailed. "That's extortion!"

"A man's gotta do what a man's gotta do," Jack said and stood up. The world spun crazily for a moment, but then he spread his legs apart for better balance.

Lights flashed on in a half dozen of the apartments facing the street, including Zoe's. He could tell which apartment was hers because her friend Amy hung out of the window, aiming a camera.

"Hey, Jack," she called gaily, as though she saw a man standing on top of a bus every day. "Shall I get Zoe?"

"I'd be much obliged if you did," he yelled. He risked a glance down at the sidewalk to make sure his two hired men were in position, then told them, "You can start as soon as I give the word."

"This is crazy," he heard the Krazy Kid say.

"Look who's talking," Jack muttered but focused on the window. It seemed like an eternity before Zoe's sweet, surprised face appeared.

"Jack Carter, what in the world are you doing?" she called down to him.

"Taking a chance," he answered and gave the two violinists the word to start playing the song they'd serenaded he and Zoe with at the zoo.

A couple of bars into the song, Jack realized he should have learned the lyrics, but it was too late now. And darn if he could think of the words.

"I'm in love with *you-ou-ou-ou-ou*," he improvised in a key he realized was off-tune.

The same bar of music repeated over and over so he sang the line a couple more times, putting his hand over his heart for emphasis.

Even though the residential street was usually quiet, traffic backed up and drivers sounded their horns. Somebody in the apartment next to Zoe's yelled that he could be arrested for disturbing the peace. In another apartment, a dog howled along with the music.

But Jack didn't care about anything except Zoe's reaction to his declaration. Standing on top of the bus, he was almost even with her second-floor apartment but he was having a devil of a time making out her expression in the light of the half moon.

He took a step forward, hoping to get a better view, and promptly lost his balance.

"Uh-oh," he said a moment before he slid off the bus. His butt hit the roof and he felt his pants catch on something and tear. He pitched forward, belly first, onto the trunk of a car parked between the bus and the curb. If it hadn't been a Volvo, he would have crushed it.

He lay there for a moment, stunned both by the fall and the fact that he hadn't broken any bones. By the time he managed to stand up, Zoe was there.

"Are you okay?" she asked, searching his eyes.

"Heck, no. He's crazy," yelled Marty Peobody.

Jack felt his lips, about the only part of his body that wasn't sore, curve into a smile. Ignoring Marty, he said, "I'm as fine as the hairs on a fire-bellied toad now that you're here."

She ran her hands up and down his arms and made him do a three-sixty so she could inspect him for damage. "You ripped your pants," she said, and he reached back to feel a tear high on the thigh of his jeans.

Her voice was breathless when she added, "I love it when you wear torn pants."

"You do?" he asked in surprise. When she nodded, he smiled. "If that's what it takes to impress you, I got a couple other pairs I can rip."

"Is that what you were doing on top of the bus?" she asked. "Trying to impress me?"

"I was trying to impress on you that I was taking

a chance," he answered. "I was about to ask if you'd take a chance on me, but then I fell on my behind. So here goes.

"I love you, Zoe O'Neill. I've loved you since college. I know I flirt with just about every female I see and I can't promise to stop. But I can promise to always be faithful and to love you forever."

"How can you promise forever?" she asked, running her fingertip down his jawline. "Aren't you forgetting why people call you K-Jack?"

"I used to wonder why I couldn't get past three dates with anyone else, but now I know," he said softly. "It's because those women weren't you. You're my home run, Zoe."

She bit a lower lip that looked like it was trembling. "You really are a sweet talker, aren't you, Jack Carter?"

"Not as sweet as I should have been. I should have told you I loved you a long time ago but I was afraid to take a chance. Please tell me I haven't made a mess of things?"

"Oh, but you have," Zoe said as tears gathered in her eyes. His heart seized as he tried to make sense of what she was saying. Had he blown it after all?

"Is it because you think I won't be able to take a chance on anything else?" he asked, then hurried to reassure her. "Because that's not true anymore. I got the coaching job, Zoe. I got it because your belief in me gave me the courage to believe in myself.''

''That's wonderful,'' Zoe said, cupping his cheeks in her hands. The tears that had been gathering in her eyes streamed down her face, counteracting the words.

''You do believe that I'll be faithful, don't you?'' he asked anxiously.

''Of course I do,'' she said as the tears continued to fall. ''You were right. I was using the ladies' man argument to keep you at a distance because I had my life all mapped out. Falling in love wasn't a part of it.''

His heart seemed to seize. ''Are you sayin' you're in love with me?''

''Yes, I love you,'' she said through her tears. ''You're my OWGA, Jack. My LOAL. How could you doubt I love you?''

''If you love me,'' he said slowly, ''then why did you say I made a mess of things?''

''Because you have,'' Zoe said.

He cocked a brow but grinned because she was giving him a watery, loving smile. ''So let me get this straight. Making a mess is a good thing?''

He had to shout the question to be heard above the blaring of the car horns, the yelling from the apartment windows, the serenading music and the advancing police siren. Not to mention the clicking of Amy's camera.

"A mess, my love, is the most wonderful thing in the world," Zoe said an instant before they ignored the one they were in and got lost in each other's kiss.

Darlene Gardner

Twice Shy

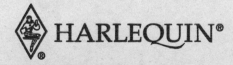

HARLEQUIN®

TORONTO • NEW YORK • LONDON
AMSTERDAM • PARIS • SYDNEY • HAMBURG
STOCKHOLM • ATHENS • TOKYO • MILAN • MADRID
PRAGUE • WARSAW • BUDAPEST • AUCKLAND

Dear Reader,

Have you ever seen that commercial where some
unsuspecting soul thinks he can eat a single potato
chip, but winds up devouring the entire bag?

I think lying is like that.

Once you get started, it's nearly impossible to tell
just one.

Amy Donatelli, the heroine of *Twice Shy,* doesn't
mean to lie to Matt Burke about the man from her
past whom she can't forget.

But if Matt has an OWGA (One Who Got Away),
she wants him to think she has one, too. Though
she doesn't count on having to tell one white lie
after another to cover up for the first one. Or the
way her invented One Who Got Away ends up
sounding more like someone any sane person
would want to avoid.

Amy's problem is that she's becoming increasingly
certain she doesn't want Matt to go anywhere at
all. Except, of course, he thinks she's in love with
someone else.

Oh, what a tangled web we weave…

Hope you enjoy mine.

Darlene Gardner

Books by Darlene Gardner

HARLEQUIN DUETS
39—FORGET ME? *NOT*
51—THE CUPID CAPER
68—THE HUSBAND HOTEL
77—ANYTHING *YOU* CAN DO…!

HARLEQUIN TEMPTATION
926—ONE HOT CHANCE

1

AMY DONATELLI RIPPED HER gaze from Matt Burke's very fine set of gluteus muscles, which were making their eye-catching way to her kitchen, and focused on the suggestion she fervently hoped she hadn't heard one of her guests make.

"What did you say?" Amy asked, already feeling guiltier than her kindergarten students at Ambrose Academy when she caught them finger-painting each other rather than their art projects.

"I said now that I've captured my OWGA," Zoe O'Neill answered, giving Jack Carter a big smile and his arm a little squeeze, "it's time you and Matt try your luck with yours."

Unfortunately nothing was wrong with her hearing. Amy's stomach pitched and rolled as she accepted the fact that Zoe really had brought up the dreaded OWGA, the acronym for the One Who Got Away.

She might have sunk to the floor in guilty horror if she hadn't already been sitting on the living-room carpet around the super-size coffee table she'd suggested the four of them use as a dinner table.

As it was, she swayed and had to grab the end of the table for support. The only thing that had gotten away from her was her common sense when she'd made up that big, fat lie about having an OWGA.

She still didn't know what had come over her, because lying was not her thing. It had started honestly enough when she, Matt and Zoe had gotten into a conversation about OWGAs a month or so ago. Then Matt had intimated that most everybody, himself included, had an OWGA.

The next thing she knew, she was inventing one for herself.

"I don't know why I didn't think of it before," Zoe continued, oblivious to her distress. "Jack and I wouldn't be together if you and Matt hadn't pushed me to look him up. I'm going to return the favor."

Before Amy could mount a protest, not that she'd yet figured out exactly what to say, Jack was speaking.

"Wait a second, darlin'," he told Zoe, "I don't think you should be stirring up trouble in paradise."

"You call this paradise?" Zoe indicated the overturned crates that served as end tables, walls festooned with print fabric and enormous throw pillows Amy had used to infuse personality into the place she was house sitting. "I've heard the term 'garagesale chic' used to describe Amy's style of decorating but never paradise."

Jack gave his fiancée a smile so slow and wide it was easy for Amy to see how her friend had fallen in love with him. "I wasn't talking about her place," he said. "I was talking about her man."

"What man?" Amy and Zoe asked in unison.

"The man who insisted on clearing away the dinner plates. I'm thinking he's probably stacking them in the sink right about now."

"Matt?" Amy squawked. "You're talking about Matt?"

"Matt isn't Amy's boyfriend," Zoe said and laughed. "Why did you think that?"

"When the two of them asked us over to dinner to celebrate our engagement, I just assumed," Jack said as a puzzled indentation appeared between his brows. "Especially when I noticed the way she was—"

Amy didn't let him finish. "You caught me checking out his butt, didn't you?"

This time, Jack aimed his grin at her. "I was gonna say I noticed you finishing some of his sentences, not that I'd seen you eyeballin' his attributes."

"Who was eyeballin' whose attributes?" Matt asked as he reentered the room, located the nearest chair and sat down. The rest of them were still on the floor but Matt wasn't a floor sitting kind of guy. Not when casual dress for him consisted of a suit sans jacket and a loosened tie.

Why, he was even wearing tails in the Ugly Cube photo she'd shot of him last year at a mutual friend's wedding. The only reason the photo had made the cube was that the lens had distorted the shape of his face, making him look loopy.

"Amy told us she was ogling your butt when you walked out of the room," Zoe answered.

One of Matt's dark-blond eyebrows rose as he looked at Amy. "Really?"

"Not ogling, looking. Can I help it if you have a cute rear end?" Amy asked and rolled her eyes when he winked at her and said, "Right back atcha."

The mischief in his light-brown eyes brightened what was, essentially, a nice face. A strong jawline complemented his high cheekbones and called attention away from a nose that was slightly too long. His full-lipped mouth, however, was perfectly formed. As was his broad forehead and thick, wavy hair the color of burnished wheat.

Okay. His face was more than nice. She'd even categorize it as handsome. But this was Matt, who'd been her platonic buddy for going on seven years since they'd met in college junior year. Matt, who was not and never had been her boyfriend.

"Jack here got the impression that we were a couple," Amy told Matt, who let out a laugh so loud that Speedy Gonzalez, the box turtle she kept in a thirty-gallon aquarium in the living room, tucked her head into her shell.

"That's a good one," Matt said. He probably would have guffawed and slapped his knee if guffawing and knee-slapping hadn't been beneath his dignity.

Amy shot him a glare. The notion of her and Matt together *was* ridiculous, but did he have to laugh so loudly?

"If you don't put a lid on that laughter in the next couple seconds, Burke, I'll come over there and do it for you," Amy said.

"Now aren't you the laugher calling the laughee black?" Matt asked, but he'd stopped laughing.

"Don't you remember the way you snorted last week when that guy at Brewster's asked us how long we'd been married?"

"I do not snort," Amy denied hotly. "I have a delicate laugh."

"Okay. Then don't you remember the way you *trilled?*"

Amy felt a snort rising to the surface so she covered her mouth with a hand and tried to turn it into a trill. It came out somewhere between a chortle and a giggle. Her laughing eyes met Matt's and her anger faded.

"Yep, we're the odd couple," she said.

"The Odd Couple," he repeated with a smug smile. "The Neil Simon movie starring Jack Lemmon and Walter Matthau."

"Darn, I thought I was going to slip one by you," Amy said.

"Slip what by who?" Jack asked, looking confused.

"It's this game Amy and Matt play with movie titles," Zoe explained. "They're both film buffs. Any time one of them mentions a title in conversation, the other has to recognize it and provide the stars."

Jack cocked his head. "You sure they're not a couple?"

"Positive," Zoe said. "Amy's impulsive and Matt's premeditated. She wants to have fun and he wants to make money. Yin and Yang. Besides, they both have their sights set elsewhere."

"We—" Matt began.

"—do?" Amy finished.

"Of course you do," Zoe said. "Matt, don't you remember telling us Mary Contrary was the woman from your past you couldn't stop thinking about?"

"Mary Contrary?" Jack cut in. "Isn't she the girl in the nursery rhyme with the seashells?"

"She had cockleshells, not seashells," Zoe said. "But Matt says his Mary Contrary doesn't have any."

"Not Mary Contrary," Matt said. "Contrary Mary. Her last name's actually Contrino."

The name sent a shiver through Amy. Probably because she had some of the windows cracked and the October chill was seeping into the house.

"You know, I have an OWGA, too," Amy said, then could have slapped herself. Why had she said that? Lying was wrong. She told her kindergarten students that all the time.

"What was his name again, Amy?" Zoe asked.

Amy swallowed. *Tell them*, her conscience implored. *Tell them you made up the name as well as the man*.

"Pier LeFrancois," Matt supplied, putting enough emphasis on the first name that Amy suspected he was deliberately misstating her nonexistent OWGA's name.

"*Pierre* LeFrancois," she corrected.

"Oh, yes. The Frenchman." Zoe clapped her hands. "You never told us how you met him."

"That's right, I didn't," Amy said slowly while her conscience screamed at her to tell her friends the truth.

"Were you high-school sweethearts like Matt and Mary?" Zoe asked, and Amy's conscience took a back seat to a brain that focused on the word "sweethearts." If Matt could have one, so could she.

"Oh, no, I only met Pierre five or six years ago." Amy's conscience made a return appearance at her fabrication, and she cringed inwardly.

"But we were in college then." Zoe shook her head as though it couldn't be so. "We were roommates. I knew the names of every guy you went out with. Unless you had a one-night stand with somebody you didn't tell me about, you didn't date a Pierre."

"Amy doesn't have one-night stands," Matt said, and his voice sounded testy. Amy sent him a grateful smile for sticking up for her. The corners of his mouth lifted in acknowledgment.

"I know she doesn't have one-night stands. It was an expression of speech," Zoe said, then pinned her gaze on Amy. "So how did you meet Pierre?"

"It was the semester I was student teaching," Amy blurted out. *Think, think.* Why on earth had she invented a French OWGA when an all-American one would have done just as well? "Pierre was...the French teacher."

"The French teacher!" Matt sounded not only horrified but angry. "What kind of creep was he? Didn't he know there are rules against teachers dating students?"

"Pierre was no creep," Amy retorted, her temper rising to match his. Did Matt really believe she'd make up a creepy OWGA? "And I wasn't a student. I was a student teacher."

Matt crossed his arms over his chest and glowered. "Same thing."

"It's not the same thing at all," Amy said, "although I don't recall saying that Pierre and I acted on the attraction."

Oh, great, Amy thought when Matt's glower turned to a glimmering smile. *He'd probably had a torrid affair with Contrary Mary and she'd invented a platonic OWGA.*

"Still, he was very sweet and romantic," Amy said. "He used to call me..." She faltered as she tried to think of a French term of endearment. *Ami* meant friend, but what was the French word for love? "*...mon amiba.*"

"He used to call you his *amoeba?*" Matt's eyebrows rose, and she wanted to scream for forgetting he was fluent in French. "Yeah, he sounds like a real romantic guy to me."

"He was romantic," Amy said, then cringed. If Pierre was so romantic, why had he referred to her as a one-celled, microscopic organism? "You know how an amoeba is constantly changing shape? Pierre said I was like that. He never knew what to expect from me and I...uh...had the power to change his life."

"His amoeba. That *is* romantic." Zoe put one hand over her heart and got a dreamy expression on her face. "Why didn't you ever tell me about him before?"

Amy sighed inwardly because she'd probably told

Zoe more secrets over the years than a priest hears in a confessional. "I suppose because what Pierre and I shared seemed so much like a...fantasy, I didn't want it examined in the harsh light of reality."

Matt gave an audible groan, erasing Amy's guilt over lying. She hadn't disrespected his OWGA—not out loud, anyway. Why was he disrespecting hers?

"How did you two lose touch?" Zoe asked, dragging Amy's attention away from Matt.

"It was one of those things," Amy muttered while the wheels in her brain spun. "I had a semester of college left after I finished my student teaching and somehow we never managed to connect."

"Didn't you do your student teaching in Northwest D.C?" Zoe asked and sprang to her feet like she'd been shot out of a cannon.

"Yes." Amy didn't like the speculative gleam that had entered Zoe's eyes. Or the way her friend was scooting down beside one of the end-table crates and yanking out a thick phone book. With a sinking heart, Amy recognized the residential white pages for the D.C. area.

"You didn't do your student teaching all that long ago," Zoe pointed out. "Maybe Pierre still lives in town."

Amy was about to claim she'd heard that Pierre had returned to France when Matt said, "Even if he does live here, Amy shouldn't have anything to do with him."

"And why's that?" Amy asked, bristling.

He shrugged his broad shoulders as though he hadn't made an outrageous, out-of-line suggestion.

"Because students develop crushes on teachers all the time and they don't mean a thing."

"And the crushes students develop on each other are meaningful?" Amy countered, setting her jaw. "Like the one you had on Mary Contrary? You're saying that was the real thing? When you were, what, all of sixteen?"

"I was seventeen." He seemed to hesitate, but there was nothing indecisive about his next words. "And it was the real thing."

"I was twenty-one," Amy retorted. "So I'm sure that what I felt was more real than what you felt!"

"I don't see a P. LeFrancois in the phone book," Zoe said and closed the book. Amy might have left it at that if Matt hadn't looked so smug about it.

"Then I'll try directory assistance," she said, marching to the phone and picking up the receiver. She waited for an operator to come on the line and supplied the city and the name.

"I'm sorry," the operator said, "we have no listing under that name."

Amy grabbed the pad she kept next to the phone, pretended to listen and jotted down a haphazard series of seven numbers. She hung up the phone and held up the pad.

"Here it is," she said triumphantly. "Pierre's phone number."

"I think you should call him," Zoe said excitedly.

"I think you shouldn't," Matt said.

Jack leaned back against the sofa as though he wished it were quicksand that would swallow him up. "No way, no how I'm offering up an opinion."

"Of course I'm going to call him," Amy said, picking up the receiver again. She hesitated as she thought about what number to call. She couldn't risk dialing her own for fear her friends might hear the busy signal.

Making a hasty decision, she punched in a series of numbers.

"Paco's Pizzeria," the harried-sounding voice on the other end of the line said. In the background, she could hear a cook shouting orders and more ringing phones.

"Hello, Pierre?" Amy made her voice low and sultry. "Oh, it's so wonderful to hear your voice again. This is..." She let her voice trail off, as though she'd been interrupted.

"This isn't Pierre's Pizzeria." The man's voice was scratchy, as though he'd been talking on the phone too long. "It's Paco's Pizzeria, and I doubt Paco exists. Supposedly he owns the chain but I've never seen him."

Amy feigned delighted surprise and covered her mouth with a hand. "Yes, it is," she said, dropping the hand. "It is your *amiba.*"

"It's real loud in here. Could you speak up?" the pizza man asked. "Did you say you wanted the pizza delivered to Amelia?"

Zoe was clapping in delight, but Amy was more interested in Matt's reaction. He released a short, harsh breath and shook his head, as though he wasn't caught up in the romanticism of it all. She'd show him! She'd make it more romantic.

"I don't know how we lost touch, either," she said

to no perceptible change in Matt's expression. "Darling," she blurted out. Matt's head snapped up.

"Look, Amelia." The pizza man didn't sound happy. "I heard you that time. It's real busy tonight. Just tell me what you want on the pizza, okay?"

"I think about you all the time, too, Pierre." She thought Matt's jaw clenched but couldn't be sure. She pursed her lips, blew three kisses into the phone and imagined steam escaping from Matt's ears. But that could have been the vapor residue from her kisses.

"This isn't Pierre's, it's Paco's." The pizza man was fast losing patience. "Didn't you hear me the first time?"

She put the back of her hand against her forehead. "Oh, how could we have wasted so much time?"

"I bet he's married," Matt muttered.

"I'm hanging up unless you tell me what you want on your pizza," the gravelly voiced man said. "I'm a happily married man."

She scowled at Matt, then smiled into the phone. "That is such a sweet thing to say, Pierre. Imagine not being able to marry anyone because you knew I was out there somewhere."

"That's it," the man said. "Customer satisfaction be damned. I'm hanging up."

"How fantastic!" Zoe exclaimed as the sound of a receiver being slammed resounded in Amy's ear.

"How fictitious," Matt mumbled.

"Of course I believe you," Amy said into the dead phone line. "Especially because…the thought of you is what's kept me from getting seriously involved with anyone else.''

"Oh, come on," Matt said. "If that were true, you would have called him before now."

"Shhhh," Zoe said like the true friend she was, defending Amy by shooting Matt a murderous glance. "You're spoiling the moment for her."

"You better listen to Zoe," Jack advised Matt. "Women like this kind of mushy stuff. That's why they're always dragging us to the movies to see Meg Ryan."

"Meg's okay, but I like Sandra Bullock better," Zoe said. "She seems more real."

Amy had been so busy paying attention to her friends' conversation that she'd lost track of the one-sided one she was conducting. All eyes turned to her.

"What's that?" She stalled for time as she tried to think of something for Pierre to say. Unfortunately she had Sandra Bullock on the brain. "Get outta here. Do I really remind you that much of Sandra Bullock?"

Amy watched Jack gesture to Zoe. "And she used to think *I* was a sweet talker. I don't have anything on this French guy."

"What's he saying?" Zoe asked Amy in a loud whisper.

Amy covered the receiver. *Think, think.* "He says Sandra never would have gotten the part in *Speed* if I was up for it, too."

Matt let out a short laugh. "Never mind that you can't act a whit. Remember *Romeo and Juliet* in college?"

"Can I help it if they cast me as Romeo because there weren't enough male actors?" Amy momentarily abandoned her imaginary conversation with Pierre for a real one with Matt. "Besides, what's that got to do with anything?"

"Everything. You heard Jack. This guy's a smooth talker who doesn't mean a thing he says."

"Hey, leave me out of this," Jack said, putting both palms up and looking horrified. "Like they say back home in Tennessee, I don't got no dog in this fight."

"They're not fighting," Zoe said, shaking her head. "Matt and Amy never fight. Besides, Amy's on the phone."

Zoe was right. She was on the phone, even if the only thing on the other end was static.

"Of course I know you're sincere, Pierre," Amy said and made a face at Matt.

"Ask him if he wants to get together," Zoe prompted, a suggestion which was, of course, ridiculous. Pretending to talk to an OWGA on the telephone was one thing. Pretending to date him was quite another.

"Don't ask him," Matt said.

"Saturday night? Why, yes, I am free Saturday night," Amy said at the same moment the dial tone blared. She turned her back on the group and jammed the earpiece against her temple to muffle the noise.

"What was that sound?" Zoe asked.

Amy called over her shoulder, "Pierre's rejoicing that I said yes." She hesitated. If they'd heard the dial tone, would they buy that explanation? "He loves the opera. When he's happy, he sings a few notes.''

''He sounds darling,'' Zoe exclaimed.

''He sounds like a weirdo to me,'' Matt said.

''Like I've said before,'' Jack said, ''I got no opinion.''

Amy's temple was starting to hurt from the way she had the phone pressed against it so she figured it was time to end the conversation.

''What time? Seven-thirty? Wonderful. I'll be there. Until then. *Adiós!*''

She reached over to the phone's cradle, pressed the disconnect button and replaced the receiver. She rubbed the imprint of the earpiece from her temple, schooled her features into an expression she hoped was rapturous and turned to face the three other people in her living room.

Except they weren't just any people. Two of them were her closest friends in the world and the third was engaged to marry one of them. Yet she'd duped them all into believing she had a date with a man who didn't exist.

She brought her hands to her cheeks. What had she done?

''*Adieu,*'' Matt said.

She frowned. Wasn't that Spanish for goodbye? Had he figured out her deception? Was he about to get up and leave? Was he so angry she'd never see him again? She had to come clean.

''I didn't mean to—''

''—say goodbye in Spanish,'' Matt finished the sentence for her but, for once, that hadn't been what she intended to say. "*Adieu* is French. *Adiós* is Spanish. I'm surprised the French teacher hasn't taught you that."

"I'm sure they have better things to do when they're together than talk about the translation of goodbye," Zoe said. "You heard Amy on the phone. This man is her OWGA."

"Actually, I—"

This time it was Zoe who didn't let her finish. "Who would have thought Amy had an OWGA?"

Not me, Amy thought.

"Or that he would sound like he's so perfect for her," Zoe continued.

"He sounds all wrong for her to me," Matt said.

Amy forgot about confessing and crossed her arms over her chest. "Is that so? And why is that?"

"Come on, Amy. He's a smarmy French guy who tries to seduce student teachers."

"Pierre did not try to seduce me," Amy said. There she went again. Making her OWGA sound as though he didn't have a sex drive. "Not that he didn't want to."

"This date is a bad idea," Matt said. "You don't know anything about the guy. Sounds like you managed to hold him off when you were student teaching but who knows what he'll do when he has you alone."

Amy bit her bottom lip, torn between wanting to be angry at Matt for his pigheadedness and wanting to kiss him for his concern. Not that she'd kiss him on the lips, of course. She'd go for the cheek. She was pretty sure of it.

"That's not fair, Matt," Zoe said. "How would you feel if Mary Contrary's friends had the same suspicions about you?"

Something inside Amy tensed at the mention of the other woman. Matt cleared his throat and seemed to think about what Zoe had said. "That's different. Mary and I go way back."

"So do Pierre and Amy," Zoe said. "It's a parallel. Mary's your OWGA, and Pierre's Amy's."

"Yes, Pierre's my OWGA," Amy chimed in, then mentally grimaced. The lie was once again on the table. "And I'm meeting him Saturday night."

"Saturday night?" Zoe said, making a face. "I just remembered. The four of us have plans to go to that new comedy club downtown Saturday night."

Indecision filled Amy, because Zoe was right. Not only had they made plans, but the plans were much more appealing than the one she'd invented. Her companions would be live, flesh-and-blood people instead of the invisible man.

Although Zoe and Jack were in that saccharine stage that made it hard for someone who wasn't part of a couple to be around them, Matt would also be there.

Sure, he was too snazzy of a dresser. And, yeah, he needed to spend a lot less time building his bank balance and a lot more time living. But he was one of her best friends. And he wasn't invisible.

She'd cancel her date with Pierre, that's what she'd do. Either that or tell her friends she'd never had a date in the first place.

"About Saturday night," Matt said before Amy

spoke up. He slanted a look at Amy before he addressed Zoe. "I've been meaning to tell you that I can't make it, either."

Zoe's face fell. "Oh, and why's that?"

"I've got a date," Matt said, and Amy's breath caught and held. She knew what he was going to say even before the next words were out of his mouth. "With Mary."

His OWGA.

Her confession died on her lips under the gnawing knowledge that Mary Contrary, unlike Pierre Le-Francois, actually did exist.

2

_____

MATT STEPPED OFF the elevator into the lobby at the law offices of Brandenburg, Brandenburg and Brandenburg—otherwise known as the Triple B or just The Ranch—to complete silence. That is, if he didn't count the name ringing inside his head.

Contrary Mary Contrino.

He rubbed his forehead, but it wasn't because of the long hours he'd put in drafting opposition to a motion for summary judgment in a corporate dispute case.

It was because he was supposedly going out on the town tomorrow night with a woman who didn't exist.

As an attorney, he understood the danger of making rash statements. He was thoughtful, deliberate and precise. So why had he plucked Mary Contrary out of a nursery rhyme and told his friends she was his OWGA?

He pictured the way Amy had looked when he'd practically demanded that she not get in contact with her French OWGA. Her olive skin had been flushed, her full lips pursed, her dark eyes flashing with defiance.

He didn't know how, but he felt sure it was Amy's fault he'd invented Contrary Mary Contrino.

The clicking noises the heels of his European leather shoes made on the marble floor cut into the silence of the cavernous building, but not as effectively as the booming voice of the night security guard.

"Lordy, Matt. Ain't you never heard of TGIF? You're supposed to be thanking God it's Friday so you can party, not so you can work late."

"Evening, Nellie." Matt stopped at the counter and regarded the woman who bore more than a passing resemblance to his mother. Her brown hair was pulled back from her strong-featured face in a bun so tight it made *his* head hurt. "I could point out that you're working late, too."

"'Course I am. I work nights, child, not days like you're supposed to." The security guard made a *tsking* sound. "Where you going now?"

"To the gym, maybe," Matt said. "Home, probably."

She folded her hands across her ample chest. "And how do you expect to meet a woman if you don't get out more?"

Matt narrowed his eyes. "Have you been talking to my mother? Because you sure sound like her."

"'Course I do. I got four grown boys of my own, not a one of which would have given me a grandchild if I hadn't pushed them to find wives first."

"I'm not getting married any time soon," Matt said dryly.

"Course you're not. Before you have a marriage, you gotta have a date."

"What makes you think I don't have a date?"

Nellie harrumphed. "You obviously don't have one tonight. The way you spend all your time working, I'd bet my bloomers you don't have one tomorrow night, either."

Matt considered telling Nellie about Contrary Mary, but lying to a woman who reminded him of his mother didn't seem wise. Besides, he definitely didn't want to see her without her bloomers.

"I'm a junior employee at a major law firm," he said. "I don't have time to date."

"Man does not live by the law alone," Nellie declared as Matt's cell phone sounded.

Saved by the ring, Matt thought. He took the phone out of his briefcase and checked the number. Amy. He hadn't been conscious of his heart beating previously but now felt its *thump-thump-thump.*

"I've got to take this call," he told the security guard.

"You got to get a love life, is what you got to get. Is that a female callin' you?"

"A female friend," Matt specified.

"You got to like 'em before you can love 'em," Nellie's voice trailed after him as he walked away from the desk and flipped open the phone.

"Hello, Dolly."

"The movie starring Barbra Streisand and Walter Matthau," she said instantly. "Honestly, Matt, you'll never stump me if you can't come up with harder titles than that."

"I thought that was hard."

"If my name was Dolly, maybe."

He smiled into the receiver. "Is it my fault you have total recall?"

"*Total Recall*. Arnold Schwarzenegger and—" she hesitated "—Sharon Stone!"

"You're good," Matt said as he walked out of the building into the Washington D.C. night. "Very good."

"That's what I keep telling you," she said.

Still cradling the phone, he headed down the deserted sidewalk toward the garage where he'd parked the BMW he was leasing. "Are you going to tell me why you're calling so late on a Friday night?"

"I left a message on your machine earlier but you didn't call back," she said. "I couldn't wait till tomorrow because I really need you."

He wished, he thought, then frowned. Where had that thought come from?

A taxi changed lanes on the adjacent street directly in the path of a PT Cruiser, whose driver laid on the horn. "That was a car horn." Her voice sounded accusatory. "Matt Burke, are you just now leaving The Ranch?"

"What do you need?" What he didn't need was another lecture on stopping to smell the roses. Not when she couldn't understand that before you could take a sniff of the flowers, you had to make enough money to buy them.

"Because it's ten-thirty and you've been working—"

"Amy?" he interrupted. "What do you need?"

The hesitation at the other end of the line was uncharacteristic. He stopped walking. *Please don't say you need a man's advice on the love life you plan to have with the French guy.*

"I need a lawyer," she said. "I'm being sued."

MATT BARELY HAD TIME to appreciate the way the morning sun shining on the fall foliage transformed the modest Arlington street where Amy was living into a red-and-gold paradise before a more riveting sight appeared in the doorway.

Amy. In jeans and a happy-face sweatshirt with her dark hair curling wildly about her shoulders.

"Good, you're here," she said, grabbing his hand and drawing him into the house.

Electricity sparked where their skin touched, shooting up his arm and zinging to his heart. Amy's dark, expressive eyes flew to his. She looked as shocked as he felt.

"Did you feel that?" she asked.

He gave a slow nod, never taking his eyes from her face. He'd always liked her long nose and eyes so dark it was hard to distinguish the pupils, but when had she become so pretty? Her skin was a gorgeous shade of olive, her lips so cherry-red that his mouth started to water.

He gulped and saw her do the same. She dropped her eyes and yanked her hand from his grasp. "Must've been static electricity," she mumbled.

"Must've been," he said, but his hand still tingled. He shoved it into his pocket. "Is Zoe here yet?"

The three of them were supposed to congregate at Amy's place this morning to come up with a solution to her problem. Matt would provide legal expertise, Zoe moral support.

"She's not coming," Amy said. "Turns out Phoebe Lovejoy is appearing at a bookstore this morning and she and Jack wanted to get a book signed."

Phoebe Lovejoy. The *Spice Up Your Sex Life* author. Matt felt a bead of sweat form on his brow. "So it's just the two of us?"

She nodded and wiped her brow. "Zoe apologized but said we didn't need her anyway. That you and me would make a great team."

"She said that?" He frowned. They'd always been a three-member team in the past. In fact, he couldn't remember ever being alone with Amy.

"She did." Amy scuffed her stocking feet, then gave a bright smile that seemed false. "We might as well get started."

He followed her past the living room, where they'd eaten plates of pasta with Zoe and her new man days before, and into the kitchen. His eyes lingered on the way her blue jeans hugged her very shapely rear end.

His comment the other day, about her having a nice backside, had been just that: a comment. But now he realized it was true. Had it always been true?

Before he could come up with an answer, she plopped down on a chair at the kitchen table and indicated he should sit, too. He sat, thinking this is where he'd wanted to be the other night at dinner.

But trust Amy to have dinner in the living room and serve up conversation in the kitchen.

"I'm ready to rumble," she said abruptly, reminding him of the way emcees sometimes announced pro-wrestling matches.

He nearly swallowed his tongue while visions of the two of them wrestling on the floor, without clothes, leaped into his mind.

"Excuse me?" he said.

"Let's go to court," she said. "I'll fight back."

He blinked to clear the naked wrestling image from his deluded mind. The rumble she'd been talking about was a court fight. Nudity didn't have anything to do with it.

He crossed one leg over the other to give himself time to compose himself. And to stop thinking of Amy's gorgeous skin bared to his gaze. She favored unstructured dresses and baggy shirts but...

"What do you think, Matt?" Amy asked.

I think that underneath it all your breasts probably look fantastic. Plump and firm, with nipples the color of your lips.

"Matt?" she prompted.

The case, he reminded himself. She wanted advice on the case, which had something to do with a complaint from a neighbor. He should have gotten more information out of her last night on the phone. But when he'd stepped into the parking garage, the cell phone line had started crackling and she'd told him the details could wait until morning.

But, of course, Amy wasn't a detail person.

He went into professional mode, clearing his throat, straightening his backbone, adjusting his tie.

"I can't believe you wore a tie," she said.

He glanced down at his tie, which featured tiny yellow triangles against a bright blue backdrop, too loud for weekday wear but perfectly suited for weekends.

"What's wrong with it?" he asked.

"You don't think you're overdressed for a Saturday morning?"

"But I left my jacket in the car," he said.

"But don't you…" Her voice trailed off and she sounded…exasperated. As though she didn't understand the significance of dressing the part when dispensing legal advice. "Never mind. Just tell me when we can go to court. I may not be innocent, but no jury will convict me."

"The point is to stay out of a courtroom," Matt said, more than a little exasperated himself. Especially when he digested her last comment. "What do you mean you may not be innocent?"

She shrugged. "Technically, I did say it."

"Say what?"

"That I didn't think the hairstyle was particularly flattering." She leveled him with a look. "It wasn't. And isn't the truth always the best defense?"

Matt absently scratched his head. "Somebody's suing you because you didn't like a hairdo?"

"Essentially," she said and got to her feet. She moved across the room to the kitchen counter with a sexy grace. Had she always walked with that sensuous little shimmy? Why hadn't he noticed it before?

She rummaged through the frightening number of papers on the counter, many of which appeared to be receipts he bet she hadn't entered in her checkbook. No matter how many times he lectured her on the importance of balancing her account, she never seemed to do it.

"Do you ever feel like you can't see something even when it's in front of your face?" she asked as she rummaged.

If she hadn't given a triumphant exclamation and held up a notepad, he would have thought she'd read his mind and was referring to her sexy shimmy.

"I wrote down the exact wording of the complaint so I could tell you." She read from the pad. "Intentional infliction of emotional distress."

She cocked a hip, and his eyes flew to the tight fit of her jeans on her long legs. He rubbed a brow, because it felt like Amy was intentionally inflicting emotional distress on him.

Yeah, right, he thought. As though she had a clue that the libido of one of her closest friends would go ballistic over the sight of her in worn jeans, white athletic socks and that happy-face sweatshirt.

He tried to concentrate on her legal problem. "It sounds like a nuisance lawsuit to me."

"You bet it is," she said and crossed her arms over her chest. The motion pulled the sweatshirt tight and hinted at the size of her breasts. She was definitely bigger than a B cup, which he must've noticed before.

"So what are we going to do about it?" she asked.

He was in favor of her flashing him but that wasn't what she was asking. The case. He had to think about the case.

"We could possibly get the case thrown out of court but I need some more details," he said.

"What kind of details?"

"About this woman who's suing you—"

"It's not a woman," she interrupted. "It's a man."

That got Matt's attention off her curves. "A man is suing you for not liking his hair cut?"

"His name's Fabio."

His jaw actually dropped. "The cover model?"

She frowned. "I don't think this Fabio models."

Matt wasn't so sure of that. After all, how many men went by the name Fabio? A mental picture of the lawsuit-threatening Fabio emerged. Chiseled features, stately carriage, flowing locks he couldn't stand to have criticized. "Tell me what else Fabio's attorney said."

"What attorney?"

"The one who claimed you were intentionally inflicting emotional distress on his client."

"An attorney didn't tell me that. Fabio did."

"You talked to him?"

"Of course I did. He lives next door."

Matt made a face. "Here's my first piece of legal advice. You absolutely can't keep speaking to this man."

"But what should I do if I go outside to get the newspaper and he says, 'Good morning?'"

"Nod."

Her face fell. "It seems unfriendly not to speak."

He raised an eyebrow. "And suing you for intentional infliction of emotional distress is a friendly act?"

She bit her lower lip, which looked…lush. His heartbeat sped up and his breath caught.

"Am I in trouble?" she asked.

Not in nearly as much trouble as I am, Matt thought.

"I'm not sure." He dragged his gaze away from her luscious lips and stood up. "It doesn't sound like this Fabio has much of a case. Tell you what. Let me talk to him and see if I can make this whole thing go away."

"Great idea," she said and made a move to get past him. "Give me a minute to put on some shoes."

"Wait."

He closed his fingers over the delicate bones of her shoulder blade and she stopped dead. The electricity was back, radiating up his arm and zinging his heart, the same as before. He released her but his body still felt charged.

"More static electricity," she said.

He nodded. Or at least he thought he did. "That's what I figured."

Their eyes held and the electricity seemed to migrate from their bodies to the air.

"Did you want something?" she asked in a breathy voice.

Did he? The way his body was springing to life, it sure seemed like it.

"Yes," he said, and her mouth parted. In invitation?

"What do you want?" asked Amy. His buddy. His pal.

"I want you…" he said and chickened out, "…to stay here."

Her dark eyes filled with disappointment. He wanted to believe it was because he'd added a qualifier to the sentence but her next question nixed that hope. "Why?"

Because if I'm in your presence another minute, I'm going to do something stupid. Like kiss you.

"I already told you why." He strove for his most professional tone, which was difficult considering the decidedly unprofessional thoughts he'd been having. "It's not advisable to speak to someone who's suing you. I'll talk to him as your representative."

"But…" Amy began, then apparently thought better of protesting and gave a meek nod. "Okay."

"Okay?"

"Okay," she repeated, her voice as submissive as the nod.

He walked to the front door, not sure whether he was more worried about his newfound reaction to her or her newfound meekness. Because Amy Donatelli was anything but meek.

He'd barely swung the door open and stepped onto her small porch when he became aware of her presence behind him. He turned to see her balancing on one foot as she pulled on the second of her sneakers.

He sighed. "I thought you were staying put."

"I didn't tell you which house was Fabio's."

"Which house?" he asked, being careful to move out of electricity-generating range as she joined him on the small porch.

"It's... Oh, there's Fabio now."

He looked right, then left, canvassing the neighborhood for a chiseled Adonis with long, blond hair. But the only people in sight were a dark-headed boy on a tricycle, a grizzled old man the size of a jockey and a tall, matronly woman whose teased hair made her head appear twice its normal size. Of the three, the woman looked most like his mental picture of Fabio.

"Where?" Matt asked.

Amy moved abreast of him, so close that he could smell her. She wasn't the type to wear perfume or to put on scented moisturizers but she smelled clean and sweet all the same. Like strawberries, which was probably the scent of her shampoo.

"There." She pointed to the little old man at the same instant the sun hit his full head of white hair and turned it...blue? "See what I mean about his hair?"

He gave a low whistle. "That's not a color nature intended hair to be."

"Exactly." She sounded self-righteous. "What was I supposed to say when he asked me if I liked the new shade?"

"Yes," Matt hissed at her. "Everybody knows you don't tell the truth if a senior citizen asks what you think of his too-blue rinse. Don't you ever think before you speak?"

She grinned. "If I did, I wouldn't tell you I think you look cute when you're mad."

"Yoo-hoo, Miss Amy." The voice calling the greeting sounded so youthful it took Matt a moment to figure out it hailed from the old man. He turned, grateful for the interruption because he very much feared his face was turning red.

Fabio raised the gnarled hand not holding the morning newspaper and gave a cheerful wave. "Hello, neighbor."

"Why is he being so friendly?" Matt asked out of the side of his mouth.

"Fabio's always friendly," she answered in a low voice before waving back.

Friendly was a good sign—even though it didn't compute. "I'd better go talk to him," Matt said and strode across the green expanse of Amy's lawn.

"Hello there, young fella," Fabio said, his smile so bright Matt had to blink. He either had his teeth professionally whitened or those were one dynamite set of dentures. "Let me say right off the bat that any boyfriend of Miss Amy's is a friend of mine."

"I'm not her boyfriend," Matt said.

The man looked puzzled, then peered around Matt to focus on a spot behind him. "Is that true, Miss Amy?"

Amy? He'd instructed Amy to stay in the house. Matt whirled in time to see the confounded woman standing only a few feet behind him vigorously nodding her head.

Fabio scratched his. "I could have sworn... Well,

never mind that.'' To Amy, he said, ''Aren't you going to introduce us?''

This time Amy shook her head back and forth, which didn't make sense. Even though she didn't know when to keep her mouth shut, Amy was usually polite.

''I'm Matt Burke, Amy's lawyer,'' Matt said, sticking out his hand to make up for her lapse.

''Her lawyer?'' The man seemed more puzzled by the information than alarmed. His hand closed around Matt's in a surprisingly strong grip. ''The name's Fabio.''

''Pleased to meet you, Mr. Fabio,'' Matt said.

''Not Mr. Fabio. Fabio. Period. I go by the one name. Like Cher, Madonna and people of that ilk.'' He looked at Amy. ''Didn't you tell him that, Miss Amy?''

She nodded but still didn't speak. Matt, however, had plenty to say.

''I was hoping… Fabio…that I could have a moment of your time to talk about the specifics of the lawsuit you're bringing against my client.''

''Oh, sure.'' Fabio flashed those whiter-than-snow teeth. ''I made some brownies last night. Why don't the two of you come inside and have some.''

Matt was about to say he'd be glad to accept the invitation but Amy had other things to do when she stepped in front of him and gave another of her perplexing nods.

''Follow me,'' Fabio said and then practically hopped, skipped and jumped up the sidewalk leading to a house that was a virtual carbon copy of the one where Amy lived.

Amy followed, leaving Matt no choice but to keep pace.

"I thought you agreed to stay home," he said in a low, annoyed voice as he trailed her.

"You advised me not to speak to him," she whispered back. "That's what I agreed to."

"That's why you're not talking?"

"Uh-huh."

"And you think you can keep it up. You?" He shook his head. "Look who's talking about not talking."

Her smile grew wider. "*Look Who's Talking*. Starring John Travolta and Kirstie Alley and some anonymous baby."

He looked up at the sky, praying for patience. "I wasn't trying to stump you with a movie title. I mean it. You can't be quiet for that long."

"Can, too," she said. "Tell you what. I just got a new pair of Rollerblades. If I can keep quiet, you have to come skating with me this afternoon."

Alarm skittered through him. "Just you and me?"

"Zoe and Jack, too. They should be free by this afternoon."

"I don't skate," he said.

"Squawk, squawk," she said, flapping her elbows and doing a truly terrible imitation of a chicken.

"Okay, okay," he said in a low, insistent voice. "The bet's on, but only if you stop acting like a chicken."

Fabio, who had made terrific time in his dash for

the front door, stopped to wait for them. Amy flattened her elbows against her sides and gave Matt an impish look.

"What are you two whispering about?" Fabio asked.

He waited for Amy to answer but she put a hand in front of her mouth, shielding it from Fabio, and made a zippering motion across her lips. He couldn't help but smile.

"Nothing," Matt told Fabio.

"Looks like sweet nothings to me," the old man said and swung the door open. "Come on in."

Denying that he was Amy's boyfriend would have been repetitive so Matt indicated that Amy should precede him and followed her into Fabio's house.

In no time they were sitting next to each other on a plaid sofa in a living room so neat Matt wondered if Fabio employed a maid service. The coffee table where he set the plate of brownies smelled of lemon furniture polish and the carpet had been recently vacuumed.

"Go ahead, eat up," Fabio said. Matt started to call upon his willpower to resist junk food when it occurred to him that Fabio would be in a more amenable mood if they partook of his hospitality.

He picked up two brownies, handed one to Amy, took a big bite and nearly spit it back out.

"Good, aren't they?" Fabio asked, as though unaware he'd forgotten to add sugar to the batter. "I wish I could have one but I'm a diabetic. Can't even do a taste test. Still, I do love to bake."

Matt made himself chew and swallow. He nodded,

hoping his eyes weren't watering too much. Milk. He needed milk. He picked up the glass Fabio had provided and washed the brownie down with a huge swallow.

He turned to Amy to try to warn her, but it was too late. Her face was going through more contortions than a gymnast vying for a gold medal.

"I wanted to talk about this lawsuit you're considering bringing against Amy." Matt hid a smile. Served her right for not staying home. "I understand you haven't filed it yet."

"No, I haven't," Fabio said cheerfully, tilting his head to regard Matt as he might a favorite grandson. "You're a lawyer. Maybe you could tell me how to go about doing that."

Matt exchanged a look with Amy, who was still in no-sugar shock. Was this guy for real? "We'd prefer it if you wouldn't file the lawsuit at all."

Amy nodded in agreement.

Fabio folded his hands together on his lap and shook his head. "I don't know about that. Miss Amy did say she didn't like the rinse I was using."

At that moment, the sun peeked out from a passing cloud and shone through the window directly onto Fabio's blue hair. Matt squinted against the sight. He didn't know the ins and outs of hair care, but he didn't like the blue 'do, either.

"That doesn't mean she was intentionally inflicting emotional distress," Matt said.

"How do you know?"

"Because I know Amy," Matt automatically retorted. It wasn't the rational legal argument he should have given but that didn't seem to matter when Amy reached over and squeezed his hand in thanks. This time he didn't feel a sparkle of electricity but a flash of warmth.

"I don't know," Fabio said, but he seemed to be wavering. Matt decided to hit him with the full legal arsenal.

"To prove intentional infliction of emotional distress, you'd have to show that the defendant, Amy, acted intentionally or recklessly and that her conduct was extreme and outrageous. You'd also have to prove you were severely distressed."

"I wore a baseball cap for almost a day."

Amy tapped Matt on the shoulder and whispered in his ear, creating an all-body shiver he tried to hide. He nodded to acknowledge he'd heard her and concentrated on defending his client.

"But isn't it true, Fabio, that you often wear a baseball cap?" he asked, feeling like Perry Mason in the reruns he used to watch of the television courtroom drama. "That you, in fact, enjoy wearing one?"

Fabio seemed absolutely delighted by the question. "Why yes, that is true. Miss Amy, did you tell him that?"

She nodded soundlessly, causing Fabio to scrunch up his bushy gray eyebrows. "Is something wrong with your voice, Miss Amy?"

"I can't talk," she mouthed, no sound escaping her lips.

"You poor dear. Why didn't you tell me you had laryngitis before now?" Fabio didn't wait for an answer but got up and started for the kitchen, calling, "Wait there while I put on a pot of tea. I think I have cough drops somewhere, too."

"What is he trying to do?" Matt asked when he was out of earshot. "Kill us with kindness before he goes in for the kill?"

"I told you he was friendly," Amy whispered back. "Keep working on him. I think you're wearing him down."

An hour later, after Fabio had plied Amy with cough drops and tea and Matt had choked down another sugar-free brownie, Fabio suddenly made an announcement.

"Okay," he said. "I won't file the lawsuit."

Another fifteen minutes passed before Amy and Matt were in the sunshine, walking from Fabio's house to hers as the little, blue-haired man waved goodbye from his porch.

"Can I talk now, legal eagle?" she asked.

"*Legal Eagles.* Robert Redford and Debra Winger," he said. "Go ahead. Talk away."

"I have my own pair of blades but we can rent you skates at the rink," she said smugly.

He closed his eyes, remembering his promise. She usually had such a hard time keeping her mouth shut that he'd been positive he couldn't lose the bet. "Trust me, you don't want to go skating with me."

"Yes, I do. I won. You lost. So you can't back out."

"And here I thought we'd both won," he said dryly. "You did notice that he's not filing the lawsuit, didn't you?"

"Of course I noticed." She tugged at his hand, halting his progress and causing the electricity to flow. Her dark eyes were sincere when they met his. "Thank you."

She rose on tiptoe to press her warm, firm lips against his cheek. An erotic thrill ran through him, powerful enough to reach his nerve endings and make him want to haul her the rest of the way into his arms. But he couldn't. She was his buddy.

Not to mention the woman he was seriously beginning to lust after. The woman who, this very night, had a date with a man she'd been lusting after for years.

Considering that he and Amy would drive each other nuts in days if they hooked up as more than friends, it was a very good thing the specter of her OWGA loomed.

He wasn't going to examine why the thought of the looming OWGA made him so miserable.

3

So what if Zoe couldn't come skating, Amy told herself as she finished fastening her Rollerblades and got to her feet in the carpeted area of the Roller Emporium.

She wasn't nervous about being alone with her good friend Matt. Sure, it had occurred to her that this was the first time they'd operated as a twosome in the years they'd known each other.

But nothing romantic was going on between them. Why, he had a date with another woman that very night. And not just any other woman. His OWGA. The blasted Mary Contrary.

"What does she look like?"

Matt glanced up from the vinyl seat where he was lacing up a pair of ugly brown skates with orange wheels that looked like they belonged in an antique shop.

"What does who look like?"

She tapped the toe of one of her Rollerblades on the thin carpet and almost lost her balance. "The Contrary One."

He paused and seemed to search his memory. "Oh, Mary's beautiful. Long, wavy blond hair. Blue eyes. Peaches and cream complexion."

Amy half expected him to add that Mary favored sky-blue dresses that tied in the back with a white sash. Then she'd not only look like artist renderings of the nursery-rhyme character, she'd dress like them, too.

The corners of her mouth tugged downward as she pictured Matt with the woman with the nursery-rhyme perfect looks.

"What does the French guy look like?" Matt asked.

"He's the most handsome man in the world," she blurted out.

Matt let out a snort. "And what does the most handsome man in the world look like?"

The description that leapt to mind was the standard tall, dark and handsome, but she needed to do better than that. Specifics. She needed specifics.

"He's six feet six. More tan than—" she paused, trying to think of the name of the actor who seemed like he had a tanning booth for a second home "—George Hamilton. And gets mistaken for Cary Grant all the time."

"Isn't Cary Grant dead?"

"I meant Cary Grant's grandson," she corrected quickly.

"So he's abnormally tall, on the verge of getting skin cancer and doesn't have his own look?"

She bristled. "I told you, he's extremely handsome."

"Sounds like it." Sounding doubtful, Matt went back to lacing up his skates. Why couldn't he ever say anything nice about her imaginary man?

"Pierre wouldn't welsh on a bet," she said as she regarded his ancient skates. "He would have put on the Rollerblades."

"The bet was that I'd go skating with you." When Matt glanced up from his orange vinyl chair, Amy realized for the first time that his eyes were the exact color of toffee. Rich, creamy toffee. "You never specified that I had to wear Rollerblades."

She thrust aside her sudden craving for toffee and focused on their argument. What was wrong with her? "That's a technicality. I meant to say it."

"Cases are thrown out of court on technicalities all the time," he said. "It only counts if you actually do say it."

She stuck out her tongue at him, glad he'd reminded her why a relationship between them would never work. Not that she was thinking of embarking on one. "Do you have to act like such a stuffy lawyer all the time?"

"I don't know many stuffy lawyers who would spend a Saturday afternoon at a place like this," he said, indicating the roller rink with a sweep of his hand.

The centerpiece of the cavernous building was an oval rink with a polished wooden floor. Overhead lights flashed down on it, creating rotating patches of red and yellow. A snack bar was off to one side of the rink, a skate-rental counter to the other.

Children were everywhere. Laughing as they zoomed around the rink at top speed, crying as they took a spill, singing along to pop music that blared from the sound system.

"I think this is a great place," she said, breathing in the distinctive scent of floor wax.

"You would," he retorted but he did it with a smile that did funny, mushy things to her insides. The corners of his eyes crinkled and a dimple appeared in his right cheek. When had he become so handsome? Her eyes dipped. And when had he developed such a great body?

His shoulders were broad, his stomach flat, his legs long and dusted with golden hair.

"Amy?"

Her eyes flew to his, which seemed to be focused on...her lips? Was he asking if it would be okay if he kissed her.

"Yes," she said, then brought a hand to her mouth. "I mean no. No. The answer's no."

"I didn't ask the question yet."

"Oh, right. I knew that. Of course I knew that. Yes, I did." She was babbling and made herself stop. "What was the question?"

"Why were you staring at me?"

"Because you look good." She nearly rolled her eyes, especially when he grinned. Maybe he was right. Maybe she shouldn't always say what was on her mind. "But then those are designer workout clothes, aren't they?"

"They're what I had in the bag in my trunk. You told me I couldn't skate in slacks and a dress shirt," he said, skirting the question.

He didn't need to answer, anyway. She could tell his name-brand black shorts cost more than her jeans and T-shirt combined. Heck, his haircut probably cost more than her clothes. And he'd obviously dished out major bucks for the Lycra-blend material that allowed his unfaded yellow T-shirt to cling to his pectoral muscles.

She wondered if he bought famous-label underwear, if he wore boxers or briefs, if she was losing her mind.

This was Matt, the original Material Boy. Who had a date tonight with his OWGA.

He put his skate-encased feet on the floor, anchored both hands on the arm rest of the chair and stood by virtue of rippling biceps. Adonis on skates wouldn't look so fine.

Help, Zoe, she thought, looking wildly about for her friend. But Zoe wasn't there the way she'd always been in the past.

"You two will make a great team," Zoe had said. Had she meant in bed or out of it?

"Shall we?" Matt held out a hand she realized he expected her to take.

"I don't think we should," she blurted out.

"Should what?" He sounded confused.

"Touch," she said, then hastily explained. "Because of the static electricity."

Never mind that the science didn't make sense. She knew perfectly well that nobody wearing skates could scuff their feet and pick up those pesky static-causing electrons.

She was having a weird physiological reaction to him that could get her into major trouble.

Even if it hadn't been for Mary Contrary, she couldn't get romantically involved with him. He made a fine friend, but his workaholism coupled with his focus on money and the things it could buy would drive her crazy in no time. So would his unwillingness to cut loose and have fun. Like Zoe said, they were yin and yang. Which was okay for friends but not for lovers.

Not that she wanted to be his lover. Not really. Her eyes rose to the sculpted beauty of his face and dipped to that hard-muscled body. Her heart beat at hummingbird speed. Okay. So maybe she did want to be his lover. That didn't mean she could.

"I should call Zoe to see if she and Jack are back yet," Amy said, and her voice cracked like an eggshell. "I bet Zoe would love to come skating."

"Zoe likes to have her feet planted firmly on the ground," Matt said. "Skating's not her thing."

"When did she tell you that?"

"On the cell phone about ten minutes ago when I was changing clothes in the locker room."

She immediately thought of him stripping down to his famous-label underwear. *Oh, boy*, she thought and fanned herself.

"Something wrong?"

"Yes."

"Are you having second thoughts about the skating?" he asked, sounding a little too eager. "Do you want to do something else? Like take in a movie?"

"No!"

Sitting beside him in the darkness, with only an armrest separating her from all that gorgeous male flesh, would be much worse than skating alongside him.

"Why not?" he asked. "You're usually up for a movie."

She was about to tell him they couldn't go to a movie unless Zoe was along to sit between them when a wild-haired girl, no older than six or seven, suddenly got up from the seat where she'd been putting on her skates and headed for the rink at full speed.

"Out of the way, people," she yelled. A demonic look glazed her eyes as she barreled through.

Matt barely moved in time to avoid being clipped, then raised an eyebrow in his trademark gesture. "You sure about the movie?"

"I'm sure," she said.

"You do realize that we're going to be in the line of fire all day, don't you?"

"In the Line of Fire," Amy said automatically. "Clint Eastwood, John Malkovich, René Russo."

And Amy Donatelli.

She hadn't been one of the stars of that movie, of course. But the way she was reacting to Matt, she very definitely was in the line of fire.

Fire that had nothing to do with combat and everything to do with chemistry.

AMY GLIDED AROUND THE outside edge of the roller rink until she caught a glimpse of Matt ahead of her.

Twenty minutes had passed since they'd taken to the rink and she'd yet to skate alongside him, but that was hardly her fault. Even if she hadn't been wary of that boomeranging electricity, she couldn't skate that slowly.

She put on the jets to get by him, did a graceful half turn and faced him while she skated backward. A half-dozen small children zoomed by Matt and past her before she spoke.

"Is there something wrong with your skates?"

He glanced down at the antiques. "Why do you ask?"

"You're not going very fast."

"That's because I asked the rental guy to tighten my wheels so I wouldn't fall."

Amy's mouth dropped open. She indicated an instructor with a group of very young children, who were marching on their skates like miniature soldiers.

"They tighten the wheels on children's skates when they're learning," she said.

"I know." Matt pointed to a child with pants so droopy his mother probably needed to think about changing his pull-up. "That little guy was in line ahead of me. That's where I got the idea."

"Why didn't you just ask if you could take the class?" she asked jokingly.

"I did." He shrugged those broad shoulders. Colored lights shone on him, casting him in red, then yellow. "But the rental guy said you had to be five years old or under."

She took his hand. That pesky electricity crackled, but she ignored it. She had more important things on her mind. "Come on, buster. Let's go get those wheels loosened."

"Okay. But if I fall, it'll be on your head," he said with more good nature than she would have expected.

"That would hurt," she said, "so let's hope I'm as good at teaching skating as I am kindergarten."

Thirty minutes later, Amy strove to keep up with Matt as his strongly muscled legs powered his grandpa skates around the rink. Darn him. He might spend the bulk of his time in a law office but he moved with the grace of a natural athlete.

"You conned me," she said, her breath more labored than she would have liked. "You can too skate."

"I never said I couldn't skate," Matt said. "I said I hadn't skated in a long time."

"The way you're moving," she said as her eyes once again took in the sleek, powerful muscles of his legs, "it couldn't have been that long."

"Guess it's like riding a bicycle. It's something you never forget."

They took a turn side by side and came up fast on a stumbling teenager trying hard to regain his balance. Amy veered right and Matt cut left, safely bracketing the boy until they came back together on the other side.

"Lucky for him we're so quick on our feet or he'd be a skate sandwich," Matt said, his eyes sparkling.

She laughed, enjoying a glimpse into his playful side. She thought about what he said about never forgetting how to ride a bicycle.

"I'll never forget skating with you for the first time," Amy said, then could have groaned. She hadn't meant to say that aloud. What would he make of it?

He turned his head, smiled and winked. "Me, neither."

Cool air rushed over her face as they skated. Along with his comment, it chased away the hot blush of embarrassment that had started to stain her cheeks. The memory, it seemed, wouldn't only be hers. It would be theirs.

When the announcer proclaimed the next skate for couples only and Matt took her hand, it felt like the most natural thing in the world. Even with the electricity crackling between them.

"Shall we?" he said and they skated off to the saccharine strains of a ballad by one of those bands that featured a quartet of dancing, singing teenage boys.

"Strike up the band," he said, "we're coming through."

She giggled. "Jimmy Connors and Judy Garland."

"Gotcha," he said. "Jimmy Connors was a character in the movie, not to mention the name of a pretty good tennis player. Mickey Rooney was the star."

"You're right," she said, not at all put out by being wrong. How could she feel disappointed at being stumped when it felt so right skating with him?

They skated in silence as she drank up the sensations: the warmth of his hand, the coolness of the air, the slow beat of the music. He skated gracefully, like a big cat.

Who would have thought she could be turned on by a cat? Or that she'd never want this day with Matt to end, as it would in a few hours? A thought struck her. Why did it have to? She didn't really have a date tonight and, with any luck, she could persuade Matt to cancel his.

What the heck. She might have a better chance of successfully getting Matt to cancel if she confessed that Pierre was a figment of her imagination. And that Matt was the man she wanted to be with tonight.

"Matt. There's something I need to ask you," she said and his toffee-colored eyes focused on hers. They were smiling, like her lips. The song ended and blood pounded in her ears, so loud she could hear it unless…

She turned in time to see at least a dozen adolescents wearing paper birthday hats and all-systems-go grins flood the rink directly into their path.

Matt let go of her hand and tried to zig. Amy tried to zag. For a pregnant moment, it seemed they'd successfully avoid crashing to the floor but then Matt's wheel clipped hers and they both went down.

Matt did a half split and spun around before landing stretched on his side. Amy hit the floor hard, her butt bouncing once.

"Ha, ha, lady. You wiped out!" one of the birthday-hat wearing brats yelled as he skated away.

Matt scrambled to his knees and half crawled to her side to help her to her feet. "Are you okay?" he asked as his strong arms lifted her.

"I'm fine," she said when she was on her skates. Her smarting backside was not uppermost in her mind. Matt was.

Her hands pressed into the solid muscle of his shoulders, his concerned eyes bore into hers. Unable to help herself, she reached up and laid her hand alongside one of his high cheekbones. They were in the middle of a rink with children zooming around them, but it felt like they were alone.

"Before we fell," he said in a low voice, "what were you going to ask me?"

It wasn't so much what she'd been going to ask him as what she'd been about to do. She'd meant to kiss him. Not right then and not at the rink, but surely tonight if he agreed to cancel the date with his OWGA.

She would have kissed Matt. Her friend. Who'd never last as her boyfriend because of his studied, materialistic view of life. For gosh sake, he drove a BMW and lived in a pricey D.C. condo. She used public transportation, happily existed on a private schoolteacher's salary and couldn't have afforded to live in Arlington if she wasn't housesitting for a fellow teacher's globe-trotting parents.

The fall, it seemed, had knocked the sense back into her. She dropped her hand from his face.

"Do you think Mickey Rooney could play tennis?" she asked lamely. "He was kind of short to be a basketball player, but tennis players don't have to be all that tall."

"You wanted to talk about Mickey Rooney?" He sounded dazed, which made her realize she hadn't yet asked him how he'd fared in the fall.

"I also want to know if you're okay," she said.

His full lips twisted. "I was doing fine, but now I feel like the man who fell to earth."

"Starring David Bowie," she supplied.

"And Rip Torn," he added, "which is appropriate because I think that's what I did to my shorts."

Not able to resist, she craned her neck to get a view of his back side and got a glimpse of his underwear through the tear. It was black, which was the last color she would have expected him to wear.

Great, she thought wryly.

Not only had she committed herself to a date with a man who didn't exist, but she'd spend the whole miserable evening fantasizing about what Matt would look like wearing nothing but his black-as-sin underwear. Or, better yet, nothing at all.

MATT HAD BEEN TRYING to hold out until 11:00 a.m. but at a few minutes past ten, he turned away from the legal briefs spread across the desk in his home office and picked up the phone.

He dialed Amy's number from heart, mentally phrasing a question about how she was feeling after the tumble she'd taken so she wouldn't suspect his real reason for calling was to find out about her date.

One ring... He pictured her moving across her small, cluttered house on her long, lovely legs.

Two rings... She'd be nearly there, hopefully unhampered by bruises and stiffness.

Three rings... She should be reaching for the receiver, eager to confide that she'd seen through the smooth-talking Frenchman's act clear to his insincere heart.

Four rings... Why wasn't she picking up? Had she stayed out so late that she was still asleep?

Five rings... Was she suffering from the delusion

that a man who'd barely refrained from seducing a student teacher actually made a worthy OWGA?

Six rings... Was she even at home? It was early Sunday morning, for cripe sake. If Frenchy had so much as touched her with his pinky finger, he would—

"'Lo." Amy's voice, heavy with sleep, came over the line.

Matt blew out a relieved breath. "You're there."

"'Course I'm here. I live here." She seemed to be making a concentrated effort to wake up. He pictured her stretched out in bed, her mouth parted, her eyes heavy-lidded, her body warm from sleep. Did she wear a skimpy camisole to bed? An oversize T-shirt with nothing underneath? Nothing at all?

"Who's this?" Amy asked.

Fueled by his imagination, Matt's breaths were coming much too hard. He struggled to get his breathing back under control so he could answer her with some semblance of normalcy.

"Is this an obscene caller?" She sounded wide-awake now. And mad. Very, very mad. "Because this heavy breathing thing won't work with me, buster. Why, I oughta—"

"Amy, it's me," he interrupted. "Matt."

There was a pause at the other end of the line. "Matt? I don't understand. Why are you breathing like that?"

"Because... I just got back from a run." He closed his eyes, praying for forgiveness. Surely telling a white lie was preferable to being thought of as a pervert. "I, uh, sprinted the last mile."

"But it's pouring outside," Amy pointed out.

Matt's condo was on the top floor of a fashionable high-rise in downtown D.C., and he became aware of the steady pounding of the raindrops on the roof. A glance at the window revealed heavy sheets of gray rain.

"I ran on a treadmill," he said. "Downstairs. In the exercise room."

"Does that mean you and Mary Contrary had an early night?"

Matt rubbed his forehead, completely unprepared for the question. He'd been so focused on Amy's date with her OWGA that he'd forgotten he'd supposedly had a date with his.

How could he tell her that the date had gone badly, or that it hadn't gone at all, when she and Pierre had stayed out so late she was asleep at ten o'clock?

"Not at all," he said. "You know me, I'm an early riser. Mary and I partied the night away."

"Mary likes to party? You mean, as in drinking and dancing?"

The way she said it, Mary sounded like a lush. "Dancing more than drinking."

"But you don't dance."

As a rule, he didn't. "I like to watch people dancing."

"You mean Mary was dancing with other men?"

He grimaced. "No. She was kind of dancing…alone."

"You mean on tables?"

"No. Not on tables. In the aisles."

"I hadn't realized Mary was so wild."

"She's not wild, just…uninhibited," he said and figured he better change the subject. The way this conversation was going, he'd probably say Mary had learned to dance at a strip club. "How did your date with Pierre go?"

"Great," she said instantly. "Make that fantastic. Stupendous, actually. Incredible even."

He cradled the phone against his ear. A powerful wave of a nameless emotion churned through him with such nauseating power it was difficult to phrase the next question. "So he's everything you remembered?"

"He's better than I remembered. Much more handsome."

Oh, yeah? "Mary's more beautiful. And sweet. Very sweet."

"Pierre's romantic."

Not in Matt's book, he wasn't. "Yeah, I remember how he calls you his amoeba."

"He's so romantic, he…wants to cook for me. He subscribes to the theory that the way to a woman's heart is through her stomach."

"I thought that was the way to a man's heart," he said, then couldn't stop himself from adding, "which I suppose is why Mary's having me over for dinner."

"Pierre's such a wonderful cook, he can prepare a feast anywhere. In fact, he doesn't want me to go to the trouble of traveling to his house. So he's going to cook at mine."

"When?" he asked through clenched teeth. Just how fast of an operator was this guy?

"When what?"

"When is Pierre coming to your house to cook the feast?"

She didn't answer for so long that he thought she wouldn't tell him. Had she picked up on the vitriol in his voice?

"Friday night," she finally said.

"Is that right?"

"That's right," she said.

Silence stretched over the line while he fought the urge to demand that she cancel the dinner date. But how could he do such a thing when he'd invented one of his own?

"Matt?" She broke the silence first, flaring hope that she'd ask him to break his date, which he'd do gladly. Even if he actually had one. "Were you calling for any particular reason?"

He felt sure he had been calling for a reason, but the disappointment radiating through him made it hard to remember what it was. He resurrected a familiar discussion.

"When did you say the people you're housesitting for are returning?"

"Just before Christmas," she answered with a heavy sigh, "which is the same answer I've given you the dozen or so other times you've asked."

"You know I'm worried about you finding another place to live that you can afford," he said. "I did your taxes, Amy. All you pay now is utilities and you're barely getting by."

"I'm getting by fine," Amy said. "I'm not worried, so you shouldn't be, either."

"But what are you going to do? What's your plan?"

"I don't know yet," Amy said. "It's two months away."

"But—"

"Did you call me up to argue with me?"

Her question stopped him, because arguing hadn't been on his agenda when he'd picked up the phone. He'd had a crazy hope she'd tell him her date with Pierre had been a bust and suggest the two of them get together. Instead she'd raved about Frenchy and he'd picked an argument.

"Of course not," he said, clearing the way for the two of them to say their goodbyes.

After he hung up, he realized he'd forgotten to ask if she was suffering any lingering effects from their fall.

He certainly felt bruised and battered enough for the both of them, except it wasn't his arms, legs or torso feeling the pain.

It was his jealous heart.

4

CHILDISH LAUGHTER and high-pitched shouts carried on the crisp, fall breeze as Matt got out of his BMW in front of the Ambrose Academy.

Despite the lofty name and its position as a private school, the Academy wasn't anybody's idea of a status symbol. Housed in a modest, low-slung brick building, it existed largely to give the children of hard-working, dual-income parents a private-school education at a cut-rate cost.

Amy had taken a job there without regard to the fact that she could have made more money just about anywhere else. He'd tried to explain the concept of getting the most buck for your bang, but she obviously hadn't been listening.

"Hey, Miss Amy, watch this!"

Matt had been heading for the office, but veered toward the playground at the back of the school when he heard a child call Amy's name.

He rounded the corner of the building to see a small boy with a shock of curly black hair standing on top of one of the slides. He had his hands outstretched like wings.

Before Matt could rush to the rescue, Amy was already there, catching the child as he launched him-

self into the air. The boy was so small that she staggered but didn't fall. She hugged him fiercely to her
for a second, then set him down on the wood chips
of the playground.

"I know you plan to grow up to be a superhero,
Timmy," she began in a patient voice.

"Not just any superhero," the boy cut in. "Super
Hawk Man."

"You need to remember that super heroes, even
ones as super cool as Super Hawk Man, don't develop their powers until they're at least teenagers."
She put her hands on his narrow shoulders and gazed
straight into his eyes. "Until then, you have to promise me not to leap off tall things."

"I promise, Miss Amy."

The boy gave her a teacher-knows-best nod, gazing at her with big, worshipful eyes. Matt didn't
blame the kid. Perhaps it was because he hadn't seen
her in five, long days. Perhaps it was something else.
But he couldn't take his eyes off Amy, either.

She was wearing one of those flowing, unstructured dresses that would have looked like a sack on
anyone else, but Amy had paired it with a chunky
necklace and funky black ankle boots that managed
to give it pizzazz.

She'd pulled her mass of dark hair back into a no-
nonsense ponytail that called attention to her great
bone structure and clear skin. She smiled at the little
boy, probably to soften her censure, and Matt's
breath caught.

She looked magnificent.

Urgent, the phone message she'd left with his secretary at the law firm had said.

He was aware of his own sense of urgency, like a stiff wind at his back, pushing him to go to her.

Because he wanted to hurry, he made himself walk slowly. The sun was high in a cloudless blue sky, and he appreciated the way it caught her dark hair and infused it with fiery highlights that matched the golds and reds in the autumn leaves. The wind whipped her unstructured dress against her body, accentuating her woman's shape, making his heart pound.

The slender young woman who worked as Amy's kindergarten aid called the dark-haired boy over to the game she was organizing. She tossed a husky blond girl a bright orange ball and positioned Timmy at a makeshift plate.

"Hey, teacher," Matt called to Amy.

Her concentration on her students had been so total that she visibly started before she turned. When she caught sight of him, her mouth dropped open.

"Oh, my gosh," she exclaimed as he walked the rest of the way toward her. "Is it safe for you to be out of the law office in broad daylight? You're not going to melt or anything, are you?"

"Very funny," Matt said, shoving one hand in his pocket. "I do leave the building for lunch engagements and appointments, you know. And I don't work late every night."

"You worked late last night."

"Only because you bowed out of happy hour so

you could go with Zoe to watch Jack coach that fall baseball game.''

"Oh, come on, Matt. You probably wouldn't have shown anyway. You work so much that, for you, a sixty-hour workweek is the norm. So when you only work fifty-five hours, it seems as though you're getting off at a reasonable hour.''

"What I think is reasonable and what you think is reasonable isn't necessarily the same thing,'' he began, mounting a familiar argument. "I—''

"Matt, watch out!'' Amy yelled an instant before the orange kickball slammed into his shoulder.

Considering it had been launched by a five-year-old, the ball hit with more force than he'd have thought possible. The ricochet sent it bouncing back toward the group of children, flying through the air like a big orange menace.

Big-eyed, dark-haired Timmy was at the plate, looking as innocent as an angel.

"Sorry, Miss Amy's friend,'' the boy said with a lisp so pronounced it was cute. "You gots to be more careful.''

Amy took Matt's arm, ushering him slightly away from the children's game. The electricity zinged him again. Judging by the way she dropped his arm, it probably zapped her, too, but this time she didn't mention it. She merely looked up at him, her pretty dark eyes questioning.

"What are you doing here, Matt?'' she asked.

"I got your message and came to see what you needed.''

"In the middle of the day?''

Matt shrugged. "I tried calling you first but the woman who answered the phone said the best she could do was put a message in your mailbox."

"You must not have gotten Barbara then. She'd do anything for a man with a sexy voice."

Pleasure skimmed through him, as refreshing as the breeze. "You think I have a sexy voice?"

"Well, yeah," she said as though it were obvious. "But, sexy voice or not, class isn't supposed to be interrupted unless the message is urgent."

"My secretary said your message *was* urgent."

Amy brought both hands to her mouth and shook her head as she gazed at him. Her eyes seemed to turn a softer brown. "Do you mean to say you left your office in the middle of the afternoon because you thought I needed you?"

He scuffed a foot and looked away from her knowing eyes. "I had to take a deposition from someone who doesn't live too far from here."

"How far?"

"Five miles," he said, then met those soft brown eyes, "give or take twenty miles."

"Matt Burke," she said, smiling at him so that her entire face glowed, "I think I might swoon."

If that wasn't a cue to tell her she meant more to him than some fictitious Mary he'd stolen from a nursery rhyme, he didn't know what was.

"Listen, Amy," he said, taking a step forward. "I...ow!"

This time, the kickball hit him in the small of the back. He whirled in time to see the dark-haired culprit's grin of triumph. The little boy wiped the look off his face faster than a teacher erases chalk from the board.

"You're out, Miss Amy's friend," the boy yelled in his innocent, lisping singsong voice. "When the ball hits you, that means you gots to leave."

"That's how you play dodgeball, not kickball," Matt said.

"It is too how you play kickball." The kid rested his hands on his skinny hips. "You're not too smart, are you, mister?"

"Timmy Carson!" Amy's assistant strode across the playground until she was standing in front of the little boy. "Remember how we talked about respecting your elders? Miss Amy's friend is an elder."

"Thanks a lot," Matt muttered under his breath.

"Just 'cause he's old don't mean he's right," the kid said petulantly.

"Timmy, I want you to apologize." Amy's voice held a warning note, and this time the message got through to the little boy.

"Sorry, Mr. Old Guy," he said, but made clear he was apologizing under protest by thrusting out his tongue, sticking his thumbs in his ears and wagging his fingers when the teachers weren't looking.

"Listen, Matt, this isn't a good time," Amy said in a low voice when the children returned to their kickball game. "We should probably talk about this later."

He refrained her with a hand on her arm and kept it there despite the jumping electrons. No way, no how was he leaving until he knew what this was about. "Talk about *what* later?"

Now that the question was out, he was aware that he was holding his breath as he waited for her answer.

"Fabio says he's going to file another lawsuit."

The breath whooshed out of him, like a bubble that had been burst with a sharp needle. He dropped her arm as he tried to make his brain process the information.

"Your urgent message was about a lawsuit?" he asked.

She nodded, tipping her head as she looked at him. "What did you think it was about?"

He'd thought she was going to tell him she'd decided to dump her OWGA so she could date him instead. His throat closed and he swallowed to make a pathway for his words.

"I wasn't sure," he said, squaring his shoulders so she couldn't tell he was fighting disappointment, "but I'm surprised Fabio is still a problem. I thought I convinced him you didn't intentionally inflict emotional distress on him."

"You did," Amy said. A gust of wind blew tendrils of her loose hair into her eyes and he had to clench his hands to keep from smoothing the hair back from her forehead. "But now he's claiming I keep him awake at night by playing loud music."

"You don't have a stereo," he said.

"When I told him that, he said I must've been watching music videos on MTV," she said wryly.

"Watch out, mister!"

This time, the warning came from a little girl with a high, sweet voice. Matt whirled in time to see the orange ball hurtling toward him, like a warning. He put out his hands and caught it.

Timmy was no longer at the plate, but his right leg was in a follow-through position, as though he'd cocked and fired from his place in the infield.

Amy clapped her hands and laughed before calling to the little boy, "Now you're the one who's out, Timmy."

Matt didn't believe it, though. Despite his over-whelming propensity to be a jealous brat, Timmy was obviously a favorite with Amy. So, for that matter, was Pierre.

Matt might be holding the ball, but he was the odd man out.

AMY THOUGHT THE STARS casting Arlington in a bright, clear light were inappropriate considering the mess she'd gotten herself into.

If her brain had been operating on even half its cylinders when Matt dropped by the school yester-day, she'd have pinned him down on when he in-tended to talk to the litigious Fabio.

But her mind had shut down somewhere between realizing he'd left the office in the middle of the day—for her—and realizing he was the most attrac-tive man she knew.

When he'd promised to stop by to talk to Fabio, she'd nodded like a bobble-head doll, only later re-alizing she'd given him carte blanche to visit on Fri-day. The same day Pierre was supposed to whip her up a culinary feast.

Her hope that Matt would show up late in the af-

ternoon, well before any self-respecting man who
didn't exist would think about starting to cook, had
died hours ago.

It was nearly seven-thirty, prime chef time, and
Matt still hadn't arrived. She was starting to think he
was timing his visit to coincide with the one Pierre
was supposedly paying her. Was Matt on to her? Did
he know there was no Pierre?

The thought sent her rushing to her bathroom mirror, prime position for a woman who was a rotten
liar. She not only needed to whip up a story explain-
ing why Pierre wasn't going to show, but she needed
to make it convincing.

"Oh, hello, Matt," she said to the mirror. "Pierre?
Oh, yes, he was supposed to cook for me tonight.
But, alas, he got tied up at the office."

She frowned at herself, then shook her head. Lawyers like Matt got tied up at the office, not French
teachers who worked out of a high-school classroom.
She tried again.

"Unfortunately my darling Pierre has been called
away on a family emergency." She put her hand to
her throat for dramatic effect. "Oh, yes. His devotion
to his family is very pleasing."

Her brows knotted as she peered into her image in
the mirror, which was suddenly full of inconvenient
questions.

"What kind of an emergency, you ask? You want
to know why, if Pierre and I are so close, that I'm
not seeing him through his time of need?"

She made a face at herself, because she didn't have
any good answers. Of course she'd stay by Pierre's

side. If, in fact, he actually had a body. The only thing that should be able to keep her away was a communicable disease.

"That's it," she told the mirror excitedly. "Pierre's sick! And so contagious he can't bear to have me near him in case he makes me sick, too."

When the doorbell rang a few moments later, Amy was still tossing around possibilities of what could have befallen poor Pierre. Pink eye, pin worms, head lice…

"Hey, Amy," Matt said when she opened the door. She barely had time to appreciate the way the cut of his suit accentuated the breadth of his shoulders and length of his legs before he asked, "Isn't tonight the night Pierre's supposed to cook for you?"

"Yes." She was ready to spit out the reason Pierre had sent his regrets when it occurred to her that he hadn't told her an important nugget of information. "When is Mary supposed to cook for you?"

"Tomorrow night."

"Does she know you're allergic to moo goo gai pan?" She remembered the way his face had flushed a couple months ago when Zoe suggested dinner at that Chinese restaurant. She'd have poured a glass of water over his head to cool him down if Zoe hadn't grabbed her arm. "Give me Mary's number and I'll make sure she's not making moo goo."

"It's the MSG I'm allergic to, not the moo goo gai pan. Besides, Mary wouldn't cook that anyway."

"Are you sure? I don't mind calling her to check." And to try to figure out what Mary had that Amy didn't.

"I'm sure." Matt leveled her with one of those serious looks that usually made her want to scream at him to lighten up. This one made her nervous.

"Pierre stood you up, didn't he?" he asked abruptly.

"Pierre would never stand me up," Amy retorted. He didn't look as though he believed her, so she felt compelled to add, "Why, the only way he'd break a date with me is…if he were dead!"

She nearly kicked herself when she realized what she'd done. If she invented an ailment for Pierre now, it'd have to be fatal.

"If Pierre's here," Matt said, leaning closer to her, "then where's his car?"

"He arrived by taxi," she said, then instantly realized her mistake when she noticed Matt's bottom lip turn slightly downward.

Like most men, Matt dug cars. He was the target audience for automobile advertisers who draped beautiful women over gleaming machines. Something about the combination screamed testosterone, which is what Matt probably thought a man without a car lacked.

How dare he think Pierre didn't have testosterone!

"Pierre has a car," she said. "A big, powerful one."

Matt cocked an eyebrow. "Does he drive it?"

"Of course he does," she said, then tried to think of the reason it wasn't parked in her driveway. She was about to claim Pierre's car was in the shop when the argument suddenly struck her as too simple. "But he hasn't gotten used to driving on the right side of the road.''

"Didn't he grow up in France?" Matt asked.

"Yes. In the…" Amy racked her brains as she tried to remember a region of France, "Countryside de la France."

"Do you mean the French countryside?"

"*Sí.*"

"*Oui.*"

"What?"

"*Oui* is the French word for yes, not *sí.*"

"*Oui* it is. Pierre grew up in the French country-side."

"Drivers in the French countryside use the right side of the road, the same as they do in the French cities," Matt said. "It's the British who drive on the left."

Amy fought to keep her eyes from closing in mortification. How could she have mixed up her left-handed countries like that?

"Pierre's mother is British," Amy said lamely. "She's the one who taught him to drive."

"Then it's a good thing he took a taxi," Matt said. He tilted his head, as though trying to look around her. She stayed where she was, which was essentially blocking the doorway. "I'd like to meet him."

"You can't," she said, stifling an urge to wipe her damp palms on her dress.

"Why not? I thought you said he was here."

"He is here." She had to do something—and fast—to wipe the suspicious look off Matt's face. "But he's in the bathroom."

"I can wait until he gets out."

"That's not such a good idea. He'll be a while."

Matt wrinkled his nose, clueing Amy as to what he was thinking.

"Oh, no," she said, waving her hands frantically. "It's not what you think. It's just that, well, the plumbing isn't working at his place."

"You can't mean he's taking a shower in there?"

"Possibly," Amy said and searched her brain for something positive to say. "Pierre likes to be clean, Especially, I would think, before he cooks."

Matt appeared speechless for a moment before he said, "Are you making this up?"

"How dare you accuse me of that," Amy spat out, hurt to the core. Matt had known her for years. He, of all people, should know what an honest person she was. "I'm not a liar."

"I shouldn't have said that," Matt said, immediately conciliatory. "I know you don't lie. Can you forgive me?"

"Oh, all right," Amy said, still miffed.

True, she didn't really have anything to forgive him for considering that Pierre was a complete fabrication. But, darn it, she never would have invented him in the first place if Matt hadn't spouted off about Mary Contrary. Anybody could see her lies were his fault.

"It's just that Pierre seems so…weird," Matt continued. "Maybe he's lying to you. Have you thought of that?"

"He's not lying to me," Amy said, leaping to the imaginary man's defense. "He's not weird, either."

"Eccentric, then," Matt said.

"In the very best sense of the word," she said with gusto, then nodded toward Fabio's house, which had so many lights glowing it looked like a giant birthday cake. "It looks like Fabio's expecting you."

After Matt had walked across the lawn between her house and Fabio's and she heard the old-timer greet him like a beloved grandson, Amy closed the door and leaned the back of her head against it.

Not only had that been way too close of a call, but it wasn't over yet. Matt was bound to check back in after he spoke to Fabio, presumably when she was in the middle of being served a French feast.

She raced to the kitchen, pulling cookbooks haphazardly from the shelves until she found one with a section on French cooking. She leafed through the pages, growing increasingly despondent until inspiration struck.

She rummaged through drawers, pulling out in turn an envelope of Bernaise sauce mix, a couple hunks of cheese and the never-been-used fondue pot her mother had bought her five years ago.

She'd plop the cheese in the fondue pot, melt a couple candy bars in a pot on the stove to make it smell as though Pierre was whipping up chocolate mousse for dessert and pop open a bottle of wine for effect.

The smells alone would convince Matt something wonderful was cooking, but she needed something more. Something to convince Matt that Pierre was doing the cooking.

She wandered around her house, searching for

anything she could dress up, prop in a chair and pass off as a Frenchman. Her gaze fell on Pandamonium, the giant stuffed animal she'd borrowed from Zoe when she'd been teaching her kindergarten students about panda bears.

Five minutes later, she stood back and surveyed her handiwork. She'd propped Pandamonium on a pot to add the illusion of great height and positioned him with his back to the door. His Hawaiian shirt, one her father had left behind on his last visit, probably deliberately, was adequate. The witch's wig she had left over from Halloween was less so, but it would have to do.

"Take that, Matt Burke," she said aloud, imagining his reaction when he got a glimpse of the panda bear in disguise.

That should teach him not to accuse her of making up things.

MATT STOOD OFF TO THE SIDE of the window in Fabio's living room, holding back the sheers so he could get a clear view of Amy's little house.

The lights were on and the blinds drawn. So far he'd gotten a shadowy glimpse of Amy moving through the living room but that was it. As much as he'd contorted his body, he hadn't been able to get a clear view into the kitchen.

"As you can see, there isn't much space between your girlfriend's house and mine," Fabio was saying. "When the wind blows this way and she has her music on, I can't hardly hear myself think."

Matt narrowed his eyes, but squinting didn't help. He still couldn't get a glimpse of Pierre.

"Do you think my lawsuit would be stronger if I said I had to wear ear muffs around the house?"

Something moved in front of one of Amy's windows, so imperceptibly that Matt wasn't sure he'd seen anything. But then it moved again and Matt cocked his head this way and that until he realized he could see the faintest outline of an aquarium. And the silhouette of Speedy Gonzales, Amy's box turtle, who was probably waking up from a nap.

"I thought about saying I had to wear earplugs but maybe that's too much? What do you think?"

Darn. What was going on in there?

"Matt."

The sound of his name diverted Matt's attention from Amy's house to Fabio. The blue rinse seemed fainter today and might not have been perceptible at all if Fabio hadn't been on a monochromatic kick. Everything he had on was robin's-egg blue, including his tennis shoes and socks.

"Yeah?" Matt said, eager to get back to the window.

"What do you think?"

"About what?"

Fabio gave him a disappointed look. "I suppose I understand you can't advise me on my lawsuit but there must be some questions you want to ask me."

"Yes," Matt said. "There certainly are."

Fabio clapped his hands. "I just knew a lawyer as good as you seem to be would want to get the lowdown from—"

"Did you see a French guy arrive at Amy's place in a taxi a little while ago?" Matt interrupted.

Fabio sat up straight. "Excuse me?"

"A French guy," Matt repeated. "Amy says he's handsome, but I'm not so sure. He's extremely tall and I have serious questions about his hygiene."

"I didn't see anyone but I wasn't watching," Fabio said. "I was baking an apple cobbler so I could offer it to you later."

"Did you hear anything?" Matt pressed. "A car horn? A greeting? A couple lines from *Madame Butterfly?*"

"Nothing like that," Fabio said, then pointed at his left ear, which was fitted with a hearing aid. "I don't hear all that well."

The fact that Fabio wore a hearing aid seemed to be important, but at the moment Matt couldn't bother to figure out why. Driven by an urge he didn't understand, Matt strode across the room until he was directly in front of Fabio.

"How's your eyesight?"

Fabio backed up a little in his seat. "Twenty-fifty without my glasses," he said slowly. "Twenty-twenty with them."

"Can you tell me, Fabio, if you've spotted other men entering and exiting Miss Donatelli's house?"

"Well, yes. There's Dylan."

Matt's heart nearly stopped. One of the most important rules of cross-examination was not to ask a question if you didn't know the answer. He'd believed Pierre was his only competition and now he'd found out that the mysterious Dylan was also in the running.

"On second thought," Fabio said, "I'm not so sure Dylan goes *inside* Amy's house, but she does come to the door to give him money, I do know that."

Matt shook his head in horror. First Amy had gotten involved with an operatic Frenchman without a functioning bathroom and now she'd taken up with a freeloader.

"Where can I find this Dylan?" Matt asked, barely containing his anger.

"He lives a couple doors down, but I wouldn't go over there too late at night," Fabio said. "His parents like him to go to bed early."

"He lives with his parents?"

"Most thirteen-year-olds do," Fabio said. "Although Dylan's more industrious than most, I personally think he charges too much to mow the lawn."

Matt rubbed his brow as the reality of the situation sunk in. He'd been jealous of a thirteen-year-old when the real threat was inside Amy's house, cooking her dinner. "You sure you haven't seen this French guy before?"

"You mean the extremely tall fellow with the hygiene problem?"

Matt frowned as it again struck him that Pierre didn't sound quite real. He hadn't even mentioned to Fabio that the Frenchman was unnaturally tanned, a really bad driver and quite possibly a seducer of French students.

"He sounds like somebody's idea of a bad joke, doesn't he?" Matt asked. "Do you know I accused Amy of making him up?"

"You think this tall guy is a figment of her imagination?"

Matt quickly shook his head. "No, no. I'm sure he exists. Like Amy says, she doesn't lie. Just because I don't want him to be over there cooking her dinner doesn't mean he isn't."

Fabio clutched his chest and let out a gasp so loud that for a moment Matt feared he was having a heart attack. "Do you mean to tell me that right now, as we speak, another man is trying to steal your woman?"

"Afraid so," Matt said, sinking into a plaid armchair across from Fabio. He didn't bother to correct Fabio's misconception that Amy was his woman, mostly because he liked the sound of that.

The little man sprang to his feet with a vigor belying his age. "Then what are you doing here? You need to knock on Miss Amy's door and fight for what you want."

"Do you really think so?" Matt asked, leaning forward on the plaid.

"I really think so," Fabio said fiercely, his blue eyes blazing. Who would have thought such a small, old man would have the heart of a warrior? "Now get up and go to it."

"I'm going," Matt said, but he was at Amy's door before he realized he didn't have the faintest notion of how to fight for what he probably shouldn't want.

5
―――――――

THE DOOR OPENED, releasing the scent of cheese and chocolate, but it wasn't Matt's sense of smell that went on alert. It was his sense of sight.

Before Amy stepped onto the porch and pulled the door shut behind her, he caught a glimpse of the back of a man sitting at one of the kitchen chairs. A very tall, very broad man with long, stringy black hair and strange ears.

"I can't believe you're already finished talking to Fabio," Amy said. "Tell me what happened. Did he agree not to file the lawsuit?"

"Not exactly," he said while he wondered not only what was wrong with Pierre's ears but how the heck he should proceed. Or, heck, if he should proceed.

Their friendship was precious to him and, he thought, to her. Would trying to change the dynamic between them ruin what they had? Especially considering the yin-yang thing?

Amy glanced at the door, then back at him. "You understand I can't talk long."

The thought that she didn't want to keep Pierre waiting obscured Matt's caution. Fabio was right, he thought darkly. It was time he fought for what he wanted, and the perfect ammunition was a compliment.

The porch light shone down on her, throwing her into a golden spotlight. She was wearing another of her unstructured dresses, this one in a tie-dye pattern. Her long, curly hair was loose and spilling down her back in a dusky cascade.

She looked so lovely that his throat ached.

"Have I ever told you what a pretty woman you are?" he asked in a soft voice, then kept his eyes trained on her face as he waited for her reaction.

"*Pretty Woman*," she said and smiled. "Starring Julia Roberts and Richard Gere."

He shook his head. "You don't understand. I mean I think you have a special all-American beauty."

"*American Beauty*. Kevin Spacey and Annette Bening," she said. "Now what do you mean by not exactly? Is Fabio going to file that lawsuit or not?"

"I'm not sure," he said while he tried to think of another way to convey he was interested in changing their relationship.

"Did you tell him that I don't watch MTV? That I don't even have a radio? That it couldn't possibly be me he's hearing?"

Matt got a mental image of Fabio, his ear fitted with a small transmitter, as the little man told him he didn't hear that well. He closed his eyes as his mind made the leap it should have made then.

"Did you know that Fabio wears a hearing aid?" he asked.

"Oh, my gosh, Matt, you're brilliant." She grabbed his arm, and an electric thrill ran through him. "Did you point out that probably all he needs to do is turn down the volume on his hearing aid?"

Matt hadn't pointed out much of anything at all except Amy having dinner with another man, but there would be plenty of time to clear up matters with Fabio later. He had more important things on his mind right now, like Amy's hand on his arm.

He glanced down at it, then into her eyes, where he saw the knowledge that she was touching him dawn. Her hand dropped away, her lips parted and confusion seemed to descend over her.

"Thanks for talking to Fabio for me," she said, her eyes suddenly darting away from his. "But I really should get back inside."

"To Pierre," he said, the words cutting into him. She nodded. "To Pierre."

"I saw him when you opened the door," Matt said before she could disappear into the house. "I knew he was tall, but I didn't think he'd be so, well, bulky."

"You thought he was bulky?" She bit her lip. "I assure you he looks more svelte when he's standing up."

"And his hair," Matt continued, making a face, "I didn't think it'd be that long. Or that stringy. Or that black."

"Pierre's hair only looks stringy when it's wet from the shower. Most of the time, it has quite a lot of body."

Matt should stop criticizing the other man's appearance, but it irritated him how quick she was to leap to the bulky, long-haired Frenchman's defense.

"How about those ears?" Matt whistled low and loud. "Have you noticed how they...protrude?"

He watched Amy's back stiffen. "Protruding ears are a LeFrancois genetic trait. It's not nice to call attention to them."

"I won't say anything about his giant ears when you introduce us." Matt braced one hand against the door and leaned over her. "Why don't you invite me in and get it over with?"

"I'm not inviting you in," Amy said, calling attention to her you're-not-getting-in-the-house stance. Her back was flush against the door, her arms at her sides and slightly uplifted.

"Why not? And don't say it's because Pierre's in the bathroom, because we've already established that I saw him sitting there in your kitchen."

"Already established," she repeated and rolled her eyes. "Do you always have to talk like such a lawyer?"

"I am a lawyer," he pointed out. "Since we already established Pierre is inside your kitchen, there's no reason I can't meet him."

"Yes, there is. He has—" she paused, then suddenly stabbed the air with a forefinger "—poison ivy. That's why he was in the shower."

"You can't wash off poison ivy."

"He didn't realize it was poison ivy until it wouldn't wash off. Now that it won't, well, he doesn't want to be seen."

"Why not?"

"Vanity," she answered quickly, then must have seen his frown. "Of course you can't blame him for that. Anyone as handsome as Pierre can't be seen at less than his best.''

Matt's frown deepened. He supposed he should be happy the Frenchman's poison ivy would prevent him from getting cozy with Amy tonight, but nothing Amy said about the guy was reassuring.

''I'm getting a bad feeling about this guy, Amy. I don't think you should see him anymore.''

She bristled visibly, as he should have known she would. But how do you tactfully tell a woman the man she thinks is the love of her life isn't good enough for her?

''Does that mean you're not going to see Mary anymore, either?'' she asked tartly.

''Mary? What does she have to do with it?''

''If I told you *I* wanted *you* to stop seeing Mary, would you listen?''

Matt took in the challenging lift of her chin, the flash of her dark eyes and the slight thrust of her lower lip.

Hell, yes, he thought. Even though he'd conjured up Mary, she couldn't compete with Amy. Amy was a vision from the top of her curly head to her…bare feet?

He frowned, reminded of the many differences between them. He couldn't imagine sitting down to dinner with his feet au natural.

''I knew it!'' she exclaimed. ''I knew you wouldn't stop seeing Mary if I told you to.''

He let out an audible sigh, because she'd misinterpreted his hesitation. How had they gotten on the subject of Mary anyway?

"Mary's not the issue here," he said.

"Why not?" She thrust her lower lip out farther, making him want to nibble on it. "If you can criticize Pierre, I can criticize Mary."

"Nothing's wrong with Mary."

"You don't think perfection's a fault?" she countered. "Nobody likes someone who's perfect."

"Being perfect is better than being as flawed as Pierre."

"How can you say Pierre's flawed? You don't even know him."

"Only because you won't introduce us." He threw up his hands. "As for how I know he's flawed, you told me. You've hardly said one positive thing about him."

"That's not true!"

"Here's your chance then. Tell me something good about him."

Amy brought her hand to her head, the better to help her think. She'd said lots of positive things about Pierre in the past, but obviously Matt hadn't been listening.

She needed to come up with something so good, something so positive it would shut him up.

"Pierre's a fabulous kisser," she told him.

"How can you tell his kisses are fabulous?" he asked in a low voice. He still had one of his hands braced against the door and she was aware of how close their faces were. So close she could pick out the faint lines around his eyes and mouth. "How do you know what a really fabulous kiss is?"

"That's a strange question," Amy said. She tried

to back away from him but found she had nowhere to go. "I've been kissed before. I can identify fabulous when I come across it."

"Maybe you haven't been kissed by enough men to tell which ones are the really fabulous kissers."

Amy's backbone straightened. "I've been kissed by plenty of men."

"You've never been kissed by me."

His voice was low and so sexy her stomach felt like it was trying to leap out of her body. Still, his presumption was so arrogant she felt compelled to point it out.

"Are you implying you're a better kisser than Pierre?"

"That's not for me to judge." His gaze moved slowly down her face until it settled on her lips. "You, on the other hand, are in perfect position to compare."

Her heart rate sped up so much she could feel the organ banging against the wall of her chest.

"That's not true." Her voice was as low and husky as his. "You and me, we've never kissed."

He braced his left hand on the other side of her body, effectively penning her in. Not that she could have mustered the will to go anywhere. She couldn't even gather the will to move.

"Maybe it's time we rectified that," he said and brought his mouth down on hers.

Amy hadn't been lying when she claimed she'd been kissed by lots of men, but she'd never been kissed like this. His lips were softer than they looked and moved over hers with such unhurried reverence that the tension seeped from her body.

He was familiar and unfamiliar at once, this man whose mind she knew so intimately but whose body she'd never explored.

Her lips explored his now, opening and closing over the entire length of his mouth. When he exhaled, she felt as though she was drawing in his breath. Her hands came up to cup the back of his head while her fingers tangled in the waves of his thick, burnished hair.

Matt, she thought dazedly. *She was kissing Matt.*

She wasn't aware she had said his name aloud until he drew back his head, smiled at her and said, "Amy."

Then he was kissing her again, his arms no longer braced against the door but around her, his tongue no longer teasing her lips but stroking inside her mouth.

Heat licked at her like flames from a bonfire, infusing her with warmth. Matt was right. *This* was a fabulous kiss, the standard by which every kiss should be judged.

Even in her wildest imagination, Pierre couldn't begin to kiss like this. Pierre, who didn't actually exist but who Matt thought was inside her house.

She wrenched her mouth away from his as an awful realization sunk into her hazy brain.

Matt would think she was cheating on Pierre.

"Amy, what's wrong?" he asked, his mouth still teasing the side of her face. "Didn't you think that was fabulous?"

How could she answer him with anything other than the truth? "Yes..."

He nuzzled her neck, creating an all-body shiver. She had a nearly irresistible urge to turn her mouth back to his but first she had to make him understand.

"...but I don't cheat," she said, more than a little unsteadily.

He lifted his head and she read passion on his face before a curtain seemed to close over it, shutting out the emotion. He drew back until they weren't touching and a coldness settled over her. It wasn't half as chilling as his voice.

"I don't cheat, either."

Pain detonated inside her at the realization that he meant he didn't cheat on Mary Contrary.

She'd been about to confess that she had no one to cheat on, but the words caught in her throat. How could she have forgotten about Mary Contrary? What could she possibly do now to save face?

"But of course we weren't cheating," she said, clearing her suddenly clogged throat. "We were conducting an experiment. That's an entirely different thing."

"Is that what you're going to tell Pierre we were doing?" His expression hadn't changed except for a slight narrowing of the eyes. "Conducting an *experiment?*"

"I'm not going to tell Pierre anything," she said, "because there's nothing to tell."

And no one to tell it to, she added silently.

"Are you going to confess what happened to Mary?"

"Like you said," Matt said, "there's nothing to confess."

"Exactly," she said, her heart breaking. How could she keep up the fiction that nothing had happened when a single kiss from him had changed her world? She prayed for the strength to get through the next few minutes.

"Well," she said, nodding toward the inside of her house, "Pierre's waiting."

"Yeah," Matt said, "and I'm sure Mary's waiting for me to call."

She couldn't stop herself from asking the question. "You call her every night?"

"Every night," he answered.

Something burst in Amy, something hot and green and ugly. "She sounds wonderful," she said insincerely.

"She is wonderful."

"So is Pierre," she said dramatically. "I should go to him. I'm sure he's missing me."

He stepped back and indicated the door with the sweep of his hand. "Don't let me stop you."

"I won't."

She opened the door and slipped into the house, careful not to let Matt get too clear of a view of her kitchen. She dropped into a chair catty-corner from the stuffed panda bear, who was having a Bad Ear Day. Even though she'd strategically draped locks of stringy hair over them, they still stuck out.

"I've gone and done it now, Pandamonium," she told the stuffed animal. "Not only did I kiss another man, but I think I may be falling for him."

She swept the hair back from her face and sighed.

"Of course I realize he's all wrong for me, but that doesn't seem to matter." She sniffed. "I'll tell you what matters—Mary Contrary. I don't suppose you have a friend we could introduce to her so she'd leave Matt alone?"

The panda's opaque black button eyes gazed sightlessly back at her.

"No?" she said, wiping a tear from her eye. "I didn't think so."

MATT DRUMMED HIS FINGERS on the desk in his cubicle, vaguely aware he wasn't getting any work done. But how could he be expected to work with Amy and Pierre LeFrancois crowding his thoughts?

Easy, the rational part of his mind answered. *Stop thinking about them.*

His fingers kept drumming.

Amy had made it abundantly clear she wanted him to stay out of her business. So stay out of her business he would. He'd stop trying to tell her Pierre was all wrong for her.

He'd stop worrying about her, period.

The phone on his desk rang and he snatched it up, eager for something else to occupy his mind.

"Matt?"

"Amy," he breathed.

"No, it's Zoe. Amy and I don't sound anything alike, you know."

He knew. If he hadn't had Amy on the brain, he never would have made the mistake. Amy's voice was deeper and sultrier, especially after she'd been kissed. He banished the image of Amy, her mouth swollen from his kisses, from his mind.

"What can I do for you, Zoe?" he asked, trying to sound upbeat.

"You can tell me everything you know about Pierre LeFrancois."

Matt made himself laugh, even though the mention of the Frenchman had his blood churning. "I'm sure you know more about him than I do."

"You mean you haven't met him yet, either?" Zoe's sigh was audible. "I don't know what's going on, Matt. You know what Amy told me when I asked if she wanted to get together with me and Jack tomorrow night?"

Matt was about to predict she'd launched into a story about the egotistical Pierre's reluctance to be seen with poison ivy but she didn't give him a chance.

"She said he doesn't like people. Isn't this guy supposed to be a teacher? How can he teach if he doesn't like people? Students are people."

"Amy says he's eccentric," Matt said.

"Eccentric? I think that's another word for defective. There has to be something wrong with him."

Matt thought of the people-hating Pierre's bulky build, enormous ego, questionable hygiene and giant stature. He doubted there was only *one* thing wrong with him.

"Amy's a grown woman, Zoe. If she wants to get involved with Pierre, there's not much we can do about it."

"But we're her friends, Matt. If we're nervous

about this guy, don't we owe it to her to check him out? It's not as though she doesn't have enough problems, what with those people she's subletting her house from coming home early.''

Matt's hand tightened on the receiver. ''How early?''

''Next month,'' Amy said. ''And we both know she doesn't make enough money to keep living in Arlington.''

She would if she got a job at the nearby Fairfax County public school district, which compensated its teachers better than most of the nation's other school systems.

He'd seen a *Washington Post* story the other day that not only detailed how much more public schoolteachers made than private teachers but also stated that Fairfax County was in the midst of a teacher shortage.

Amy was a qualified applicant. Because he'd helped her compose her résumé, he had it on the hard drive of his computer.

''But I can't think about that right now,'' Zoe went on, oblivious to the plan that had started to form in his mind. ''Not when I'm so worried about her and Pierre. What are we going to do about him?''

Nothing, Matt's common sense advised him. *Remember, you promised yourself to stay out of her business.*

''Do you remember where Amy did her student teaching?'' he asked as another, less advisable plan kicked around in his head.

''Herbert Hoover High. Why?''

"Didn't Amy say Pierre still works there?"

"Yes."

He took a deep breath, trying to hold in the words, but they came spilling out anyway. "I could pay Pierre a visit and find out for sure if we have anything to worry about."

"Oh, Matt. That's a great idea," Zoe exclaimed. "You're the absolute best."

"No, I'm not," Matt said after he hung up the phone. "I'm an idiot."

Two hours later, as he walked down the wide hallway that led to the office at Herbert Hoover High School, he felt like an even bigger idiot.

Now that he was here, on the verge of meeting Pierre LeFrancois, he wasn't sure what he'd do or say.

Challenge him to a duel at sunrise to determine which one of them was more worthy of Amy?

Tell him to stay away from his girl, disregarding the fact that Amy was not now and never had been his?

Order him to get the hell out of Dodge?

By the time he entered the office and approached the school secretary's desk, he was convinced this confrontation was a very bad idea. He started to turn around.

"May I help you?" the secretary's voice stopped him. She was a middle-aged woman with an air of competency and one of those cheerful, round faces made for smiling.

"No," he said.

The woman's smile lost some of its wattage but

didn't entirely disappear. "Excuse me for asking, sweetie, but why did you come in here if you don't need help?"

Matt wondered how to appear as though he did indeed have a brain, especially because he might as well go through with his plan now that the secretary was speaking to him.

"It's not help I need," Matt said. "It's information."

The woman's brows drew together and her smile faded a little more, clueing Matt that his attempt to convince her he was an intelligent life-form had failed.

"I can help you by giving you information," the woman said, slowly and distinctly pronouncing every word.

Matt tried to smile but his muscles felt so stiff he probably looked like he was grimacing. But he'd gotten this far. He might as well try to salvage something from his visit.

"Can you tell me about the French teacher?"

The secretary's smile disappeared completely and wariness clouded her eyes. "May I ask why?"

He was about to cite public information laws when it occurred to him that might not be the smartest way to go.

"My daughter's thinking about taking French and I want to make sure the teacher's qualified."

The secretary cocked her head. "You don't look old enough to have a daughter in high school."

"I started young," Matt said.

The woman eyed him critically, obviously trying

to gauge how young he would have been when his daughter was born. A daughter, Matt realized for the first time, who would have to be at least fourteen or fifteen.

"You must have been *very* young," the secretary said.

"I'm precocious," Matt said, alarmed by how easily the lie slipped out. Now he not only had a phantom girlfriend, but an imaginary daughter as well. This didn't bode well for the credo of honesty he'd vowed to live by.

"Still," the woman said, examining him critically, "your wife must be quite a bit older than you."

"I'm not married," Matt said.

The woman's hand flew to her throat. Her smile was long gone and it was clear that he horrified her.

"Could you please just tell me what you know about Pierre LeFrancois," Matt said before she could ask him about the imaginary mother of his non-existent daughter.

"Who?"

"Pierre LeFrancois," he repeated, "the French teacher."

"Our French teacher's name is Brigitte LeFevre."

Matt started. "Are you sure?"

"Of course I'm sure. But even if I mixed up my LeFrancois's with my LeFevre's, I can tell the difference between a man and a woman. Our French teacher is a woman."

A woman and not a conceited giant who was not only seriously weird and possibly illiterate but who was lying to Amy about where he worked. Matt wouldn't be surprised if he'd been fired, possibly for trying to get it on with a student.

"Do you know what happened to Pierre Le-Francois?" Matt asked. "He would have been a teacher here about five years ago."

"I've only been here for two years," the secretary replied before her features hardened. "You don't have a daughter, do you?"

Her expression was so fierce that he backed away from the desk. He'd been about to ask if she could direct him to someone who might know why Pierre had been fired, but that idea disappeared in her cloud of suspicion.

"I'd like to have a daughter someday," he said truthfully.

"You better leave," the secretary said, "before I call security."

Matt left, figuring he had enough information.

If Pierre wasn't telling the truth about his place of employment, God only knew what other lies he was feeding Amy. He could be married, in the country illegally, on the lam from the law.

And it was Matt's duty to warn Amy about him.

6

AMY POPPED A BEER NUT into her mouth and regarded Zoe and Jack from across the booth in the
midst of the happy hour madness at Brewster's, their
Wednesday night hangout.

"I don't understand it," Amy said. "This call
comes out of the blue asking me when I want to
come in for an interview with the Fairfax County
school district. But I never applied."

"That sure is strange," Jack said.

His arm was flung over Zoe's shoulder and his
fingers were playing with her hair. Add the besotted
look on his face whenever he looked at her friend,
and he seemed like a man very much in love.

Amy ruthlessly stamped out the envy trying to take
root in her soul, because she was genuinely thrilled
that her friend had found love.

It wasn't Amy's fault, or Jack's, that Matt didn't
throw his arm over her shoulder and play with her
hair.

"Maybe you applied years ago and forgot about
it," Zoe said. "They could still have your application
on file."

"Uh-uh," Amy said. "You know how I feel about

the large class sizes in public schools. No way I sent in an application.''

''It sure is a mystery then,'' said Jack but Amy was only half paying attention because Matt had suddenly appeared in her peripheral vision.

She'd been not so subconsciously watching for him for an hour even though she'd convinced herself his ridiculous work schedule would keep him away. Again.

''Well look who's here,'' Zoe said, grinning up at him. ''The missing piece.''

''Hey, Zoe,'' Matt said with a smile every bit as charming as the ones Jack Carter bestowed on the female population. Privately Amy thought Matt was even more attractive than Jack, who was about as good-looking as men came. Of course, to cast your vote with Matt, you had to get past that clean-cut thing he had going on and his maddening insistence on being well dressed.

''Amy.''

Amy probably wouldn't have noticed that Zoe was addressing her if her friend hadn't clapped her hands three times. Amy's head jerked around.

''Aren't you going to move over so Matt can sit down?'' Zoe asked.

Amy looked back at Matt so see him regarding her with a twinkle in his eye. ''It's okay with me if you don't move over and I sit down anyway.''

''Hey, Matt,'' she said with studied nonchalance, completely ignoring her embarrassing mental lapse and his flirting.

He made to sit down and she moved over fast. It

was either that or risk that spontaneous sexual combustion that ignited every time he touched her.

She wasn't even going to think about what happened when he kissed her.

Amy kept her eyes trained straight ahead, afraid to look at Matt unless her body remembered what her mind was trying to forget.

"What did I miss?" Matt asked and she took a quick peek at him.

How could anybody be so clean-cut that he showed no trace of chin stubble even though it was nearing seven o'clock? Why did she want to press kisses to his face to make sure he was as smooth shaven as he looked?

"We were trying to solve a mystery," Zoe said. "Amy got a call from Fairfax County schools asking her to come in for an interview."

"When did you schedule it for?" Matt asked Amy.

Amy swung her eyes to his, not so much because she felt compelled to look at him, even though she did, but because of his ridiculous question.

"I didn't," Amy said. "I don't want to work for Fairfax County schools."

"Why not?" He actually looked puzzled. "You'd make double what you're making now."

"I've told you this before, Matt. Money's not important to me."

"Come on, Amy. You won't find another place you can afford to live if you don't start making more money. Why do you think I sent in your résumé in the first place?"

"You submitted my résumé!" Something hot bubbled inside her but it had nothing to do with attraction. "What gave you the right to do that?"

"The certainty you weren't going to do it yourself."

"When I submitted Jack's résumé for that coaching job, he was happy abut it," Zoe chimed in, but Amy ignored her.

She glared at Matt. "You're missing the point. If I'd wanted to apply, I would have."

"Of course Jack secretly wanted to be a baseball coach," Zoe cut in, "while I'm getting a very strong impression that Amy doesn't want this job."

"She should want it," Matt countered. "It could be the only thing that stands between her and homelessness."

"Homelessness!" Amy cried. "Of all the ridiculous things to say, that one takes the booby prize."

She stared at him, appalled he had the nerve to look angry when he was the one who was interfering in her life.

"I think—" Zoe began, but Amy was vaguely aware of Jack interrupting her friend.

"Hey there, Zoe darlin', why don't you dance with me?"

"We've gone through this before. There's no dance floor," Zoe said.

"Then how 'bout you come away with me," he said, grabbing her by the hand and leading her from the booth so that only Matt and Amy remained.

Matt broke their stare-down silence first.

"Okay, maybe I shouldn't have implied you'll be

on the streets if you don't get another job. But the people you're housesitting for are coming back next month."

"Zoe has a big mouth," Amy muttered.

"When they do come back, where are you going to live?"

Amy threw up her hands. Could he be more obsessed with details? She was tangentially aware of a waitress approaching their booth, putting on the brakes and reversing directions.

"Something will work out," she said. "It always does."

"Like what?" he pressed.

"I don't know." Did he have to be so anal? "Maybe I'll live with some other girls like I did after college."

"News flash. There's a reason your foursome broke up. Your roommates got jobs that paid a decent wage. Do you really think you'll be able to find other women your age who want to live four to a house?"

Ooooh, he made her so angry. Implying that she wasn't grown up enough to take care of herself. All because she wasn't a slave to the almighty dollar like he was.

"Then maybe I'll live with Pierre," she blurted out.

His jaw tightened, his skin paled and she was immediately sorry. How could she have said such a thing? Of course she wasn't going to live with Pierre. Even if he had existed, he was turning out to be no great prize. This had gone too far. She needed to confess right now.

"You can't live with Pierre," Matt stated forcefully, as though prepared to stop her.

She changed her mind about confessing. "I can do anything I darn well please. Including working for what you think is peanuts and moving in with Pierre."

"But this guy—" Matt rubbed his forehead, trying to think of a tactful way to say what he needed to tell her "—this guy isn't what he seems. Maybe he doesn't even have a job."

"Sure, he does. He's a French teacher."

"At Herbert Hoover High? Isn't that what you told Zoe?"

"Yes," she said slowly. "Why are you asking?"

"The school secretary says no Pierre LeFrancois works there."

"How would you know what the school secretary says?"

He took a deep breath and released it, knowing he had to confess but really, really not wanting to. "Because I went to the school to ask about Pierre."

She made a disbelieving noise. "I can't believe you checked up on me."

His mouth twisted as he thought about how to reply. Didn't she understand that he cared about her? Didn't she know this thing with Pierre was killing him?

"I'm your friend, Amy," Matt said. "That's what friends do."

"Friends do not spy on each other," she said. "How would you like it if I spied on Mary Contrary?"

"There's nothing to spy on," he said. That, at least, was the truth. Which he really should tell her.

"You mean because Mary's so perfect? Maybe you only think she's perfect. Maybe Pierre's the one who's perfect."

He put his intention to tell her about Mary on hold because they had more important things to discuss. "If Pierre told you he taught at Herbert Hoover High, he's not perfect."

She bit her lip as she seemed to digest that. "Maybe I misunderstood him. Maybe he was talking about where he used to teach."

Matt tried not to roll his eyes. If Pierre's first language was French, it was possible Amy *had* misunderstood him. But he wasn't willing to give the guy the benefit of the doubt. Not with Amy's happiness at stake.

"Maybe you understood him perfectly. Maybe he's unemployed. Hell, maybe he's married."

"Maybe Mary is a closet transvestite," she said.

He thought of the woman he'd conjured up from the nursery rhyme, in her garden with her silver bells and cockleshells, wearing her pretty blue dress.

"That's ridiculous," Matt said.

"So are the things you've said about Pierre."

"Then introduce him to me."

"Not unless I can meet Mary, too."

Again, he thought about telling her there was no Mary. But then he took in that stubborn lift of her chin and that glimmer in her eyes.

She'd have a hard time forgiving him if he made

the confession now. She'd probably even be angry enough to refuse to introduce him to Pierre.

"What do you have in mind?" he asked.

Her chin lifted higher. "A double date next week."

Matt swallowed his misgivings. He had to make sure Pierre wasn't playing Amy. For Amy's sake. And maybe for his own.

"Fine," he said. "Next week it is."

He watched her pick up her mug of beer, which had been sitting neglected on the table as they argued. She downed a third of the frothy liquid in a single gulp and set it on the table with a thump.

"Fine," she said.

Except it wasn't fine. Not by a long shot.

"MY GOODNESS, CHILD." Nellie, the night security guard at The Ranch, put her hands on her hips as Matt walked toward her. "Don't tell me you're working late on another Friday night?"

Matt stopped at her counter and gave her a tired smile. "Okay," he said, "but I am."

"Still no woman?"

Matt thought of the way Amy had retreated after their kiss, how she hadn't understood he'd sent in her résumé because he was worried about her, how she'd probably never want to see him again if she found out there was no Mary Contrary.

"Still no woman." He recognized the irony in his answer. Not only didn't he have a woman of his own, but he'd committed to a double date with a date who didn't exist.

"Like I've told you before, you won't find a woman unless you get out more." Nellie snapped her fingers. "Hey, do you like plays?"

"Sure do," Matt said, although he couldn't remember the last time he'd made time to attend one.

"Starting next weekend, my niece is starring in a play over in Northeast Washington. *St. Andres' Fault.* It'd do you good to get out and see it."

"Your niece is an actress?" Matt asked as the wheels in his head started to turn. "Is she, by any chance, blond?"

"Last I saw her, she was," Nellie said, giving him a strange look.

Excitement coursed through Matt. He felt as though the gods had dropped a gift into his lap. Nellie's niece could be the answer to his problem.

"Could I have her phone number?"

Nellie retreated a full step. "I know I told you to find a woman, but I didn't think you'd take me so seriously."

"It's not what you think—" Matt began, but Nellie wasn't listening.

"Lordy, Lordy, Lordy," she said, shaking her head. "Understand, I love my niece. I'm not against blind dates, neither. But I can't see the two of you hitting it off, what with you and your lawyerly ways. Trinity's a little...unusual."

"But she is an actress?"

"Been an actress all through high school and beyond." Nellie narrowed her eyes as she regarded him. "You don't have some weird hang-up with blond actresses you want to tell me about, do you?"

"Of course not," Matt said, hastening to reassure her. "It's really very simple."

I need to hire an actress to portray a woman who doesn't exist, he thought.

Aloud, he said, "I know a part that's available and thought your niece might be right for it."

"A part in a play?"

"Yeah. That's right," Matt said. He figured the real-life drama he'd gotten himself into by agreeing to double-date with Amy could qualify as a reality play.

"I didn't figure you for the theatre type."

"We all have hidden facets," Matt said. "Can I have her number? Please?"

"Well, okay," Nellie said, reaching under the counter and pulling out pad and pen. "Trinity's always looking for work." She glanced up at Matt before writing down her niece's number. "But don't say I didn't warn you about her."

Matt immediately discounted her words. So what if Trinity was a little unusual. An actress played a role and that's what Trinity would do for him.

Nellie didn't understand that, in actuality, what she was doing was saving him.

AMY PLOPPED DOWN ON THE SOFA and regarded the stuffed panda bear she had propped in an armchair. "Have I told you yet that you and me are double-dating next week with Matt and Mary Contrary?"

Pandamonium stared back at her through his blank black eyes. He was still dressed in her father's Hawaiian shirt and the Halloween wig. Although the getup had fooled Matt once, she had little hope the pretense would work again. Especially considering Matt would be justified in expecting her date to walk and talk.

"I know," she said, leaning her head back against the sofa back, "I've made a real mess of things."

Speedy Gonzales chose that moment to stick his head out of his shell. For a moment, the box turtle appeared to be nodding.

"I feel bad enough," she said. "You don't have to agree with me."

Out of the corner of her eye she noticed that the light on her answering machine was blinking.

"This better not be Fairfax County public schools again," she told Speedy Gonzales and Pandamonium. "After I withdrew my application, they still called about me coming in for an interview."

She scooted forward on the sofa cushion, gazing at the stuffed panda and the turtle in turn.

"You guys don't think Matt submitted another résumé, do you?" When neither of them answered, she reached over and hit the play button on the machine.

"Amy, it's Matt. You really need to get a cell phone."

At the sound of his voice, her heartbeat sped up. But she still managed to stick her tongue out at the phone to veto, yet again, the suggestion that she get a cell phone.

"It's important you call me whenever you get this message," he continued and her heart beat even faster.

Could he be calling to apologize? Or, better yet, to suggest they nix the double date and date each other?

"Something's come up with Fabio," he said, killing her hope. "He's threatening to file another lawsuit. I hoped I could talk to you before I went to see him but he insisted I come over tonight. Call me as soon as you get this."

Did that mean Matt was at Fabio's now? She searched her brain and couldn't think what she could possibly have done this time to get herself sued. There was only one way to find out.

She picked up the receiver and dialed Matt's cell phone number. He answered after the first ring.

"Burke here."

"Matt, it's Amy. What's going on?"

"Give me a minute, okay," he said and she overheard him telling someone he needed to take the call in private. Within seconds, he was back on the line.

"I'm over at Fabio's," he said. "He claims you're decreasing the property value of his house."

"What! How?"

"He said you're damaging his curb appeal by encouraging litter from your yard to drift into his."

"That's ridiculous," Amy exclaimed. "That's even sillier than suing me because I didn't like his blue hair."

"He says he has the evidence to prove it. I need your side of the story before I can proceed."

"Okay," she said. "I'll come over there and tell it."

"No. Remember what I told you about having contact with someone—"

Amy didn't hear the rest of what he said because she'd already hung up and headed for the door.

Fabio could make his ridiculous claims to her face.

"Why, Miss Amy, how nice it is to see you," Fabio said a few moments later as he held the door open wide in welcome. His wizened face was split into a white-toothed grin so huge it looked like it belonged on a much bigger man.

"Don't give me that." Amy stomped into the house and whirled to confront him. "If you're so glad to see me, you wouldn't be threatening to sue me."

She was so focused on Fabio's never-wavering smile that she didn't realize Matt was standing next to her until he touched her arm. The electricity was so potent, she nearly jumped.

"Amy, as your attorney, I'm advising you to go back home and let me handle this," he said.

She channeled the electricity to her rapidly heating temper. "I will not. I know you're on my side, Matt, but I want to hear what Mr. Let's-Sue-Amy is saying about me."

"Now, now, dear," Fabio said, patting her arm. "There's no need to get testy. You're among friends."

"But you're threatening to sue me!" Amy said. "That's not a friendly action."

"Amy, go home," Matt said.

"There's no need for Miss Amy to leave." Fabio gestured to his living room. "The three of us can sit down and have a nice chat. Would anybody like a scone? I made some this morning.''

"No, I don't want a—'' Amy began.

"We'd love some scones,'' Matt interrupted, giving her a pointed look. "Wouldn't we, Amy?''

"Oh, wonderful.'' Fabio clapped his small, wrinkled hands. "Sit down in the living room and I'll be right out with them. I'll bring tea, too. Tea would be nice.''

"I don't want a scone,'' Amy practically hissed at Matt when they were seated side by side on the sofa. "Why did you tell him we'd eat scones?''

"If you're going to ignore attorney-client advice, you're going to eat a scone.'' Matt's tone wasn't quite harsh but it was clear he was annoyed. "I don't want you antagonizing Fabio.''

"Me antagonize him? He's the one who's antagonizing me. I don't understand it. It's like he's this lovable puppy who's eager to please to your face, then bites you in the rear when you walk away.''

"That kind of analogy will not get him to drop the lawsuit.''

"But it's a stupid lawsuit!''

"He can still file it. Then it will be up to a judge to decide whether it has merit,'' he said, bringing his head close to hers. He smelled faintly of cologne, which usually turned her off, but of course Matt would choose a scent that appealed to her. "Since you refuse to leave, it's in your best interest to be quiet and listen to what he has to say. Can you do that?''

He reached across the chasm and took her hand,

never letting his toffee-colored gaze waver from hers. When he touched her and looked at her that way, she'd do anything he asked. That didn't mean she had to be docile about it.

"I can try to do that," she snapped.

His smile caused her heart to flip-flop. "That's my girl," he said, squeezing her hand.

But she wasn't his girl. Mary Contrary was.

Maybe she should learn by Fabio's example and sue Mary for unintentional infliction of emotional distress. If she won the suit, she could ask for Matt as compensation.

From the way he was scowling at her, though, he'd probably insist on filing an appeal.

7

MATT WAS GOING TO THROTTLE her.

Amy gave her hair an imperious toss, exposing said neck to view. It was long and lovely, definitely not something he could bear to throttle.

Okay. So what he wanted to do to her neck—hell, her entire body—was cover it in kisses. That didn't mean he wasn't angry at her for completely disregarding his legal advice.

"Here we go." Fabio entered the living room carrying an intricately designed tray holding a teapot and what looked to be irregularly sized rocks. "I've got scones."

Matt knew Amy well enough to recognize the stubborn set of her lips meant she was about to refuse to dine with the enemy. He shot her a warning look as he plucked a scone off the tray, took a bite and nearly cracked his teeth.

"They were in the refrigerator so they're a bit cold," Fabio said, pouring tea into their teacups. His pinky finger was *not* extended and he didn't seem to know that scones were best served warm from the oven with butter. "I dare say my Delia's scones were much better than mine."

They couldn't possibly have been worse, Matt

thought, taking a gulp of tea. If he let the tea sit in his mouth, maybe it would soften the scone enough that he could chew it.

"Who's Delia?" Amy asked. She had a scone in her hand but not in her mouth.

"My late wife. Sometimes I can't believe it's been three years since she's been gone." Fabio's bright expression momentarily dimmed before he resurrected it, and Matt saw the same flash of sympathy cross Amy's face that he felt reflected on his own. "I hope the two of you enjoy my scones as much as I enjoyed hers."

Matt nodded but Amy wasn't as compliant. She was hardening her jaw, obviously trying to wipe out whatever sympathy she may have felt. For a soft-hearted woman, she could be incredibly hard-headed.

"That sweet, little old man act won't work with me, buster," she said. "I know what you're about."

Matt nudged her with his elbow to remind her to be tactful. He supposed he should be grateful she was flinging words at Fabio instead of scones. The one in her hand might kill him.

"What did you say, Miss Amy?" Fabio asked, pointing to his hearing aid and leaning forward.

"She said she thinks you're sweet," Matt said loudly and clearly.

Fabio beamed and folded his hands in his lap. "Oh, thank you. I think you're sweet, too."

"Don't you sweet talk me, you rabble-rouser, you," Amy hissed through her teeth. "You're just trying to get me to drop my guard so you can stick it to me."

Again, Fabio cupped a hand to his ear and looked questioning.

"Now she says she doesn't understand why someone as sweet as you is filing a lawsuit against her," Matt answered.

"I haven't actually filed it yet, dear," he pointed out, addressing Amy.

"Don't call me dear," Amy said. Unfortunately she'd gotten the hang of speaking loudly and clearly.

"Amy, stop it," Matt said in a low voice but she was past listening to him. Her eyes were sparkling with temper, her chest heaving with it.

"Matt said you're claiming I'm decreasing your property value by depositing litter in your yard."

"Oh, no, dear. I didn't say you were depositing litter in my yard," Fabio said with a shake of his head. "The word I used was *contaminating*."

She shifted the scone from one hand to the other, but incredibly didn't let it fly. "That's the stupidest thing I've ever heard," she said with heat.

Matt uncrossed his legs and blew out a heavy breath. Stupid was not a word he advised his clients to use when speaking to the parties who were suing them. He usually advised his clients *not* to speak at all.

"What Amy means is she considers your claim to be unreasonable," he said, trying to be diplomatic.

"And very, very stupid," Amy added.

"You said you'd be quiet and listen to what he had to say," Matt told her out of the side of his mouth.

"I said I'd *try* to be quiet," she corrected.

"What Amy meant to say," Matt addressed Fabio, but slanted her another warning look, "is that she didn't generate the litter."

"It was still transported from her yard to mine," Fabio said.

"But I wasn't the one who transported it," Amy blurted out. "If you're going to blame something, blame the wind."

"The method of transportation might not matter in the eyes of the law," Fabio said.

"Then again," Matt said, consideringly. "It might. We could prove that Amy wasn't deliberately—"

"More scones, anyone?" Fabio interrupted, still with that cheerful lilt to his voice. Instead of picking up the plate of scones, he pointed to it. Considering how heavy it must be, Matt didn't blame him.

"How can you talk about scones at a time like this?" Amy asked.

"We don't have to talk about scones," Fabio said. "We could always talk about something else. How 'bout those Redskins?"

"You want to talk football?" Amy's mouth was practically hanging open. "I don't believe it."

"If you're not into sports, I'm also conversant on other subjects. Politics. Movies. Religion. I'll talk about anything you like."

"If that isn't the most..." Amy began but surprisingly allowed her voice to trail off when Matt lightly squeezed her arm.

"Let me ask you something, Fabio." He leaned forward, his elbows resting on his knees, his mind forming a theory. "You said the litter in your yard was hurting your property value. Are you thinking about selling?"

"As a matter of fact, I am," he said.

"But you told me you've only lived here for three months," Matt said, watching the other man closely. "Why would you want to sell after so short a time?"

The little man pursed his lips, as though he didn't want to reveal the reason. Matt gave him a nod of encouragement and, after a moment, Fabio spoke. "I don't know anybody here."

"Aren't you from this area?" Matt asked.

"I'm from upstate New York. Lived there all my life until I moved here."

"Do you mean you left behind everything you knew?" Amy asked, sounding incredulous. "Your home? Your friends? Your family?"

"Wasn't much family left after Delia was gone," Fabio said. "My brother, her sister. We always loved children but God didn't bless us with any of our own." He smiled at them in turn. "If Delia and I had had children, I like to think they would have turned out as well as you two did."

"Thank you," Matt said, recognizing the honor of the compliment. "But there's something I still don't understand. If your life was in New York, why did you move to Arlington?"

"No special reason," Fabio said, but Matt noticed the flush of red that started to form under his skin.

"You moved because of a woman," Amy declared.

Fabio's startled expression told him Amy had hit

the mark. It also told him Fabio didn't particularly want to admit that.

"Now that wouldn't have been a particularly smart thing to do," Fabio hedged but the red flush deepened.

"Doesn't matter if it was smart. You still did it," Amy said with typical bluntness. "Who is she? Where is she?"

Fabio put a hand to his blue-tinged hair and let out an audible sigh. "I can't believe I'm going to tell you this."

"Tell," Amy ordered.

"Her name's Helen Primrose, although she may still go by her married name of Helen Clark. She was widowed a few years ago. Like me."

"Does she live in Arlington?" Amy asked when Fabio paused. She sounded exactly like a reporter on the trail of a story. Since she was no longer talking about the lawsuit, Matt sat back, content to let her take the lead in the conversation.

"She lives in Alexandria." Fabio named a community not more than five miles away. "I thought she might think I was stalking her if I moved too close."

"What does she think of you moving to Virginia to be with her?" Amy asked.

Fabio avoided her eyes. "I don't know."

"Oh, my gosh." Amy laid a hand on Matt's arm but kept her eyes trained on Fabio. He endured the sparking electricity until he could enjoy the warmth of her touch. "You haven't told her, have you?"

The little, blue-haired man looked so uncomfortable Matt felt compelled to come to his defense. "It's not easy to tell a woman how you feel about her."

For one charged second, Amy's eyes met his and he wondered if she knew he was talking about much more than Fabio and Helen. But then she swung her gaze to Fabio, who was speaking again.

"I haven't told Helen anything at all," Fabio said. "I've picked up the phone to call her a dozen times, but I can't make myself dial."

"Why not?" Amy asked.

"I'm not sure she'll remember me."

The space between Amy's eyebrows narrowed. "How exactly do you know her?"

Fabio looked sheepish. "She's the cousin of a friend. I met her at a dance when I cut in on her partner."

"Then surely she'll remember," Amy said, and Matt could have hugged her for injecting encouragement into her voice. "When was this dance? A year ago? Two?"

"Fifty-two years ago," Fabio said. "It was my senior prom. I meant to call and ask her out afterward, but she lived in Virginia and I was in New York. By the time I got her phone number from her cousin, she was already married."

"Oh, my gosh," Amy exclaimed. "Helen's your OWGA."

"My what?"

"O-W-G-A," Matt spelled. "It stands for the One Who Got Away."

"She did get away at that," Fabio said. "Understand, I loved my wife with all my heart. But I never stopped thinking about Helen. When I heard she was widowed, I got it into my head that I could move here and start courting her.'' He sighed. ''I should have stayed where I was. It would have saved me the trouble of having to move back to New York.''

''No,'' Amy said forcefully. ''You're not going anywhere.''

''Excuse me,'' Fabio said.

''You heard me,'' Amy said. ''You're not moving back to New York. Not until you at least phone Helen.''

''I don't know if I can do that, Miss Amy. What if she doesn't want to see me?''

''What if she does?''

''Even if she does, that won't change the fact that I never should have moved here where no one knows me and no one talks to me.''

A switch went off in Matt's head, illuminating what he should have seen all along.

Fabio wasn't threatening to file lawsuits against Amy because he had it in for her. He was doing it because he was lonely. Could there be a more sure-fire way to get your neighbor to pay attention to you than threatening legal action?

He was about to ask Fabio to excuse them so he could share his insight with Amy when she leaned forward and said, ''You said you liked kids, didn't you, Fabio?''

''I love kids,'' Fabio said.

''And you like books, too,'' Amy said, gesturing at the overflowing bookcase against the wall. ''Well,

I just happen to work at a school that has kids and books."

"What's that got to do with me?" Fabio asked but Matt already knew, just as he knew that stubborn, opinionated, quick-tempered Amy also had a kind heart.

"I'm proposing a deal." Amy's face was so open and animated that something softened in Matt's chest. "We need help in the school library. You stop threatening to sue me, and I'll arrange it so you can come into school and work in the library as many afternoons as you like."

"Do you mean it?" Fabio asked, looking as though he was afraid to believe what she was offering.

"Of course I mean it," Amy said, "but there's a condition."

Fabio hung his head, like a kid whose mother had confiscated his candy. "There always is," he said.

"You have to agree to let me hold your hand for moral support when you call Helen," Amy said.

Fabio's expression changed from disappointed to awed in an eye blink. "You'd do that for me?"

Amy swung her dark eyes to Matt and gave him a slow smile that did devastating things to his heart. "Only if my lawyer approves of the deal."

"Oh, yes," Matt said softly. "Your lawyer approves."

AN HOUR LATER, A SCONE sitting in her belly like a slab of cement, Amy gave Fabio a final wave as she and Matt crossed the yard to her house.

"Can you believe Helen still has the flower he gave her on prom night pressed inside a book?" Amy asked, putting a hand over her heart at the romance of it all.

"I'm still having a hard time believing Fabio plucked a petal off his date's corsage to give her," Matt said, chuckling. "They must have made quite an impression on each other."

Amy was about to ask if Mary Contrary had made that kind of impression on him but she didn't want to bring the other woman into the conversation. Not when she was still riding the high of having Helen agree to a date with Fabio.

"Who would have believed the evening would turn out this well after the way it started?" she asked. "All this time, I thought Fabio didn't like me and all he wanted was to be my friend."

"I believe it," Matt said. "I don't know of anyone who doesn't like you."

She turned halfway around and walked backward so she could see his expression in the light of the crescent moon. The moonlight bathed him in a golden glow.

"You didn't like me earlier tonight when I insisted on talking to Fabio about the lawsuit."

"Correction," he said. "I like you all the time, even when you make me crazy."

She laughed. "Then you're about the most calm crazy man I've ever seen."

"Crazy waters run deep," he quipped.

"For the record, I like you, too," she said, aware that was a colossal understatement. "That's why I've decided to forgive you for sending in my résumé. But only if you'll forgive me for not following your advice."

"Tell you what." He pretended to think but he was so sharp she knew he already had it all figured out. "I'll agree if you'll agree my agreement doesn't mean you can ignore me the next time I give you legal advice."

She made a face at him. "Do you always have to be such a lawyer?"

"Yep," he said, nodding slowly. "I always do."

"Then I'll agree to your agreement," she said, "as long as you realize it goes against my basic instinct."

"*Basic Instinct,*" he said. "Michael Douglas and Sharon Stone."

She stopped walking and put her hands on her hips. "You really are as good as it gets, aren't you?"

"You're never going to stop trying to stump me, are you? *As Good As It Gets* starred Jack Nicholson and Helen Hunt."

"What I wonder is when a fancy lawyer like you found time to go to all those movies," Amy said. "I can't quite believe you made the time when you were in law school."

"You're right," he said. "But I did have a VCR and a video store around the corner. Once a week, I rented a movie. But only if I'd met my study quota."

"You had a study quota?" Amy rolled her eyes. "You, Matt Burke, are the most anal person I know."

"The world needs anal people like me to keep free spirits like you in line."

"Oh, yeah?" She poked him in the chest with a forefinger. "Well, the world needs free spirits like me to make sure people like you have fun."

"What kind of fun are you going to make sure I have?" he asked, his voice as soft as the night breeze.

Come to bed with me, she thought.

But because she thought she might have imagined the sexual innuendo in his question, she said, "Come to the movies with me."

When he hesitated, she realized how much she wanted to prolong the evening. Even if they weren't doing the prolonging in bed.

"The night's still young," she continued, "and there's a new movie theatre in Alexandria with stadium seating and monster buckets of popcorn and…"

She stopped talking when she noticed his lack of enthusiasm. She closed her eyes, desperately trying to recover her composure so she didn't embarrass herself.

"Don't say anything," she said when he started to speak. "It's okay. I just thought that seeing as how I'm not getting together with Pierre tonight, maybe you weren't seeing Mary. But I should have realized that—"

"Amy, I would love to go to a movie with you," he interrupted. "But not tonight."

Amy swallowed her disappointment and forced herself to shrug. "I understand. I shouldn't have expected you to be free considering that you and Mary—"

"It has nothing to do with Mary."

His comment was so puzzling it rendered her speechless while she tried to figure out what he meant, but nothing came to her. Finally, he sighed.

"Some of the lawyers in my office are performing in a charity talent show later tonight to raise money for the victims legal defense fund."

"Oh," Amy said, biting her lower lip to hide her disappointment. "And naturally you're going with Mary."

"I'm not going with Mary," he said. She didn't understand the play of emotions that crossed his face any better than his next comment. "If you promise not to tell anybody what you see there, I'd like you to come with me."

She felt the smile start in her eyes before it spread to her lips.

"I'd love to come with you," she said. "But I don't understand. Why are you pledging me to a vow of silence?"

It took him a full five seconds to answer her.

"Because I'm not going only to watch," he said with a wry twist of his lips. "I'm going to perform."

A HALF HOUR LATER, Matt guided Amy inside a chrome-and-glass bar in Northwest Washington D.C. called Slap Happy's when what he really wanted to do was cut and run. Really fast and really far.

He'd dodged her questions about the nature of his act but he couldn't keep it a secret forever, not when he had to take the stage within the hour.

He knew why he'd agreed to perform. He could

no more refuse the law-office partner who'd pressured him to do the act than he could deny that he wanted to make partner one day himself. What he didn't know was why he'd asked Amy to witness what was sure to be the most excruciating ten minutes of his life.

She picked that moment to glance back at him and smile. He smiled back. Maybe he did know why after all.

"How on earth are they going to have a talent show in here?" she asked, raising her voice to be heard above the noisy crowd.

"They're using the dance floor as a stage," he said, nodding in the direction they were walking. "They were originally going to hold the show at an auditorium but the organizers must've thought the audience would be more receptive if they were drinking."

Come to think of it, a stiff drink sounded like a very good idea. It might take the edge off his burgeoning anxiety about performing in front of the crowd.

The establishment spanned two stories, with the focal point a dance floor visible from both levels, and every inch of it was packed. On the ground floor, tables fanned out from the dance floor in a circular pattern.

Matt moved his hand from the small of Amy's back to her elbow, stopping her progress so he could search for the co-workers saving a place for him. Her back came flush against him and he got distracted by her softness.

She glanced back at him, her smile as soft as her skin. "Matt," she said, and it sounded like an invitation.

To hell with the talent show and to hell with the crowd, Matt thought, and lowered his head. A piercing whistle stopped his progress shy of her lips.

"Burke, you dog, you," a voice he recognized called. "Where have you been hiding her?"

Matt reluctantly raised his head and turned toward the speaker, who was a table away surrounded by his co-workers. Quincy Boggs was fresh-faced, clean cut and famously outspoken.

"No wonder you never come out on the town with us," Quincy continued. "If I had a lady as fine as yours, I'd keep her to myself, too."

"I'm not Matt's lady," Amy said so quickly Matt thought he must have imagined her disappointment when he hadn't kissed her.

The bar was so noisy that it was obvious no one at the table had heard her. He should second her statement that they weren't involved but instead took her hand and led her over to the table.

"Everybody, this is Amy Donatelli," he said, but he couldn't bring himself to add the qualifier he usually used whenever he introduced her.

My friend.

After identifying all his co-workers by name, he pulled out a chair so Amy could sit down, then sat himself. He moved his chair so close to hers he could have flung an arm around her the same way Jack was always draping his around Zoe. What the heck, he thought, and flung.

The eyes that met his appeared startled, which wasn't a good sign. But she didn't move away, which was. Within moments, the electricity his touch had sparked turned into a pleasant current.

"We were taking bets on whether you'd show," said Sumner Faraday after his post-cigarette hack. Nobody would ever guess his specialty was health-care litigation. "Consensus was running against you."

"Don't be so hard on him, Sumner," said Mandy Drake, a cool brunette who specialized in product liability litigation and flirting. "It's not easy to stand up in front of a crowd and do what our Matt's going to do."

"What's she talking about?" Amy asked Matt but an emcee took the stage and asked for quiet, giving him an excuse not to answer.

He spent the next half hour trying to take comfort in Amy's presence while the minutes ticked away. He managed not to shudder when a grandmotherly woman performed an unaccompanied rendering of the Broadway song Annie and didn't flinch while a middle-aged man break-danced. He knew well that his act had major flop potential.

"Our next contestant is comedian Matt Burke," the emcee finally announced, sending his heart to thundering.

"Comedian," Amy squeaked when Matt took his arm from around her. "Since when are you funny?"

"I'm not." Matt gave her a tight smile. "But hopefully I will be in about two minutes."

He started for the stage, feeling as though he were

on a gangplank headed for the fathomless, blue sea. A drumroll had begun and he could feel the vibrations inside himself, like the rumblings of impending doom.

How could he possibly have allowed himself to be talked into this? Even if it was for the good of his career?

He positioned himself in front of the microphone, looked out into the sea of faces and felt his vocal chords freeze. But then he picked Amy out of the crowd and she gave him an encouraging smile and a thumbs-up sign. He took a deep breath and plunged into the familiar routine.

"Did you ever watch a football player spike the ball after a touchdown?" he asked, afraid that had been a crack he'd heard in his voice. "Or notice a hitter windmill his arm after a homer? Or see a basketball player posture to the crowd after draining the game winner? Society could learn a lot about celebrating from athletes."

His jaw had clenched the way it did when he was nervous and he made a concerted effort to loosen it. This was hell on earth, but it was a hell of his own making. Amy nodded, giving him the impetus to continue.

"Did you get that promotion you've been angling for? What the heck. Chest bump the boss. The worst that could happen is he could fall down."

He cast a look around at the crowd. Nobody was laughing, but he thought, hoped, he detected a glimmer of a smile on a few faces.

"Or maybe you're an accountant going through

your company's books who finds a multimillion dollar error in your company's favor. Why not spike the calculator? They'll buy you another one.''

Laugh, damn it, he ordered the crowd, but it didn't do any good. When he cleared his throat, the microphone magnified the sound.

''Are you a research scientist who discovers the genetic marker for a terrible disease? Forget that laboratories aren't any noisier than libraries. Thrust your arms in the air and shout, 'I'm the man!'''

To illustrate his point, Matt raised both arms high and punched at the air.

All was silent until he heard a deep, rumbling laugh as familiar as his own. Amy put a hand to her mouth, her eyes crinkling with mirth. Around her, a few others joined in her laughter.

He saw her look left, then right, then heard her let a second laugh rip with enough volume to reach the upper tables overlooking the makeshift stage.

Then a wonderful thing happened. Another audience member laughed, then yet another and another, until the entire place was rumbling with it.

The most wonderful thing of all was that the laughter didn't stop until Matt left the stage.

8

AMY MUST BE OUT OF HER MIND, because only insanity would explain why she'd agreed to come to Matt's place for a nightcap.

His high-rise building of fancy condominiums was only a mile or so from Slap Happy's but she knew better than to trust herself alone with him.

She'd been at his place before, of course, but Zoe had always been with them. Zoe, her friend. Her lifeline. Her assurance that she wouldn't do something she might regret. Like jump on Matt and tear his clothes off.

"Maybe I should call Zoe to see if she wants to come over," Amy said as he opened the door to his place and waited for her to precede him inside.

"Amy, it's after eleven," Matt pointed out after glancing down at a watch as expensive as everything else he was wearing. At least it wasn't a Rolex. "I don't think Zoe will be up for visiting at this hour."

So what am I doing here? Amy asked herself while she hesitated on the threshold. She was about to tell him she'd changed her mind and wanted to go home when she remembered the purpose that had seized her while she'd listened to his comedy routine.

She needed answers and the only way she'd get

them was by asking questions. Tonight, preferably, before he put his guard up and pretended the stage show had never happened.

She took a deep breath and stepped across the threshold into the lair of temptation. She looked around his place, with its gleaming white tile floors and sleek masculine furniture in shades of black and burgundy, and almost laughed at her choice of words.

His place looked more conducive to repression than temptation. Satisfied she wasn't in immediate danger of succumbing to the passion that simmered under her skin whenever she was with him, she eased into the subject of his comedy.

"I still can't believe you got up in front of all those people and told jokes. You! Of all people."

Amy's heart thudded when the door clicked closed behind them, rendering them truly alone, but she ignored the thudding.

"You say that like you think I'm humorless," he said dryly.

"Not humorless exactly but not ha-ha hilarious." She noticed the corners of his mouth tug downward and thought he might be misinterpreting what she was trying to say. "Not that your jokes were bad. Some of them were even funny."

"People did laugh," Matt said dryly as he loosened his tie and ran a hand through his thick hair. She wet her lips. What was it about a mussed man that was so much sexier than a perfectly groomed one? "Of course, it helped that I planted a designated laugher in the audience."

That was news to her, but it made sense. Laughter

was contagious. She'd figured that out herself when her laughs—okay, her tremendous chortles—had caused the people around her to laugh with her.

"I didn't know there was such a thing as a designated laugher," she said.

"Oh, yeah," he answered casually. "There's even another name for it—Amy."

Disconcerted that he'd figured out she'd laughed so the audience would laugh with her, she walked through his condo to his wet bar. The only sound in the place was the ticking of a sleek black wall clock and the heels of her ankle boots clicking on the tile floor. She hoisted herself up on one of the tall stools in front of the marble counter.

"How do you know it was me laughing?" she asked.

"I only know one woman who laughs like her vocal chords have been dipped in whiskey," he said.

Her gaze shot to him and locked on his eyes. In the reflected light of the tile floor and white walls of the condo, they were a lighter, richer, sexier brown. A whiskey-colored brown. A couple of weeks ago, he'd accused her of snorting when she laughed. But she liked this description better.

"Are whiskey-coated vocal chords a good thing or a bad thing?" she asked.

"A very good thing," he answered. "Especially when, up to that point, I was afraid nobody was going to laugh at all."

"Like I said, you were sort of funny." She glanced away from his eyes lest she get drunk on them. "Although I still can't understand what possessed you to enter yourself in a talent show."

She watched him open the small refrigerator behind the bar and take out two frosted mugs and two different brands of beer. He set the domestic ale she preferred in front of her.

"I didn't enter myself," he said as he uncapped her bottle and poured beer into her mug. "One of the partners at the firm entered me."

"Why?" Amy asked.

"It's one of those bizarre coincidences," Matt said as he filled his own mug with an expensive, imported brand of pale ale. He took a swig of the beer before he continued. "He saw my dad perform a long time ago."

"Perform what?"

He took another swallow of beer, seeming to avoid the question. After long moments, he answered, "My father liked to think of himself as a stand-up comedian."

Amy cradled her hands around her cool beer mug while her mind tried and failed to process the information. "Why didn't I know this?"

His shrug appeared nonchalant, but the rigid set of his shoulders told her he was tense. "Because I never tell anyone about it. It's not easy to admit that your father dragged your family from place to place because he was searching for an audience that would laugh at his jokes."

"I don't understand," Amy said, shaking her head. "I thought your dad was in plastics."

"He was for a time. He sold plastic wrap and dental floss and ladies' lingerie. He was even that guy who comes to the door and tries to get you to let him dump dirt on your rug so he can demonstrate a super-powered vacuum cleaner. But he only did those things in between gigs.''

"But I thought—'' she looked to him for help but he was silent even though she suspected he knew very well what she'd thought "—I thought you came from money.''

"I never said I came from money.''

"But you dress like it. You talk like it. You act like it.''

"That's because now I have money.''

She finished his thought for him. "And then you didn't.''

"We didn't,'' he said. "It was just my mom, my dad and me, thank God. Mom did the best she could but it was tough to find a job when we were always on the move.''

"So you didn't grow up with the country-club and caviar set?''

He laughed. "More like the cafeteria and hot-dog set.''

She was silent while she let the information digest. She'd known him for years yet hadn't known this crucial piece of information that had helped form him into the man he was. No wonder money and job security were so important to him.

"Those jokes you told tonight, were those yours or your father's?''

"It was my father's basic routine, although I modernized it a bit,'' he said. "Unfortunately that was the comedy routine my boss saw all those years ago. It was one of the only ones Dad got a laugh from.''

"There's another thing I don't understand," Amy said, regarding him over her beer mug. "Why did you let that partner in your office talk you into performing when you so obviously didn't want to?''

"I wanted to help the charity," he said, sincerity shining out of his eyes. "But that wasn't the only reason. I wanted to help myself too. I'd like to be a partner one day and the little things might give me a nod over someone else.''

"Making partner is that important to you?" she asked, and he nodded without the slightest hesitation.

As recently as yesterday, she might have upbraided him for the admission. The hard facts were that he'd reluctantly performed a comedy act mainly because he thought it would be good for his career. But yesterday, Amy didn't have all the facts. Yesterday, Amy didn't completely understand why career was so important to him.

"Being a teacher is important to me," she said, trying for once to find the similarities between them instead of the differences.

"I know," he said, coming around the wet bar and sitting down in the tall stool next to her. He was so close she could have reached out and touched him. "What I don't understand is why you have to work at a low-paying private school.''

He looked so earnest that she figured maybe it was time to explain why she'd been angry at him for sending in her résumé instead of just being angry.

"You know my mom was a public schoolteacher,

right?" she asked, and he nodded. "The thing that cut into her soul was that the class sizes were so large she couldn't give any child enough of her time. Paying extra attention to one student meant neglecting another. I didn't want to neglect any child. Ever."

"Did you ever consider that you're a strong enough teacher that those children would be better off with part of your time than with all of someone else's?"

She reached out and covered his hand with hers. A jolt of awareness hit her but so did a wave of tenderness that he had such faith in her.

"I decided long ago I'd rather make a real difference to a dozen children than half a difference to double that many."

"Even if you'd make double the salary at a public school?"

"Even if I'd make triple the salary. The money's not important to me, Matt. The children are."

He brushed back a lock of hair from her face with his free hand. "You're a special lady, Amy Donatelli," he said, his eyes intent on hers.

"Does that mean you finally understand why money's not important to me?" she asked softly.

She was unprepared for his grin and for the charming way his whiskey-colored eyes crinkled at the corners.

"Hell, no," he said. "I understand why your students are important to you but it still drives me nuts that you make so little money."

She wrinkled up her forehead and pursed her lips. "You think I drive you nuts," she shot at him. "I'm friends with a guy who wears ties on the weekends and works all the time. *You* drive *me* nuts.''

Instead of taking offense, he slipped his right hand from under hers and looped his loosened tie over his head before dropping it on the floor. He slid a thumb over her cheek, and his eyes locked on hers.

''I'm not wearing a tie now,'' he said. The indirect lighting in the room cast shadows over his face, softening his high cheekbones and square jaw so that he was almost achingly handsome.

''Yeah,'' she rasped, ''but you still drive me nuts.''

''I was hoping I had that effect on you.'' His low, soft voice set off tremors inside her because he was talking about so much more than what turned them off about each other.

He was talking about what turned them on.

''Opposites attract,'' she said in a voice every bit as soft and low. He didn't move, just kept staring at her, and she realized how much she'd admitted. She swallowed. ''I think that's the title of a TV movie.''

''I haven't seen it,'' he said, moving inexorably closer to her, ''but I'm willing to find out if it's true.''

Amy wasn't sure whether she leaned forward, whether he did or whether they both did. But she was sure the electric excitement that pulsated through her when their mouths met couldn't have been generated by any other man.

He kissed like a man straight out of a dream, as though she'd conjured him up just for her. His hands had moved from her face to cup the back of her head, holding her in place, almost like he thought she might pull away.

But how could she think of retreat when his soft lips were moving over hers, when her nose was filled with his scent, when her heart was overflowing with tenderness?

This wasn't just any man. It was Matt, who she'd known and loved for years. How much different it was to kiss a man who was already in your heart than a stranger who might never get there.

She'd tried to convince herself in the last few days that her reaction to the kiss they'd shared on the porch had been a fluke. But then she'd have to deny that liquid heat was spreading through her body and weakening her limbs.

He coaxed her lips apart to deepen the kiss. She sighed into it, first anchoring her hands on the starchy fabric of his shirt and then winding them around his neck—and losing her balance.

The tall bar stool shot out from under her and their mouths disengaged as she toppled the rest of the way into his arms. His back slammed against the marble counter of the wet bar as he caught her to him.

For a moment, she stayed there in the circle of his arms, both of them breathing hard from both the kiss and the close call.

"You don't have to throw yourself at me," he said finally, a twinkle in those eyes that she could get drunk on. "I'm perfectly willing to indulge you."

"Oh, you are, are you?" she teased back. "Well, maybe I'm waiting for you to sweep me off my feet."

He was off the stool almost before she finished the sentence, hooking a strong arm under the back of her legs and lifting her into his arms.

''Consider yourself swept,'' he said, and she buried her face against his strong, warm neck and giggled.

She couldn't see where they were going but felt the cool texture of leather against her back when he lowered her and figured he'd laid her on his sofa.

She opened her eyes and saw him standing above her looking impossibly sexy with his disheveled clothes, ruffled hair and a question in his passion-dark eyes.

She smiled and opened her arms. That was all the answer he needed. He was beside her, his hard-muscled body stretched against the length of hers, before she could blink.

She didn't want to blink, didn't want to miss even a second of the incredible thing happening between them. This time she was the one who kissed him, who coaxed his lips apart, who slid her tongue against the rough texture of his.

She rubbed against him, feeling her nipples harden, her breasts ache, her sex pool with heat.

Was this really happening?

Was she really wrapped up in Matt's arms—heck, wrapped up in Matt—on his sofa, on the verge of making love?

Alarm bells should be resounding like the bells of St. Mary's, but they weren't. Although she definitely was hearing something.

She broke off the kiss and Matt stared at her, his

eyes questioning and perhaps a little desperate. "What is it?"

She listened more closely. "I think it's the 'Battle Hymn of the Republic'."

He groaned. "It's my doorbell."

"Your doorbell plays the 'Battle Hymn of the Republic'?"

"What can I say," he answered. "I'm patriotic."

She started to pull his head down for another kiss but the battle hymn kept playing and she read hesitancy on his face. She knew he wanted her—she could feel the evidence against her thigh and see it in the strained muscles of his face—but she supposed he couldn't help it that he was so anal he had trouble ignoring the doorbell.

"Maybe you should answer it," she suggested.

"I want to ignore it."

"*I* want your full attention, and I'm not getting it until we send whoever's at the door packing," she said as the tune of the song marched on. "Besides, there's too much vengeance in that song to ignore."

He hoisted himself up on his elbows and away from her, running his hands through his hair, looking so adorably frustrated that a surge of feminine power coursed through her.

"Give me a minute and I'll get it," he said.

"No, *I'll* get it." She sat up and rearranged her clothing. "No offense, Matt. But I bet I'm way better at telling people to scat than you are."

She was composing a reasonably tactful way to say get lost when she opened the door to a petite woman with short, spiky hair bleached so blond it was almost white. She was wearing a tight black leather skirt and matching halter top. The dark circles that rimmed her eyes were accentuated by the pale foundation she wore, the latest in Goth makeup. A golden ring pierced her nose.

"Can you please tell me if Matt is in," the woman requested in a formal voice with a cultured British accent.

"Who are you?" Amy asked, tact forgotten. Pinpricks rose on the back of her neck, signaling a silent warning.

"I'm so very pleased to make your acquaintance," the woman said in the same gracious tone. "My name's Mary Contrino."

MATT BOLTED OFF THE SOFA at the sound of the fictitious name and hurried to the door only to encounter a woman he'd never seen before in his life.

"Matt, my love," cried the pale-faced pixie with the hair that looked as though it could kill, or at least maim, if she used her head as a battering ram. "Oh, these hours apart have seemed like years."

Without waiting for an invitation, she entered the condo, bypassing a shocked-looking Amy and launching herself into his arms. One of her hair spikes jabbed his chin, probably leaving a puncture wound. Matt had heard of people being struck speechless, but he'd never experienced the phenomenon himself until that moment.

"How am I doin' so far?" the woman whispered in his ear with an odd lisp before she drew back and asked Amy, "Isn't my Matt divine? I so adore a man in a starched dress shirt."

Matt might have mistaken the stranger for a high-class, society lady if not for her black leather getup, hair, makeup and piercings. She almost seemed like a top-notch actress giving a performance in a play staffed by a truly terrible costume department.

An actress.

The identity of the woman hit him so hard he nearly staggered. Trinity. The actress niece of the security guard at his law office.

The one he'd called that afternoon and who said she was busy with *San Andreus Fault* but might have time to squeeze in an audition after one of her performances. But he hadn't realized she meant tonight. And he certainly hadn't foreseen that a woman hailing straight from a play about an earthquake would be dressed like that.

"Who are you, dear?" she asked Amy in an upper-crust voice at odds with her spiked hair and stiletto-heeled, knee-length black boots.

"I'm Amy Donatelli, Matt's..." Amy's voice trailed off as she gazed across the room at him. Her hair was in wild disarray and her lips were swollen from his kisses. He thought he saw them tremble before she finished her sentence. "Friend."

A *friend!*

Something broke inside Matt's chest at the sheer inadequacy of the label and he strode across the room toward the two women, intending to straighten out this whole mess. Trinity-masquerading-as-Mary-Contrary immediately took his arm.

She was holding on too tight to shake off, so he ignored her and addressed Amy. "You and I are much more than friends."

Trinity placed the back of her free hand against her forehead, looking for all the world as though she was about to swoon. With her eyes closed, the makeup made it appear as though she had two over-large black buttons for eyes. "Whatever are you saying, my love?"

"I'm saying that Amy and I are—"

"Very good friends who have known each other for years," Amy interrupted. She seemed to grow taller, and he realized it was because she'd straightened her spine. "You don't have to worry about me and Matt, Mary. I'm…in love with someone else."

Trinity brought her hand down off her forehead. The color seemed to return to her face but it was hard to tell because of the Goth makeup. "How very nice for you," she told Amy.

Matt felt as though he'd been kicked in the solar plexus. The kisses they'd shared obviously hadn't meant a fraction as much to Amy as they had to him.

He was in love with her and, as she had so baldly stated, she was in love with someone else.

"I know it's gauche to gush, but I am delighted you're not the competition," Trinity said, addressing Amy. "I couldn't bear it if Matt was in love with someone else. Did you know we're ogres?"

"OWGAs," Matt corrected absently.

"Whatever we are," Trinity said, putting a leather-clad arm around Matt's waist, "I'm glad we're together."

"Pierre and I do everything together," Amy said, smiling brightly. Did the smile not quite reach her eyes or was that Matt's hopeful imagination? "He's my OWGA."

"You have an ogre, too? How delightful," Trinity said with enthusiasm. She looked up at Matt as she talked and he noticed that not only her nose was pierced. Her tongue was, too, which probably accounted for the lisping. "Matt, my love, is Amy and her ogre the couple with whom we're going to double-date?"

"Yeah," he said softly, aware he hadn't said much at all since Trinity had interrupted what had quite possibly been the best moment of his life. Shock—and the realization that he'd fallen into unrequited love—could do that to a man.

"When are we dining?" Trinity asked in an accent so authentic she sounded as though she actually was British.

"Next week some time," Amy said vaguely and smoothed the hair his fingers had been tangled in not long before. He had to clasp his hands together so he wouldn't reach for her.

"Let's set a date and time," Trinity said. "We'll have a perfectly marvelous time."

Amy looked doubtful but Matt wasn't about to bypass a chance to meet Pierre LeFrancois. Not after the trouble to which he'd gone to procure a Mary Contrary. Not when that trouble had arrived at a most inopportune time.

Or maybe, he thought wryly, his trouble had arrived just in time. Otherwise, he would have spilled his guts to Amy about how he felt about her and made a tremendous fool of himself.

"How about seven o'clock Wednesday at Serenade, that new place on Connecticut Avenue," Matt said. "Pierre can tell us how authentic the French cooking is."

"But we always meet at Brewster's on Wednesday for happy hour," Amy said.

"That's why I suggested Wednesday. I know you're free," Matt said.

"But Zoe and Jack—" Amy started.

"—will understand," Matt finished. "They know how much I want to meet Pierre. So we're on for Wednesday, right?"

Amy hesitated. "Right," she said.

She sounded resigned, which wasn't surprising considering Pierre was an unemployed loser. But maybe there was another reason Amy didn't want him to meet the other man. Maybe she didn't want LeFrancois to find out what they'd been doing on the sofa.

"I can hardly wait," Trinity said. Even though she was holding on to his waist, Matt had forgotten her existence.

"I should get going," Amy said and headed for the door.

"I'll drive you home," Matt offered.

"No, don't bother. I'd rather take the Metro."

"Then I'll come with you," Matt said firmly.

"Isn't he the perfect gentleman?" Trinity piped in. "Arguing with him is fruitless. My Matt will not take no for an answer."

Trinity had been talking to Amy's back but, at her comment, Amy turned and pinned her with a penetrating look. "Don't *you* argue with him? Isn't that why he calls you Mary Contrary?"

"Oh, yes indeed. I am a contrary one." Trinity paused, as though unsure of what to say next. "Neither Matt nor I take no for an answer. That's why he'll agree to allow me to accompany you."

"Great," Matt muttered sarcastically under his breath a few minutes later as he followed the two women out of his condo.

A woman masquerading as a woman who didn't exist was helping him to escort home the woman he loved. Who was in love with a loser who, unfortunately, was all too real.

9

AMY CAST A WORRIED LOOK across the table, afraid she'd made a terrible mistake in her choice of men to portray Pierre LeFrancois.

Not that she'd had much choice.

She'd phoned five theater companies before she'd found an actor who met her criteria: a tall, handsome, long-haired man fluent in French who worked cheap.

At six feet five, her impostor certainly was tall. He was also handsome in a windswept, soul-eyed kind of way. With his massive build, he even fit the size requirement of someone with proportions roughly equivalent to a stuffed giant panda.

The sticking point was that her impostor's real name was Lee Bob King and he hailed from the great state of Alabama.

"Something wrong, sweetheart?" he asked with a southern twang as thick as flies on a pecan pie left too long on the ledge to cool. He yawned and stretched out his beefy arms so enthusiastically Amy was afraid he'd pop the seams of his giant suit jacket. "Sorry. The days sure get long when you're working construction."

"You're a construction worker?" She leaned forward in her chair, trying not to get any more alarmed than she already was. "I thought you were an actor."

"I am an actor, but I gotta eat," he said, patting the substantial girth of his stomach. "Construction pays the grocery bills."

"Then you do work for the theater company that told me about you?"

"I wish," he said. "I call 'em often enough. But after that first audition, they keep saying they don't have any parts right for me. Except maybe Harvey."

"You mean Elwood P. Dowd's sidekick? In the play *Harvey?*" Amy asked, and he nodded. "But he's a pooka."

"What is that exactly?" Lee Bob asked. "I never got around to asking."

"It's from old Celtic mythology. It's like a fairy spirit in animal form. Always very large. Harvey the pooka is a rabbit. He's invisible."

"Might not be a hard part to play then," Lee Bob said, tapping his chin. "What do you think, sweetheart?"

She thought he was verging on desperate if he was considering playing a large, invisible rabbit but she didn't think it would be wise to say so. Not now. Not when she needed him to give a grandiose performance.

She dodged the question with a more important one of her own. "Do you think you could remember to call me *mon amiba* instead of sweetheart?"

He scrunched up his face so hard his dark eyebrows touched above his crooked nose. "Now why would I be wanting to do that?"

"I'd explain but it'd take too long." She darted a quick glance at the door. "Matt and Mary will be here any minute."

He looked pained. "I thought you wanted me to be believable. Frenchmen are smooth operators. They're romantic. They don't go around calling women amoebas."

"Could you just call me your amoeba and be done with it?"

"Do I have to?"

"Yes," she said, then frowned. Maybe Lee Bob wasn't getting roles because he was one of those difficult, temperamental actors. "Are you sure you can pull this off?"

He raised his eyes to the ceiling and shook his head so hard his long, black hair swung. "Why does everybody think I can't pull off a role? I'm an actor. Trained in the art of illusion."

"You have training, then?" Amy asked.

"'Course I have training." He sounded offended. "I'll fool this fella for you, don't you worry."

Amy clamped her lips together before they started to tremble as the enormity of her deception struck her. Because it wasn't just any fella they were trying to fool. It was the one she'd fallen in love with.

How pathetic, she asked herself, *was that?*

About as pathetic as showing Matt how she felt about him with her enthusiastic response to his kisses and then having Mary Contrary show up at the door.

Her heart hadn't merely broken. It had shattered. The only consolation was that she'd been able to save face by bringing up her supposed love for Pierre.

The drawback to the consolation was that she'd had to come up with a Pierre.

"There they are now," Amy told the faux Pierre when she spotted Matt and Mary at the hostess's stand.

Even though she'd seen the other woman once before, Amy was struck by how different the real Mary was from her preconceived notion of a tall, cool blonde.

She was so tiny that the top of her spiky blond head barely reached Matt's armpit despite her platform shoes. She'd left the Goth makeup and black leather at home tonight but her tight, blue minidress was almost as risqué.

Amy used to think that she was Matt's polar opposite but she'd changed her mind since meeting Mary. Pairing Mary with Matt was like putting together a neon light and a moonbeam.

"You don't mean you think that sexy, little blonde over there is Mary, do you?" Lee Bob, aka Pierre, asked.

"You're not supposed to think other women are sexy," Amy said as the pair started walking toward their table. "I'm your amoeba, not her. You have to remember that."

"Yeah, but that's—"

Even if he had finished his sentence, Amy wouldn't have heard because it was Matt who commanded her attention.

"Hey, Amy," he said, looking dreamy despite his

supershort hair and stuffy gray suit. "You remember Mary." He paused, as though expecting the other woman to utter a greeting, but she appeared shell-shocked. Matt's gaze swung to Lee Bob and hardened. "I take it this is Pierre."

"But that's—" Mary began.

Amy didn't let her finish. "Yes, this most certainly is Pierre. My OWGA."

"I hope you don't think that's French, *mon amiba,* because it's Greek to me," Lee Bob said, but he wasn't speaking in his normal voice. He was putting on a heavy accent that sounded like a weird hybrid of Alabaman and French. Oh, Lord. Where had he gotten his training? Acme Acting Academy?

"I explained what it means, Pierre," Amy told Lee Bob, pretending as though she didn't find anything unusual about his awful accent. "You're the one who got away from me. That's why I tracked you down."

"Mary's the one who got away from me," Matt said, putting a verbal stake through Amy's heart. "This is Mary Contrino, and I'm Matt Burke." He stuck out a hand to Lee Bob.

Amy waited for Lee Bob to get out of his seat and shake Matt's hand, but he'd returned his attention to Mary. In fact, he was staring so intently that Amy doubted he'd seen Matt's offered hand.

"Pierre," Amy said, giving him a sharp elbow in the ribs. He yelped. "Matt wants to shake your hand."

"*Oui, oui, oui,*" he said, sounding like the little piggie who cried all the way home. He stood up, topping Matt by a good three inches and seventy-five pounds. "*Bonjour,* pal."

He slipped his hand from Matt's before Matt could return the greeting and took one of Mary's in both of his.

"*Bonjour* to you, too," he said, not letting go of her hand until she was sitting in the chair next to him. Matt took the one next to Amy.

"Excuse me for saying this, Pierre," Matt said before they'd even sat down, "but you don't look like any Frenchman I've ever seen."

"Why's that?" Lee Bob asked, cracking his knuckles and running a hand through his long hair.

"I don't think of the French as being so—" Matt said and paused "—large."

"I think he looks heavenly large," Mary cut in, her chin in her hands, her eyes on Lee Bob. Amy could barely believe it. The woman was with Matt, and she was mooning over Lee Bob. How dare she do that to Matt!

"That's not the point," Matt said, obviously failing to realize the love of his life thought the fake Frenchman was eye candy. "The point is that the French, as a rule, aren't a giant people."

By Matt's comment and the way he'd been staring at Lee Bob's ears, which weren't nearly as large as the ones he'd seen when he'd gotten a glimpse of the big-eared stuffed panda, Amy feared he was becoming suspicious of the ruse.

She turned her attention from the fickle Mary to the pickle she was in. If she couldn't convince Matt that Lee Bob was French, the game was over.

"There's an exception to every rule," Amy said, quickly trying to think of a reason Lee Bob should qualify as one. "His mother's American. From Alabama. She's very tall. Amazonian, even."

The faux Pierre, the one reportedly born of a Frenchman and an Alabama amazon, didn't say anything to back her up. All he could do, it seemed, was smile stupidly at Mary Contrary.

"I thought you told me his mother was British," Matt said. "Isn't she the one who taught him to drive on the left side of the road?"

Amy forced herself to think. "That was his godmother," she said. "His family are devout Catholics. Isn't that right, Pierre?"

More silence. She gave him another elbow.

"Right," Lee Bob said, then seemed to remember his acting assignment. "I mean *oui*."

"Amy tells me you're a French teacher," Matt said when the waitress had taken their drink orders and handed them menus. His was lying on the table unopened. "Where do you teach?"

"He teaches high school French." Amy wrapped part of her hand around Lee Bob's extremely large biceps, the better to claim his attention away from Mary. "He's very good."

"I didn't ask *what* he taught," Matt clarified. "I asked *where* he taught."

"High school," Lee Bob answered.

"What high school?" Matt persisted, the way they probably taught him to do at law school. "And don't say Herbert Hoover High like you told Amy because I already know you don't teach there."

"Teachers leave jobs all the time," Amy pointed out with heat. How dare he interrogate Lee Bob as though he was lying to her. *She* was the one who'd made up the lies.

"I'm not so sure he left the job," Matt said. "I'm willing to bet he got fired."

"Of course he's never been fired," Amy retorted, then figured she better involve Lee Bob in the conversation. "Have you, Pierre?"

"Fired? *Bien sûr non.* Except if you count that one time when I was seventeen and Mr. Jones didn't like the way I was driving the cotton picker."

"I didn't know there was cotton to pick in France," Matt said, sounding even more suspicious now.

"He meant Monsieur Jones didn't like the way he picked grapes off the vine," Amy said. There. That sounded more French. "For the wine."

"I distinctly heard Pierre said cotton, not grapes." Matt turned his lawyerly gaze on Lee Bob. "Did you or did you not say cotton?"

"Give him a break," Amy said, then inspiration struck. "Of course he's going to get confused when he spent half his time in France and half in Alabama. Remember, his parents are divorced."

"I thought they were devout Catholics," Matt said.

"I thought they were happily married," Mary added.

Amy swung her gaze to the other woman. Mary's eyes had lost the Goth look but her lashes were heavily slathered with navy-blue mascara. Instead of a nose ring, she was wearing a diamond—or was that a cubic zirconia?—stud. "How would you know anything about Pierre's parents?"

Mary's painted lips formed an O, which she quickly covered with fingers that had nails painted black. "I don't."

"She doesn't," Lee Bob confirmed.

All eyes flew to Mary, who seemed to figure out that more of an explanation was expected from her. "Sometimes, I just know things. It's a talent I have."

"But Pierre's parents aren't together," Amy insisted. They couldn't be for her latest fabrication to hold any merit.

Amy seemed to think about that for a moment. "I didn't say the things I know are always true."

None of this, however, seemed to placate Matt. He was still bent on interrogating Pierre.

"Which part of the French countryside are you from?" he asked Lee Bob.

Lee Bob got such a puzzled look on his face, it was obvious geography hadn't been his best subject in school. He finally waved a hand.

"The fat part," he said. "Over by Switzerland."

Amy closed her eyes, wishing she could disappear as easily as she'd shut out her surroundings. It was going to be a very long evening.

MATT FINISHED OFF THE LAST of the wine in his glass, wishing he could get rid of Pierre LeFrancois as easily.

They'd somehow gotten through a gourmet dinner, with Pierre waxing poetic about the superiority of

French wines and the divinity of French cuisine, and he neither liked nor trusted the other man.

He didn't accept for a second that LeFrancois was French although he had no trouble believing that he'd been born in Alabama of an Amazonian mother.

Matt was pretty sure, in fact, that LeFrancois was a pathological liar out to bamboozle the far-too-susceptible Amy.

He still hadn't gotten an admission of unemployment from the other man, but he vowed he'd bleed the information out of the burly Frenchman before the night was through.

Maybe then Amy would see what a fraud Pierre was.

"I love a good Tuscany wine," Pierre said, kissing the tips of his long, fat fingers.

"Tuscany is in Italy." Matt impaled him with his stare. "I'd think a Frenchman like you would know that."

"You can't expect Pierre to know everything," Trinity, aka Mary Contrary, said. "It's our imperfections that make us human."

When it came to imperfections, Trinity knew of what she spoke. He no longer had to wonder why Nellie, her security-guard aunt, had tried to warn him about her. Nellie must have realized he wouldn't have much in common with a dyed blonde sporting a nose ring and a pierced tongue.

Actually, maybe imperfect was the wrong word for Trinity. Eccentric, peculiar and odd would all be more accurate.

He was still amazed that Amy had bought Trinity's

acting job the other night considering the actress had been decked out in black leather. But he couldn't blame Trinity for that. Not when it turned out he'd gotten the name of her play wrong.

She wasn't performing in *San Andreas Fault,* a play about an earthquake. She was playing the role of a vampy woman in *St. Andres' Fault.*

Trinity was the saint's fault.

"Spoken like a wise woman," Pierre said, reaching across the table to cover Trinity's hand with his.

Matt's thoughts zeroed in on LeFrancois with a vengeance as he glared at their linked hands. Obviously it wasn't true that Pierre didn't like people, because he seemed to like Trinity just fine. That the Frenchman had paid far more attention to Trinity than he had to Amy, in fact, was yet another strike against him. What kind of way was that for an OWGA to behave?

"What exactly are your intentions toward Amy?" Matt asked abruptly.

"Who, me?" Pierre asked, pointing to his broad chest. As quickly as his dreadful accent disappeared, it reappeared again. "Darn. I meant who, *moi?*"

"Yes, you." Matt glared. "What are they?"

"Pierre's intentions toward me are none of your business." Amy's dark eyes glittered as they met his. The color on her cheeks was high, making her look vibrantly alive.

A part of him knew he had stepped over a line but he didn't care. Amy's happiness was at stake.

"As somebody who's been sitting here for the last

hour watching your OWGA flirt with a woman who isn't you, I decided to make it my business,'' Matt said.

"You're complaining about how my OWGA's acted?'' Amy sounded incredulous. "How about yours? If she batted her eyelashes at him any more, she'd kick up a windstorm.''

"Distracting me from the point I'm trying to make won't work.'' Matt didn't care in the slightest who Trinity flirted with. The only woman he cared about was Amy. "I'm a lawyer. I know every trick in the book.''

"And what point are you trying to make?'' Amy challenged.

"That Pierre's not only an unemployed loser but a womanizer to boot.''

"He's no womanizer. He's totally devoted to me.'' Amy grabbed Pierre's hand, forcing him to let go of Mary's. "Aren't you, Pierre?''

"Oh, *oui*.'' Pierre said. Unconvincingly, Matt thought.

"We're perfect for each other,'' Amy continued as though she were thoroughly convinced of the faithless Pierre's devotion. "In fact, remember how I told you we might move in together? Pierre asked me to live with him and I agreed.''

"You two are going to live together?'' Trinity asked Pierre in a high-pitched whine.

Matt might have taken the actress to task for showing such obvious disappointment if he weren't nearly debilitated by the pain that covered him like a thick blanket.

Striving to get control of himself, he flung an arm across Mary's shoulders. He pulled her close, ignoring the way her spiked hair poked his chin.

"Oh, yeah," he said, meeting Amy's glittering eyes. "Well, I asked *Mary* to live with *me* and *she* said yes."

"You're going to live with him?" An obviously unhappy Pierre asked Trinity, jerking a thumb at Matt.

Matt would have pointed out to Amy the inappropriateness of the jerk's reaction if she hadn't leaned close to him.

"I'm moving in with Pierre next week," Amy said.

"Mary's moving in with me tomorrow," he retorted.

"Pierre and I are going to be deliriously happy," she snapped back.

"Mary and I will be happier."

Peripherally he was aware of Trinity slipping out from under his arm, but he couldn't worry about that.

"I give you three months before you remember how conservative you are and realize her spiked hair and pierced tongue drive you nuts," Amy predicted.

"I give you three weeks before you realize you can't live with an unemployed teacher who's about as French as one of McDonald's fries."

They were nose to nose, their eyes locked on each

other, their breaths coming hard. They'd reached an old-fashioned standoff.

Because he didn't want to break eye contact, he was annoyed to feel a tapping on his shoulder. He ignored it, hoping it would stop. It didn't.

"Matt." Trinity's voice accompanied the tapping.

"Go away," he said under his breath.

"Cool. I'm glad you're okay with it," she said, "because going away is exactly what we're gonna do."

We? Maybe it was time he heeded the tapping. He turned to find Pierre and Trinity looming over their table. The actress was huddled close to the French impostor, who was holding her to him with a beefy arm.

"Lee Bob and I are leaving," Trinity announced.

Matt could barely believe it. He knew LeFrancois couldn't be trusted and wouldn't have been surprised to learn he'd run off with another woman. But he never imagined the louse would cheat on Amy in front of her eyes.

His right hand balled into a fist, the better to punch out the disloyal Frenchman for daring to hurt Amy, when the name Trinity had used registered on him.

"Who's Lee Bob?" he asked.

Trinity gazed up at Frenchy, a worshipful expression on her elfin face. "A really hot guy who helped me get through Acting Like Olivier class," she said, all traces of her British accent gone. "Like, I don't even remember why we split."

"Must've been temporary insanity," said the big

man, who sounded like he was from the deep south now that he'd lost his pseudo-French accent.

"What was the word the two of you used before?" Trinity asked, pausing to search her memory. "Ogre. That's it. Lee Bob and I are each other's ogres."

"Wait a minute," Matt said as something raw and angry bubbled inside him. "Are you saying Pierre's name is actually Lee Bob?"

"Uh-huh," Trinity said cheerfully. "Lee Bob King."

"That's not a French name," Matt said as the bubbling got more raw and angry.

"I don't know about that," Trinity said. "What if you put the accent on the first syllable and pronounced it *le* Bob?"

Matt ignored her and asked the other man through clenched teeth, "Are you French or not?"

"Not," Lee Bob said, "but I like the sound of *le* Bob. It has flair."

Matt sprang to his feet and advanced on the French fraud, ire fueling his steps, uncaring of the other diners who stared at them. "How dare you lie to Amy like that. I oughta—"

"Stop!" Trinity said, thrusting herself in front of the big jerk. She was so petite that her body shielded, at most, about fifty percent of his. "Lee Bob wasn't lying. He was acting." She craned her neck so she could see around Matt to where Amy still sat. "Tell him I'm right, Amy."

Even though Trinity addressed Amy, Amy looked at Matt. She hesitated before speaking, which was as atypical as the guilt imprinted on her face. Slowly she nodded.

"I hired Lee Bob to convince you he was Pierre LeFrancois." Her voice dripped with the same guilt that twisted her expression.

"I knew it!" Trinity squeezed the huge arm of the man at her side and beamed up at him. "See, you can't be as bad as our drama coach said, Lee Bob. Look how surprised Matt is that you're not a Frenchman."

Matt swallowed the lump that had formed in his throat. Despite Trinity's delusions, it came as no surprise that Lee Bob had been putting on an act. The surprise was that Lee Bob had been trying to fool him instead of Amy.

"If this guy's an actor," he said, jerking a thumb at Lee Bob, "where's the real Pierre LeFrancois?"

Amy's eyes dropped to the table and her long, dark hair fell into her face. "Pierre doesn't exist," she said so softly he barely heard her. "I made him up."

The confession was so unexpected, and so staggering, that Matt dropped back into one of the chairs. All this time, he'd been agonizing over the thought of Amy with another man. *And the man didn't exist.*

"I didn't mean to lie to you," Amy rushed on to explain. "But Zoe started talking about OWGAs and you said you had one and before I knew it, I had one, too. I meant to tell you a hundred times but..." Her voiced trailed off. "But somehow I never did."

"I don't understand," Matt said, shaking his head.

"I saw a man at your kitchen table that night when we were on your porch."

That had been the night of their first transcendent kiss, which Amy had abruptly cut off, supposedly because of that man.

"That wasn't a man," Amy said in the same strangled voice. "That was a giant stuffed panda wearing a wig."

"Cool," Lee Bob said.

"Inventive," added Trinity. "I love wigs."

"How could you have done it, Amy?" Matt asked, hearing the raw pain in his voice. "How could you have kept lying to me like that?"

"Hate to interrupt but Lee Bob and I are gonna blaze," Trinity said, leaning over the table. Her dress was so tight that her breasts looked in danger of popping out of it. "Sorry about how things worked out, Matt. I'd give your money back if I hadn't spent it already."

Amy's head jerked up and Matt got a premonition of doom. "Matt pays you to date him?"

"No, silly." Trinity said, giggling. "I'm an actress. He paid me to play a role. Just like you paid Lee Bob."

"Your name's not Mary Contrino?"

Trinity smiled. "Trinity Doppelheuer. Pleased to meet ya. Who would have thought I could play a nursery rhyme character, but casting against type really works sometimes. Bye, all."

Matt didn't bother to watch the acting OWGAs

leave the restaurant because the real drama was right in front of him.

"You snake! You lied to me." Amy bit out in her customary let-it-all-hang-out way. She thrust her chair back from the table and stalked out of the restaurant, seemingly oblivious to the stares of the other diners.

Matt got out his wallet, threw down some bills to cover the check and gave chase. The night was dark and blustery with storm clouds gathering overhead, a stark change from the weather when they'd entered the restaurant. Trying not to take the impending storm as a bad sign, Matt broke into a run. He caught Amy a block away, walking swiftly down a city sidewalk.

"You lied to me, too," he pointed out but his comment didn't seem to register on her.

"There is no Mary Contrary, is there?" she muttered angrily. "I should have known it as soon as you started talking about cockleshells."

"There is no Pierre LeFrancois, either," he said. Rationally.

"*Ooooooo,* you make me so mad," she said. Irrationally.

"I wasn't the one who pretended a stuffed panda with poison ivy cooked me dinner."

"I wasn't the one who hired an actor!"

"Yes," Matt said, "you did."

"Only because you hired one first. Anybody can see this whole mess is more your fault than mine."

Matt sighed, which came out more like a heave

since he was practically chasing her down the block. "Would you please stop?"

She did so with such abruptness that he nearly plowed into her. He was close enough to get a face full of hair when the wind kicked up so he took a step back. She held the hair back from her face and he wished it was flogging him again. At least that way, he couldn't see the glare she was directing at him.

"It's both of our faults," Matt said as calmly as he could with his blood racing and his temper boiling. "I shouldn't have invented Mary. But you shouldn't have made up Pierre, either."

"You're right," she said, and he watched some of the anger drain from her face. In its place was sadness. "We were both wrong. Friends don't do things like that to each other."

"No, they don't," Matt said glumly as he stared back at her. He couldn't imagine a scenario in which he'd conjure up an imaginary girlfriend to fool Zoe. Or any of his other friends.

For a moment, neither of them said a word. The street was nearly deserted in light of the impending storm, and the night seemed to grow darker.

"It's a wonder we ever became friends in the first place," Amy continued, looking so despondent he wanted to reach out and comfort her. Instead he forced his hands to remain at his side. "We're like Zoe says—yin and yang."

"Complete opposites," he said when what he really wanted to do was tell her that he'd developed a taste for yin.

"Maybe not as opposite as you and that actress you got to play Mary Contrary," she continued softly, "but opposite enough that we don't make sense together."

"What are you trying to say?" he asked, but he already knew he didn't want to hear her answer.

He saw her swallow and watched her eyes turn glassy, as though she were fighting tears. "That we shouldn't see each other anymore." She cleared her throat. "It won't be so hard. You, me and Zoe, we've always been a trio. But she's all wrapped up with Jack now."

She shuffled her feet, looked at the sidewalk, then back up at him. "You agree, don't you?"

No, his heart screamed. The wind howled, and it sounded like weeping. He couldn't make himself speak so he merely nodded.

Their eyes held for long, heart-wrenching seconds and he had to fight to keep his hands at his side, to keep from reaching for what he shouldn't want.

"Then I guess this is goodbye," she said.

He shook his head against the horror of the word, wanting her to take it back. He imagined he glimpsed hope in her eyes, but her silence belied it. His own eyes grew misty, but he wasn't sure whether it was with nature's tears or his own as the heavens opened up.

"I'm still going to insist on driving you home," he said over the pounding of the rain.

"You would," she said, but walked beside him in silence to his car. Despite the drenching rain, neither of them hurried. Maybe, Matt thought, because they couldn't get any more miserable than they already were.

The silence grew deeper on the drive to Arlington, broken only by the swish of the windshield wipers and the sound of the rain. Matt wanted to break it, but he couldn't think how.

Finally, he pulled to the curb in front of her small house. She turned to him, her hair dark and wet against her pale, oval face. He tried to memorize each feature to hold him for the days to come.

"Goodbye, Matt," she said and got out of the car. This time, he feared the goodbye was for good.

10

AMY TURNED TO HER ASSISTANT with her customary bright smile, which had gotten more and more difficult to affix in the past two Matt-less weeks.

It was the end of a long day in which Timmy Carson, pretending to be Super Hawk Man, had leaped off one of the desks. He might have broken a bone if his fall hadn't been cushioned by Rachel Mahoney, who had bawled so hard half the students had mistaken the wails for the fire alarm and headed for the exit.

Rachel's main injury had been a caterwauling-induced sore throat, but Amy hadn't the heart to talk to her about histrionics. Especially when she had longed to throw back her head and howl with her.

She'd been so depressed she hadn't even been able to bring herself to put the photo she'd taken of Pandamonium wearing the wig and Hawaiian shirt in the Ugly Cube.

"Did you ask me something, Victoria?" Amy gathered up some papers as she spoke and tossed them in the trash can beside her desk. "My mind must have been somewhere else."

Victoria's brows drew together in a frown. A pretty blonde close to finishing her degree in early childhood education, she usually wore an open, cheerful expression.

"I wanted to know if you were okay," Victoria said, the frown growing deeper.

Amy made her brilliant smile grow brighter, which made her cheeks ache. "Why wouldn't I be okay?"

"Because you threw away the pictures the kids drew today of their notion of paradise."

"I did?" Amy got up and rushed around the desk to the trash can. The drawing on top was of a cartoon mouse serving cheeseburgers at a fast-food restaurant that featured an indoor swimming pool. "Oh, my gosh. I did!"

After Amy dug the pictures out of the trash, she looked up to find Victoria still watching her with the same worried look.

"I'm fine, Victoria," Amy said, but the words didn't sound convincing even to herself. "Just a little..." Heartbroken, she thought. "Preoccupied," she said.

"Is that because you're thinking of leaving Virginia?"

Amy's mouth dropped open. She didn't think anyone knew about that. "Who told you?"

"Fabio did," Victoria said. "When he was here yesterday in the library."

"Fabio has a big mouth," Amy muttered but privately conceded hers was even bigger for confiding in him. Victoria was obviously waiting for an explanation, so she continued, "I'm about to be out of a house and, well, I don't know if I can find another place around here I can afford."

Victoria tilted her head inquiringly. "Can't you move in with your boyfriend?"

"What boyfriend?"

"That good-looking guy who was here the other day. Matt, I think his name was."

"Matt's not my boyfriend," Amy refuted. The truth in the words hurt like a physical blow.

"He's not?" Victoria looked shocked. "But the way you two were looking at each other, I could have sworn—"

"He's not my boyfriend," Amy repeated. Why, she wondered, did everybody always make that crucial mistake? "We have next to nothing in common."

"So you two are just friends then?"

"Well, no," Amy said, and those words hurt, too. She missed Matt so much it felt like someone had cut out a vital piece of her soul. "Not exactly. Not anymore."

Because Victoria was fairly new to Ambrose Academy, she and Amy had yet to exchange many details of their personal lives. Now, however, she seemed ready to quiz Amy about the severed friendship. The way Zoe and then Fabio had quizzed her. Amy couldn't let that happen—especially because nobody understood the necessity of their break.

"The bottom line is that moving in with Matt is not an option," she said, cutting off Victoria's questions.

"In that case," Victoria said slowly, "you could move in with me and my roommates. One of them is moving out, and I'm sure it would be okay with the other two once I vouch for you.''

It was the kind of thing that always happened to her, exactly as she'd told Matt when he'd grilled her on where she planned to live. Solutions arose. Problems got solved.

But she wasn't sure she wanted to work out her problems in Arlington. She'd been thinking about moving back to her small, Pennsylvania home town, where the pace of life was slower and she wouldn't have to worry about running into Matt. Who she wanted but couldn't—and shouldn't—have.

"Thanks, Victoria," she said, "but things are complicated here. It might be better if I just moved."

"Why don't you take a couple days and think about it?" Victoria suggested. "It's not like we have anybody else waiting to move in."

Amy hesitated. "Thanks. I will," she said, although she'd already made up her mind.

She was leaving Virginia. And Matt. If circumstances had been different, she wouldn't consider abandoning her kindergarten students during a school year. But Victoria, who was taking night classes, was due to get her degree in two months. If the principal had the good sense to hire her, which Amy would make sure happened, Victoria could take over after the Christmas break and the transition would be an easy one for the children.

"Oh, I almost forgot to tell you," Victoria said. "Barbara says she took a message for you about an hour ago."

Amy rolled her eyes. "It's probably from my

friend Zoe. You wouldn't believe how many times she's called to remind me I'm supposed to meet her at Brewster's tonight. I can't take it anymore."

"Unless your friend has an unusually deep voice, I don't think she's the one who called." Victoria made her eyebrows dance. "Barbara said the caller was a man who sounded very intriguing."

Amy's breath snagged. Barbara, the man-crazy school secretary, had to be talking about Matt. He had a low, sexy, *intriguing* voice. Who could be more intriguing than Matt?

She got up so fast, she left most of her blood at her feet, making her feel light-headed.

"Let me see what that's all about," she said, trying to sound casual. She ruined the impression by rushing out of the classroom and down the hall to the office.

"Hey, Barbara," she said when she was barely past the threshold of the office. "I hear you have a message for me."

"I certainly do." Barbara pulled a pink slip off the pad in front of her and emitted one of her trademark *tsk-tsking* sounds. "I can't believe you didn't tell me you knew him."

Amy had no doubt Matt was making himself known in legal circles, but she didn't think his reputation had extended to scholastic ones.

"Imagine not telling me something like that," Barbara said, shaking her bleached-blond head. "Imagine keeping to yourself that you're acquainted with Fabio."

Amy's spirits sank to the floor as she took the slip

of paper from the secretary. Matt hadn't called her. Fabio had.

"I guess you weren't here Wednesday when he came to work in the library," Amy said.

Barbara shook her head, a thunderstruck expression on her face. "What a time to take a mental-health day. Quick. Fill me in. What was he wearing? More importantly, how did his hair look?"

Amy thought for a moment. "I think he was wearing a plaid jacket and polyester pants. And his hair looked blue."

"Really?" Barbara appeared horrified, then thoughtful. "I guess somebody must fix him up before they pose him for those romance-novel covers."

Barbara looked so disenchanted that Amy knew she had to come clean. "My Fabio isn't a cover model," she said as she glanced down at the slip of paper in her hand to the message Barbara had jotted down.

If you want to convince me why I shouldn't file a lawsuit against Matt, be at 8989 Holly Lane at eight o'clock.

"Who is he then?" Barbara asked.

Amy gritted her teeth so hard her jaw hurt. "He's a little, old blue-haired man who better turn his hearing aid down when he sees me coming."

CARS PACKED THE DRIVEWAY and lined the curb in front of 8989 Holly Lane, which turned out to be a two-story brick colonial on a tree-lined street in a quiet residential section of Alexandria.

Make that a formerly quiet residential section, because the house at 8989 Holly Lane was rocking. Make that crooning. Matt recognized the song streaming from it as an old Frank Sinatra tune.

"After you take care of business, we can head on back to Brewster's, right?" Jack asked Matt when they paused on the sidewalk to take stock of the strange surroundings. Jack muttered the next words under his breath, "Because if we don't, Zoe's not gonna let me hear the end of it."

"Zoe was supposed to meet us at Brewster's?" This was news to Matt. When Jack had asked him to meet for drinks, he assumed it was so the two of them could get to know each other better. That's why he'd driven out of his way to spend a half hour at the bar before he'd had to leave. "Then you should have waited for her. You didn't have to come with me."

"But if I'd let you go off without me, what in tarnation was I supposed to say to her if you didn't come back?" Jack asked as though the question made sense.

Another time, Matt might have tried to figure out why Jack was talking in riddles, but he had other things on his mind. Such as the reason Fabio had asked him to meet here.

At the thought of Fabio, he got angry all over again at the message the little man had left at his law office.

If you want to convince me why I shouldn't file a lawsuit against Amy, meet me at 8989 Holly Lane at eight o'clock.

He'd picked up the phone immediately, hardly

able to believe Fabio was threatening to file yet another lawsuit. But the old-timer hadn't answered his repeated calls or the door when Matt had stopped by his house to demand answers.

His only recourse was to show up here at Holly Lane as directed. He hadn't counted on showing up with Jack.

After a grinning woman with long, white hair and total disregard for the rule of fashion that said seventy-year-old women shouldn't wear miniskirts let them inside the house, things made even less sense.

A *Congratulations, Lovebirds* banner was strung across an elegant room filled with septuagenarian and octogenarian couples, some of them swaying together to the Sinatra beat in the open spaces of the room.

The banner depicted in cartoon form what looked to be an aging jockey and a tall, gray-haired woman beautiful enough to model senior-citizen fashions.

"That there couple looks like Jack Sprat and his wife if Mrs. Sprat would put on about seventy-five pounds," Jack said, gesturing to the banner. After Frank Sinatra stopped crooning and the couples broke apart, he let out a low whistle. "Well, I'll be. There they are in the flesh."

Matt didn't hesitate, his steps eating up the floor until the little man—and the very tall woman with whom he'd been dancing—was in front of him.

"How could you even think of suing Amy after what she's done for you?" Matt asked Jack Sprat. Er, Fabio.

"Hello to you, too, Matt," Fabio said in his boyish

voice with his ever-welcoming, white-toothed smile. He took the tall, gray-haired woman by the elbow. "Helen, I'd like to introduce you to Matt Burke, a very good friend of mine. Matt, this is Helen Clark, my fiancée."

"I'm so very glad you could share in our happiness by coming to our engagement party," Helen said, sticking out a long, elegant hand.

Despite her age, Helen Clark was a stunner. Her face was lined and softened with age, but still beautiful. Her carriage was stately, her figure still good. She looked about as suitable for Fabio as Matt was for Amy.

"Congratulations," Matt said. Politeness compelled him to introduce Jack, who was greeted with the same effusiveness. Not to mention the story of how Fabio and Helen had gotten back together.

"I just got engaged myself," Jack told them. "Once I saw Zoe again, didn't take me long to figure I wanted her for keeps, either."

"You can't wait around to act on love," Helen said. "You've got to trust that when it's right, it's right."

"That's what I—" Jack began.

"Could we cut to the chase," Matt interrupted, earning surprised looks from both Fabio and Jack. Although neither knew him well, they obviously realized he usually used more tact. He didn't often glower, either, but he directed one at Fabio. "I want to know what you're threatening to sue Amy for this time."

"Do I know this Amy, Fabio dear?" Helen asked

instead of the question that should have been upper-most in her mind: *What in the heck am I getting myself into?*

"I told you about her, sweet thing," Fabio said. "The teacher who lives next door to me. In fact, there she is now."

Even though the strains of a Dean Martin song were now shaking the rafters, Matt might have heard Amy coming if he hadn't spotted her first. She was punishing the hardwood floor with thundering steps, stalking through a crowd that had parted for her like the Red Sea.

Her sights were set so squarely on Fabio that Matt doubted she noticed anything, or anybody, else.

For his part, after his brain registered that Zoe was trailing after her, he couldn't see anybody but Amy. Her brown eyes sparkled with temper and her long, curly dark hair swung behind her as she stalked. Despite her long, floaty dress, she looked gorgeous.

"You've got ten seconds to convince me why I shouldn't gather my kindergartners together in your yard and teach them how to toilet paper trees," she told Fabio in a low, furious voice.

"Why, Amy, how lovely it is that you could come." Fabio stepped forward to take both of Amy's hands in his. She ripped them out of his grasp. To Helen, he said, "Helen, this is Amy Donatelli. Amy, Helen Clark."

"I've heard so much about you," Helen said in a gracious voice. She turned her regal head to include Matt in her next comment, and Amy seemed to see him for the first time. Every one of her muscles appeared to freeze. "And might I say that the two of you make a perfectly lovely couple."

"We're not—" Amy began.

"—a couple," Matt finished.

Jack reached around Amy and pulled Zoe toward him, introducing her as he did so. "Me and Zoe, we're the happy couple," he said, hugging her to him with one arm.

"Amy and Matt are the pigheaded couple," Fabio added cheerfully.

"Whatever you are to each other," Helen said, looking from Zoe and Jack to Amy and Matt, "I think both pairs of you look perfectly darling together."

"Oh, for goodness' sake," Amy muttered, then turned on Fabio. "What's going on here?" she demanded with typical bluntness. "What kind of suit are you threatening to file?"

"I don't have the wording down pat yet," Fabio said, "but I was thinking of something along the lines of failure to keep a fine friendship going."

"What?" Matt and Amy asked at virtually the same time.

"That's utterly—" Amy began.

"—ridiculous," Matt finished.

"I think it's brilliant," Zoe countered, beaming. "Much better than my plan to get the two of you together at Brewster's."

"What?" Matt and Amy asked, again in unison.

"Don't look so shocked," Zoe said. "It's no secret you've been miserable without each other. I thought all you needed to get your friendship back on track is talk. Obviously Fabio thought the same thing.''

"There's nothing to talk about," Amy said but Dean Martin's singing nearly drowned out her words. "Besides, nobody could hear me even if there was something to discuss.''

"You've got a point there," Zoe said, then crossed to Helen and whispered something in her ear. Before Amy realized what was happening, she and Matt were ushered—no, herded—to a door adjacent to the kitchen.

Helen opened the door and switched on a light, revealing a small space with a washer and dryer jammed against the wall. "You'll have all the privacy you need in there," she said before Amy felt hands pushing at her back.

As soon as she and Matt were inside, the heavy door slammed shut, muffling the noise of the party. Amy tried the doorknob, but it wouldn't turn, leaving her alone with Matt, a box of detergent and some prewash spray.

She pushed aside the knowledge that alone with Matt was exactly where she wanted to be and hoisted herself up on the washing machine so that her legs dangled.

"Would you believe they locked us inside the laundry room?" With a heavy sigh, she blew out a breath that ruffled the fine hairs around her face. "This gives new meaning to the words interfering bunch of do-gooders.''

"They're only trying to help." Matt sounded deflated as he anchored his hands on either side of the dryer to hoist himself up beside her. The motion made his muscles ripple under his fancy clothes, but she tried not to notice. "They don't understand why we can't be friends anymore."

Amy pushed her hair back from her face. "You'd think they'd realize by now that our friendship never should have worked in the first place because we're—"

"—complete opposites," Matt finished. "Yin and yang."

"Felix and Oscar," Amy countered.

"Mickey Mouse and Daisy Duck."

"Yeah," Amy began, "so what if strangers mistake us for a couple and we—"

"—finish each other's sentences. That doesn't mean we—"

"—should be friends."

"It sure doesn't," Matt said, but his denial didn't sound convincing. "So don't give another thought to Fabio's lawsuit. It's nonsense. He can't sue you for failure to keep up a friendship."

"Sue *me?*" Amy looked at him sharply. "I came over here to stop him from suing *you*."

"Fabio's message distinctly said he was going to sue you," he said thoughtfully. "Unless…he was trying to make a point."

Amy really looked at Matt for the first time since she'd come into Helen Clark's house. He was wearing his customary suit, but everything about him looked a little off. Dark circles rimmed his eyes, his mouth tugged downward and his hair didn't even look immaculate. Still, the sight of him seemed to fill up a primal part of her. Like water quenches a thirst. How was she going to live without him?

She made herself speak normally. "What kind of point would he be trying to make?"

Matt shrugged, but the motion looked anything but nonchalant. The gaze that met hers was piercing. "That we'd rush to the other's rescue."

"Of course we did." Amy should be angry at the way Fabio had manipulated them, but she couldn't be. Not when Matt was beside her. "We l—" she hesitated on the word love and substituted another "—care about each other."

"We always have," Matt said.

She gulped and forced out the words. "But that doesn't mean a friendship between us works."

"No, it doesn't," Matt agreed, and something broke inside her and spilled. She'd wanted him to say that it would work, that he'd move heaven and earth to make it work. The way she just realized she would.

"We won't have to endure their meddling much longer," Amy said, trying to sound upbeat. But how could she sound upbeat when leaving the man she loved? "I'm leaving Ambrose Academy after Christmas break."

His head snapped around. "You took that job in Fairfax?"

She shook her head. "I should have said I was leaving Virginia. I've decided to move back to Pennsylvania."

"You can't leave," he blurted out, levering a hand on the washing machine and leaning closer to her.

He was so close, she could smell him. Or was that fabric softener? She breathed in again and got that slight whiff of cologne plus an intoxicating something else. No, it was Matt she smelled.

"You were right," she said, trying not to let the smell go to her head and muddle her brain. "I need to be more practical. I can't give up teaching at a private school so I have to move. I don't make enough money to live in the D.C. area."

"But you said something would work out," he protested, his eyes wild. She refrained from telling him she had a solution to her living problem because she couldn't take it. Not when it hurt this much to be near him.

"You can't leave," he repeated.

"Why not?"

"Because…because if you do, who's going to nag me for working too hard?" He hopped down from the dryer and came to stand in front of the washer. "Who's going to talk me into being spontaneous and doing something silly like rollerskating or flying a kite? Who's going to tell me money's not the most important thing in life?"

She swallowed. "Those aren't good enough reasons for me to stay."

"Then who's going to nag you to balance your checkbook? Who's going to make you think about life's details? Who's going to tell you to be more tactful?"

"What are you trying to say, Matt?" Amy asked, her voice breaking.

"That together we're stronger than we are apart."

He put his hands on her shoulders and the warmth of them began to seep through the cold misery of the last two weeks. "I don't know why I didn't see it before."

She shook her head, denying what she wanted to believe. "We're a disaster together. Look at the way I lied to you about Pierre. The way you lied to me about Mary."

He took her hand and held it over his heart. Sincerity shone from his light-brown eyes. "Do you know why I lied?"

"Why?" she asked softly.

"I lied..." he said and took a breath. She could hear the indrawn rasp of it, feel the beating of his heart. "Because I didn't want you to think I was pathetic for being in love with someone who was in love with someone else."

The implication of what he'd said made her heart jerk. "You're in love with me?"

He nodded. "Madly, passionately in love. I must've been all along but I didn't know it until the first time we kissed."

She was silent while she tried to digest the incredible news. Matt loved her. Joy burst in her like water from a broken dam, but he mistook her silence for something else.

She watched his Adam's apple bob as he swallowed. "Don't move away. Please. I couldn't bear not to have you in my life," he said in a raw voice. "Even if you don't love me back, we can go back to being just friends."

"What if I wanted to be friends and lovers?" she

asked in a soft voice. She saw the quick leap of joy in his eyes but it was quickly banked and replaced by caution.

"*Friends and Lovers* is a movie title," he said slowly, "but if you're playing the game, you win. This moment's way too important for me to remember the stars."

"Amy Donatelli and Matt Burke," she whispered, reaching out to touch his cheek. "This moment's important to me, too, because that's what I want us to be. If you can forgive me for not telling you about Pierre."

"Why didn't you tell me?"

"I wanted to, a hundred times." She frowned. "But then you'd say something about Mary and I was so crazy in love with you that I'd get jealous and blurt out some wild untruth."

He smiled, slow, sexy and devastating. "You're crazy in love with me?"

She expelled a short breath. "That's what I've been trying to say for the past five minutes."

"Just making sure," he said as he lifted her off the washing machine and brought her flush against his body.

She rolled her eyes. "Honestly, Matt, this premeditated thing you do drives me absolutely nuts. I don't understand why you can't be spontaneous for—"

His clever mouth cut off the rest of her sentence, effectively making her forget what she'd been about to say. Then her arms were around him, her hands fisting in his hair, her heart bursting with love of him.

They didn't break apart until a long time later when someone unlocked the door and opened it. Zoe stuck her head in the room. Her grin started small and grew wider and...baffled.

"Oh, my gosh," she exclaimed. "This is wild. I just wanted the two of you to be friends again. I never thought..."

Words failed her, but Amy had exactly the right ones. "That two people who fill in each other's blanks are—"

"Perfect for each other," Matt finished, never taking his eyes off Amy's. "In fact, she's so perfect for me I was just about to ask her to marry me."

"I was just about to say yes," Amy said, smiling up at the man who'd claimed her heart long ago. "There's no way I'm letting this one get away."

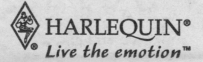

Harlequin Romance®

is delighted to present a brand-new miniseries
that dares to be different...

TANGO

FRESH AND FLIRTY...
IT TAKES TWO TO TANGO

Exuberant, exciting...emotionally exhilarating!

These cutting-edge, highly contemporary stories
capture how women in the twenty-first century
really feel about meeting Mr. Right!

Don't miss:

July:
MANHATTAN MERGER
—by international bestselling
author Rebecca Winters (#3755)

October:
THE BABY BONDING
—by rising star
Caroline Anderson (#3769)

November:
THEIR ACCIDENTAL BABY
—by fresh new talent
Hannah Bernard (#3774)

*And watch for more
TANGO books to come!*

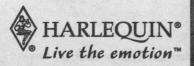

HARLEQUIN®
Live the emotion™

If you enjoyed what you just read,
then we've got an offer you can't resist!

Take 2 bestselling
love stories FREE!

Plus get a FREE surprise gift!

Clip this page and mail it to Harlequin Reader Service®

IN U.S.A.	IN CANADA
3010 Walden Ave.	P.O. Box 609
P.O. Box 1867	Fort Erie, Ontario
Buffalo, N.Y. 14240-1867	L2A 5X3

YES! Please send me 2 free Harlequin Duets™ novels and my free surprise gift. After receiving them, if I don't wish to receive anymore, I can return the shipping statement marked cancel. If I don't cancel, I will receive 2 brand-new novels every month, before they're available in stores! In the U.S.A., bill me at the bargain price of $5.14 plus 50¢ shipping & handling per book and applicable sales tax, if any*. In Canada, bill me at the bargain price of $6.14 plus 50¢ shipping & handling per book and applicable taxes**. That's the complete price—what a great deal! I understand that accepting the 2 free books and gift places me under no obligation ever to buy any books. I can always return a shipment and cancel at any time. Even if I never buy another book from Harlequin, the 2 free books and gift are mine to keep forever.

111 HDN DNUF
311 HDN DNUG

Name	(PLEASE PRINT)	
Address	Apt.#	
City	State/Prov.	Zip/Postal Code

* Terms and prices subject to change without notice. Sales tax applicable in N.Y.
** Canadian residents will be charged applicable provincial taxes and GST.
  All orders subject to approval. Offer limited to one per household and not valid to current Harlequin Duets™ subscribers.
  ® and ™ are registered trademarks of Harlequin Enterprises Limited.   DUETS02

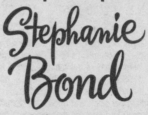
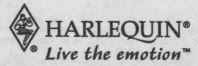

COMING NEXT MONTH

HARLEQUIN®

Duets™

#103

ARE MEN FROM MARS? by Candy Halliday

When Dr. Madeline Morgan is whisked away in a mysterious craft near Roswell, she almost buys into all those crazy UFO reports. But wait, these little green men are wearing army fatigues! And hunky Captain Brad Hawkins isn't all that *little*.... How is Maddie to know that she's stumbled upon a top secret military base and innocently threatened national security? And how can she control herself under house arrest—with Brad?

VENUS, HOW COULD YOU? by Candy Halliday

Mary Beth Morgan has finally hit the big time—a gig on a hot new soap opera, a home on the beach and enough star power to show her face with confidence at her upcoming high school reunion. But Mary Beth can't believe her high school sweetheart, Zack, has the nerve to show *his* face—gorgeous as it is—after what he did to her, or that he's trying to win her back! How can she forgive the guy who left her at the altar?

#104

A REAL WORK OF ART by Samantha Connolly

Seeing double? That's what Sam Harrison thinks when his uptight co-worker becomes easygoing, flirty and funny—overnight! Megan Dean has a job to do impersonating her twin sister, but she can't fake her feelings for Sam—he's the hottest, handsomest guy she's ever met. If only he knew which Dean he was actually dating!

THICK AS THIEVES by Jennifer McKinlay

When his best friend asks him for a favor, Jared McLean has no idea he'll end up breaking the number one best-friend law—no falling for your friend's sister! But driving across the country with the very tempting Cat Levery—in a *very* small van, no less—makes him forget all about best friends! By the time they reach their destination, they seem to have broken a few other laws, too. How else to explain the thieves that seem to be following them...?

HARLEQUIN®

Duets™ 2 ROMANTIC COMEDIES

Once Smitten Darlene Gardner
The One Who Got Away!

That's who Jack Carter is to Zoe O'Neill—the one who got away. Sure, she denies it, but Zoe must contact her onetime college crush just to prove her point. However Jack's got his own point to prove—he may be one hot jock, but he strikes out potential mates before the fourth date. Now he's determined to break the streak... with Zoe!

Twice Shy Darlene Gardner
The One Who Never Left!

That's who Matt Burke and Amy Donatelli are to each other—the ones who never left. Since their friend Zoe found true love, these two best buds are on their own for the very first time. How will such a workaholic lawyer and a free spirit ever get together? Easy—someone's suing the free spirit, so it's full steam ahead for this duo!

Talented author Darlene Gardner delivers a double dose of fun!

Visit us at www.eHarlequin.com

ISBN 0-373-44167-3